Liar Thief

First published in 2025
by The Black Spring Press Group
Maida Vale, London W9,
United Kingdom

Cover design by Matt Broughton
Typeset by Edwin Smet

All rights reserved
Copyright © 2025 May Rinaldi

ISBN 9781917788205

The right of May Rinaldi to be identified as author of
this work has been asserted in accordance with section 77
of the Copyright, Designs and Patents Act 1988

This book is a work of fiction. The characters, incidents, and
dialogue are drawn from the author's imagination and are not
to be construed as real. Any resemblance to actual events or
persons, living or dead, is entirely coincidental.

BLACKSPRINGPRESSGROUP.COM

Liar Thief

May Rinaldi

THE **BLACK SPRING**
PRESS GROUP

May Rinaldi
is a crime writer from the South-West of Scotland where she lives with her Norwegian husband, and two decrepit cats.

She recently retired from her consultancy job in Health and Safety and, in the past, has worked as a taxidermist, mycologist and lab technician, all useful in crime writing – not only can her protagonist poison her victims, she can turn them into an interesting, mounted specimen afterwards.

She is the co-founder of Moffat Crime Fest, bringing top crime authors to the Dumfries and Galloway town of Moffat. She also runs writing retreats in her secluded home where visiting authors are only disturbed by sheep, cows and the dinner gong.

She spends her spare time travelling between Scotland, Norway and Gozo, and uses her travels as settings for her books. She is currently working on a Gozo trilogy; the Mediterranean island is as much one of the characters as the people who inhabit it. *Liar Thief* is the winner of The Black Spring Crime Prize 2024.

This book is dedicated
to May Hamilton Paterson —
my mum who gave me my love of
reading and some great plot points.

Chapter 1
GINNIE

2016

My name is Ginnie.
I am a serial killer.

Not your common-or-garden, run-of-the-mill serial killer. Am I a sociopath or a psychopath? Perhaps a narcissist? According to the shrink who examined me thirty years ago I was sane and fit to plead but is this the story of a sane woman?

I'm not motivated by sexual yearnings, nor was I abused by my parents as a child, at least not physically. I've never killed an animal, not even tortured a daddy longlegs by pulling off those dangly, catch-in-your-hair legs one at a time.

I've had several husbands, one of them mine.

I use a different MO each time I kill. I've read the books, I've seen the films, so I know the terms.

I have only one rule. I kill people who wrong me. You might think they deserved to die. On the other hand, you might think they are innocent souls who just crossed my path at the wrong time.

Ghost writer Fiona Taylor has championed my cause, making her readers understand why I am what I am, why I do what I do.

The Killer Inside, my story, is number one in the charts even before release, the follow up to *The Child*

Inside and *The Woman Inside*. Psychology made easy by being written as a work of fiction. I am the subject. My confessions covered by the press thirty years earlier had piqued her interest, making me the ideal subject.

And what made me the ideal subject? Perhaps the fact that no one could understand what I had done. Fiona would give them the explanation they crave.

Why would I confess to crimes I had never committed? Why would I continue to insist that I had killed nine people?

Fiona isn't a qualified psychiatrist or psychologist but her books, films, and TV programmes, examining individuals with convoluted psychological behaviours, have made her a media 'expert'.

I inhale the heady scent of the new book, always one of my favourite smells. Placing it in my bag I glance round the bare room which has been my home for thirty years. I'll miss it.

Fiona and I have spent the past two years across a bare wooden table; her taking copious notes and recording each word I say. She has spent at least the same time with Tom – the retired Detective Inspector Tom O'Brien, that is – collecting his memories and his side of what happened. Tom is my best friend; he knows me better than anyone else.

Even when I shot him, he understood why.

'Take care out there Ginnie.' The words of the warder echo in the clash of the closing gates, a throw-back to an old TV programme. I'm blinded by flashes and deafened by the clamour of questions. Fiona covers my head and hides my face with a large black umbrella and hustles me into the waiting limousine.

She has arranged a series of interviews and talks where my story will unfold, the first of these events being the book launch. The press can wait for their bite of this particular pie. I can see the looks of disappointment on the faces of the vultures through the blacked-out windows of the car. They have been standing in a torrential downpour for the best part of an hour, hoping for a glimpse of me or the words they can use for their publicity-grabbing headline. Their efforts thwarted by the beautiful, grey- haired author.

She has recorded my story and has transcribed each word, melding my words with those of Tom. She has waited a long time, knowing inherently that releasing her book when I was freed would garner most coverage.

What she isn't aware of is that there'll have to be a sequel, or an addendum to the second print run, because I'm not finished.

I haven't forgiven the thief.

Chapter 2
FIONA
2015

I first read about Ginnie almost thirty years ago. A few paragraphs in a Sunday paper, ridiculing her "confessions", a germ of an idea forming in my brain. Now I sit in the private visiting room of Cornton Vale prison, waiting to meet the woman who will be the next protagonist in my series.

My research on her life shows that we were at school at the same time. I scoured the photograph of the sixth year of 1974. There, partially hidden behind a boy with a feather cut, was the tiny, blonde figure of the girl who says she had killed five people by that point. I can't say she was memorable. The face is familiar, but I'm not sure if that's because of the photographs I've seen in the newspapers. She was never in my circle of friends, wasn't a prefect and would have been in a different house to me. Her record shows she was top in science and maths; I studied languages and arts so we wouldn't have shared classes except in first and second year.

I stand as she enters and we shake hands, a formal gesture meant to ensure that our relationship will be merely professional.

I am writing her memoir. And if my instincts are right, it'll be very lucrative for us both.

Her grasp on my hand is firm, stronger than I expect from the tiny, waif of a woman who stands in front of me. She is staring up at me with piercing blue eyes, a look of determination in the set of her mouth.

'Pleased to meet you finally, Ginnie. I have been looking forward to this.'

'Me too. I've read your other books. I think we'll get on just fine. You were an Airdrie Academy girl too, weren't you?'

She takes a seat opposite me. We have been allowed the use of the small lounge for our meetings. Ginnie is due for release in two years-time, and this has been seen as part of her rehabilitation. Her time in prison has been extended a few times but the psychologists who have examined her and the prison manager say she is a reformed character. For several years she's been the ideal prisoner and her release is all but guaranteed. I explain that I will record her story and take notes as she speaks. I need her to relax and just be herself. I want my readers to empathise with her.

She looks at me from under the mop of greying blond curls which fall over her eyes. 'Thank you for taking on my story,' she says 'No-one else seems to believe me but I'm sure you'll understand. Everyone I've killed has deserved their fate. Their behaviour warrants my actions and I need you to explain this to the readers. If more people were like me then we'd rid the world of the liars, thieves and cheats out there.'

I'm keeping an open mind. Her story sounds implausible. I aim to get to the root of her actions, but I may not form the conclusion she wants me to. There's a reason why she is sticking to the story she told the reporters and police thirty years ago. She has never wavered from her confessions that she has killed nine people. Why this is the case is my task. I'm eager to listen to all she will tell me over the next few months and to write her story. My fans and my publisher are demanding the next in my series. There's even been early talks of a film or TV deal.

'I was at Airdrie Academy from '68 to '74. I'm sorry, but I don't think I knew you. We were a big year group.' I want to gain her trust and decide to be totally honest.

'Really?' she asks. 'You don't remember me?' A smile plays at the side of her mouth. 'Perhaps I'll be able to jog your memory.'

Chapter 3
GINNIE'S TRANSCRIPT
1966

Francis, Tom and I spent hours down at the tinker camp. They were travelling people, handymen, sharpening knives, collecting metal and rags, selling horses. The latter is what drew us to their camp. Wherever there were horses we'd be there grooming, feeding, cleaning out the ramshackle huts which housed the three piebald ponies. The owners were happy for us to spend time there, it helped them get to know the Buffers in the town; the non-travelling folk who bought the wooden clothes pegs, had their knives sharpened and passed over bags of vegetables, home baking and hand-me-down clothes for the camp children.

Their strong Irish brogue and strange words picked up easily by us resulting in a clip round the ear by our mums and a warning to 'speak properly'. Travelling from area to area, they worked in the fields of soft fruits, apples and potatoes depending on the time of year. They showed us how to strip thistles to reach the tasty crunchy nut in the centre, how to tickle brown trout in the burn amid screams of fear and laughter when something brushed our fingers as we felt gingerly under rocks for the elusive fish. They taught us songs, beautiful tunes and stories passed down through generations accompanied on fiddle and tin whistle.

On the outskirts of the camp sat an old caravan. When we passed by, we would see a gaunt figure watching us, a girl about our age. Her lank, dark hair hung over her face, like a screen keeping her from our view. She wore baggy jumpers, her bony elbows poking through the threadbare material. Her name was Christine. I had sat beside her at school. She kept to herself, everyone said she had nits and she smelled. Some days she didn't appear at school, and the truant officer would be sent round to the camp to talk to her family. When she did talk at school, she told me tales of her life with the travelling community. How she spent summers picking fruit in the berry fields, October was 'tattie howking' time, picking potatoes by hand in the farms round Airdrie. She spoke about working from dawn 'til dusk, hard physical labour hardly suited to a wraith of a girl. She fascinated me, I'd sit with her at break time at school, a pair of misfits finding each other. But she wasn't part of our gang; no room for anyone else.

Francis, Tom, and me. Only separated during school days by religion as they were both Catholic and attended the primary school at the bottom of our road while I, brought up very loosely in the Church of Scotland, had to walk a mile into town to the local non-denominational, or Proddy school. Running home when the bell rang, I dodged the groups of children coming from St Serf's who were intent on bullying and harassing anyone from Chapelside Primary. 'Proddy dogs eat the frogs,' they'd chant, and we would reply with an equally erudite, 'Catholic cats eat the rats,' in our sing-song Lanarkshire voices.

That enmity ended when I got home. Francis, Tom, and I would meet up and play in our gardens or nearby fields until we were called in for dinner. We hardly ever spent any time indoors, on wet miserable days we would adjourn to the back of Tom's dad's lorry which in our imaginations we transformed into a wild west wagon, forming circles to fight off marauding Sioux and Cherokee.

The long summer holidays were our favourite time as we could spend hours playing rounders in the road. I would take the blame when Tom struck the ball into Mrs McIntyre's garden. I didn't care if she ratted on me to my parents, I needed to protect Tom, didn't want him to get in trouble and be grounded.

We were our own version of the Q-Bikes, riding the streets of the new Holehills estate, solving crimes and catching baddies. Until my bike went missing. I'd only had it eight months, the top of the range Raleigh was my pride and joy, a Christmas present aimed to make up for my parents missing my appearance in the nativity play.

'I think I saw Tom with it,' Francis said when I had appeared at his door, angered that someone had appeared to have broken into our shed and taken it.

'But Tom's got his own bike. Why would he want mine?'

'Yours is better. His is too wee for him, he looks daft

on it.'

Tom had put on a growth spurt at the start of the holidays, and Francis had laughed at his big knobbly knees sticking out to the side on his hand-me-down bike. But to steal my bike? That was unforgiveable. I'd have given it to him is he'd asked. I trudged across the road to the field in silence. Tom would have to pay for this. Liars and thieves; two groups of people I hated.

My best friend had no idea how dangerous it was to wrong me.

I sat at the top of the bing, scanning the road below for any sign of Tom and my bike. The sound of someone blowing through a stalk of Timothy grass behind me made me turn. Tom appeared over the crest of the hill dragging his bogie behind him. Sliding down the bing on our home-made carts was one of our many games. He dropped the cart near the edge and plonked himself down on it then swung round to face me.

'What's up?' Tom could read me like no-one else.

'What do you think? Francis told me.'

'Told you what? You look like you could kill someone.'

He had no idea how close he was to the truth. 'Where is it?'

'Where's what?'

'My bike. Francis said you took it.' I shuffled closer to him, leaning my foot on the side of the bogie. If I shoved hard enough he'd go careening over the edge of the bing backwards.

'That bike?' He pointed towards the main road that ran along the base of the hill to where Francis was doing wheelies on my bike.

'Bastard. He lied to me.' Worse still he had almost made me do something I would have regretted. A few more seconds and Tom would have been plunging down the scree. I could hardly breath. Tom looked shocked. I don't think he'd ever heard me swear before.

'He was probably just joking. Come on, let's go get him.' He swung round on the bogie and indicated for me to jump on behind him.

'On you go. I'll be down in a minute. Tell him to put my bike back in the shed.' I didn't want to speak to Francis. I had to think of a way to make him pay.

'Lying bastard,' I hissed.

Chapter 4
TOM
2015

Ex DI Tom O'Brien picked up each of the plastic wallets in turn, laying them in rows on the table in front of him, smallest in bottom row, largest at top. He sent up a silent thanks to his old colleague who had provided the files, risking her job but paying back a long-term debt. Although Tom had been party to the statements made by Ginnie when she had first confessed to killing a range of people who had crossed her, his closeness to the case had meant that he hadn't had access to a lot of the paperwork thirty years previously. At the time he had persuaded his boss to let him hear what she had to say. He had sat in the room next to the interview room and listened as she confessed to the two officers taking her statement. He had been concerned for her mental health. The woman who had protected him throughout his life, the woman who had saved his life as a teenager ... she couldn't be a killer. He had never thought ill of Ginnie, until she had shot him. Even then he knew she had her reasons. Now he had access to all the files, he was no nearer reaching a conclusion.

On a chair beside him lay three A4 folders containing photocopies and the notes the investigating officers had made into the deaths surrounding Virginia Queen; the deaths that she had said she was guilty of causing but which had been thrown out by the Procurator Fiscal due to lack of physical evidence. The PF had even threatened to charge Ginnie with wasting police time, adding more years to her sentence. The teams who had examined each of the deaths had recorded them as accidental or suicides; nothing at any of the scenes had raised any suspicion of foul play. Medical records backed up their conclusions.

He lay his diaries to the right of the pile of wallets and opened the first one marking the page with one of his wife Maria's bookmarks. 1966. Every year he had been given a diary, into which he had poured his innermost thoughts. His brothers had laughed at him and teased him, but it had been his way of centring his thoughts. If he wrote down what was uppermost in his mind he could sleep at night, able to shut down the compartment which sought to make sense of any unusual occurrences or feelings. Putting things in 'boxes' was his way of coping with multi-tasking. Whether it was lists of things to do, or physical piles of notes or mail, if it was in a neat line, he could deal with it.

TOM'S DIARY

August 13th 1966

Francis took Ginnie's bike and blamed me. She called him a B. I think she was really mad at him. I wouldn't want to be in his shoes when she catches up with him. Her face *was purple.*

We're going to gran's tomorrow, it's her birthday. I'd rather stay here and go fishing with Ginnie and Francis but mum says I have to go.

He picked up the transcript of Ginnie's story Fiona had given him and read the first chapter. The smell and sounds of that summer engulfed him. The fresh greenness of the Timothy grass, the dried earth, parched under a relentless sun. The feeling of freedom they had shared as children.

He had been protected by the other two throughout his childhood. They didn't care that he had one blue eye and one brown one although it seemed to bother the bullies in the school playground. He was just Tom, their quieter, shyer friend. When Francis and Ginnie had stood on the edge of the roof of the local flats, daring each other to jump he had kept back, terrified that their game would go wrong and one or both would plummet the eight floors to the concrete below, brains oozing onto the pavement. But they never fell.

When Fiona Taylor had approached him to get his view on the child Ginnie, and the adult she had become, he had agreed readily. He had hoped that re-opening the case files with time and distance to examine them thoroughly would maybe reveal something new, something he had missed.

Ginnie had never been charged with the killings

she had confessed to. There was no evidence that any crimes had been committed. A person's word that "they killed someone" was not enough for the Procurator Fiscal to agree to a trial, which resulted in her only being charged with the two crimes enacted on Tom's family; crimes that had impacted on his and Maria's lives.

Since Ginnie's arrest and subsequent incarceration, he had wondered if he had missed the signs. If she was telling the truth and *was* a serial killer, how could he not have noticed the sociopathic behaviour? Surely if he had any inkling that his friend was capable of killing anyone, his detective-trained brain would have spotted it?

For almost thirty years he and Maria had shut Ginnie away from their thoughts, seldom talking about her. They, or at least Maria, had decided that it would be better for all involved, not least their son Joe, to allow the events of the past to dissolve into their memories. Now everything had been raised into the forefront of their lives again. He had decided that it was better to confront the past and, against Maria's wishes, had agreed to help Fiona.

His wife had always had doubts about Ginnie's friendship with him and now they had transformed into hatred.

He hoped that the book would unlock the secrets that made Ginnie what she was.

Chapter 5
GINNIE'S TRANSCRIPT
1966

'Go and get your bike. Tom's at his gran's,' Francis yelled from the bottom of our steps.

It was a hot Sunday afternoon. He and Tom had been to chapel, confessing their sins as they did every Sunday. Any lies Francis had told would have been absolved with a couple of Hail Marys. Oh that life could be that simple.

'OK. On you go, I'll catch up. I'll meet you at the quarry.' I watched as he cycled off, his fishing net jammed along the crossbar of his bike.

'Mum. I'm going down to Christine's,' I shouted through the kitchen door.

'Hang on.' She came to the door, dusting off the flour from the scones she had been baking for her friends and handed me a jam sandwich. 'OK. Be back at five for dinner.' She seemed pleased I'd made a female friend. I had always preferred the company of boys, not interested in dolls or playing houses, the one time they had bought me a pram for Christmas they had been horrified to see me hurtling down the hill in it as a makeshift bogie, the doll which had come with it discarded, hanging by one leg on the garden fence: its blue gingham dress already torn and dirty. The doll and pram had disappeared soon afterwards.

Christine's mother wasn't around. I never knew if she had died or just left, I never asked. Christine lived with her older brother and her father. They were both surly, emaciated men with poor hygiene. She told me she'd had to grow up quickly and did all of the housework and cooking at home, trying to keep the caravan and herself clean. She was hardly ever at school, but I'd occasionally knock at the caravan door and take her treats stolen from mum's baking trays. She'd take them, stuffing them into her mouth, and listen while I rambled on about school. She was always distant, always looking over her shoulder, jumping when she heard a noise outside the caravan and would chase me away if her father appeared. I didn't tell my parents any of this and they never checked.

I set off in the direction of the camp, in case mum was watching, but swung through the lane half way down the road and headed, instead, to the quarry. Francis was already collecting minnows in a jam jar when I peddled up. The quarry was an old water filled pit, the sheer white edge rising above us to the bottom of Dalmacoulter farm. Everyone said the farmer tipped his dead cattle and sheep over the cliff edge and into the depths of the quarry. No-one knew how deep it was, you couldn't see the bottom from anywhere round the edge. Francis was standing on an overhang which jutted out over the water. As I approached, he knelt on the edge, peering over the side, dipping the small red net into the murky, weed-strewn water.

'What kept you? Look at what I've caught.' He held up a large jam jar. In it were three fish and an enormous black beetle. The beetle's pincers snapped open and shut as it tried to escape the confines of its prison. He passed the jar and net to me, 'Here hold these a minute.'

'Why did you lie about Tom?' I set the net down, wrapping the string of the jar round my fist.

'What?'

'You told me he had stolen my bike, but it was you. I saw you.'

'I didn't lie.' A wide grin spread across his face, 'It was a joke. You're an eejit. Who would have believed that Tom would steal anything?'

'I believed you. You've never lied to me before. Why would you lie about that?'

He laughed. He didn't realise how much he'd upset me. He picked up the net and went back to fishing from the edge of the quarry. 'Pass me the jar,' he called over his shoulder.

I swung the jar at his head as hard as I could, making contact with the back of his skull. The minnows spilled out, gasping for air, their bodies twisting and flapping in the grass; the beetle scurried away. The force of the glass hitting his skull caused a loud crack which echoed round the quarry sides. His legs buckled, and he fell into the stinking, black water. I grabbed a branch which had fallen from an old ash tree and pushed his body under the surface. He was unconscious and didn't struggle. The edge of the quarry was unstable, shards of slate and grass sods dislodged and fell into the water, some landing on his back, some splashing into the depths. I dropped the jar at my feet and picked up a large slab of slate and threw it at his head. The weight as it struck him caused his body to turn slightly and his cool, blue eyes stared at mine, but there was no spark in them, no sign of the force that had been Francis. I stomped on the edge, causing more of the platform he had been standing on to collapse, nearly tipping into the water beside him. I peered over the edge. His body hung lifeless, suspended among the tangle of weeds at the water's edge, dozens of earwigs and slaters floated round his body, clambering on to his shorts and tee-shirt, seeking refuge from their watery grave. Maybe they'd start eating him, crawling into his ears and nose and nibbling the soft flesh. The thought made me smile.

High above a buzzard circled, riding the thermals, its keening mew rang out, lamenting the dead boy.

I placed the jar in my bike basket. I could keep my pencils in it. It seemed like the right thing to do, something that would link me to Francis forever.

'Served him right. Liar. Thief,' I muttered as I rode away on my bike, heading towards Christine's house.

*

At 5pm I left Christine's, she had been busy when I had arrived, cooking Sunday dinner for her family. I had watched her as she chopped the meat into cubes and stirred it into a big, black stew pot on the small gas stove in the caravan. I had never cooked anything; mum would chase me out of the kitchen while she prepared our meals.

'Dad and Kev will be back soon. You'll need to go before they get back. They don't like me mixing with you Buffer kids. They think I'll get ideas above my station.'

Christine's dad and brother had barely ever said a word to me. They'd glower through their dark fringes if I turned up when they were at home and would watch Christine and me as we sat and did homework.

'I don't think your family like me.' I patted one of the lurchers which was mooching under the work bench hoping for scraps to fall into its slavering jaws. 'Why don't you just tell them to get their own food, clean up after themselves.' I don't remember ever doing any housework as a child, mum just seemed to do everything.

'Aye that'll be right. I'd get a belting if I said anything like that to them. They expect me to be mum and wife to them. I know my place; you haven't got a clue Ginnie. They...' A shadow drew across her eyes. She turned towards the cooker, sniffing and wiping her hand across her face.

'They what?' She seemed to want to tell me more.
'Nothing.'
'Fair enough,' I said. I didn't press her for more, she'd had her chance.

As she filled another pot with water for the potatoes, I slipped the knife she had been using into the waistband of my trousers. It was sharp and pointed with a carved wooden handle and there was nothing like it at home. I excused myself, desperate to get out of the kitchen before she noticed the knife was missing. 'I need to get home. Mum'll have dinner ready.' I said.

'OK. See you at school,' she replied but I was already back on my bike. I transferred the blade to the basket, beside the jam jar, hiding both on a shelf in the shed when I got home.

As I stored my bike, Francis's brother Kevin stuck his head round the shed door, 'Have you seen Francis? Mum's looking for him.' Kevin was seventeen, the oldest of the six Hyslop children. He, and Tom's brother, Jim, were expected to keep an eye on their younger siblings. I was glad I was an only child, no-one to bother me or stick their nose in my business. I shook my head.

'I was at Christine's. He's maybe at Tom's?'

'No, Jim says the rest of the family are out. I'll kill him,' said Kevin. I knew he'd be annoyed that he had been tasked with finding his younger brother. I smiled.

By 8pm the whole street was out looking for Francis. It was still light, the late summer sun still warm. I joined some of the younger children searching the back courts, checking sheds and coal bunkers. The older boys were sent to the quarry. Despite being told to never go there alone, everyone knew that Francis never did as he was told. His bike was missing so he could be anywhere. His father and mine drove to the Bluebell woods, another favourite haunt. I stayed at home, ordered to get on with my homework while my mum sat with Francis's mum, reassuring her that they'd find him soon.

They did. I was shooshed off to bed when they returned with a pale, limp form cradled in Kevin's arms. I could hear his mother's screams from my bedroom.

Bastard wouldn't lie to me again.

Chapter 6
FIONA
2015

I watch Ginnie closely as she speaks. Each lift of an eyebrow, twitch of a lip or pick of a nail adds to her story. She pierces her tale with penetrating glances at me. She sees me as an interrogator, not a transcriber. I have to stop myself jumping involuntarily each time my eyes meet hers. I try to control the reaction; years of interviewing psychopaths and sociopaths for my books have hardened me, but I'm only human and have the same automatic responses as anyone else. My psychiatrist friends have taught me to remain impassive. I don't want my interviewees thinking they are getting to me, don't want to feed their egos. I need to keep in control of these interviews, but Ginnie has other ideas, she seems to be trying to shock me. I know she would relish any response on my part, any clue that she was getting to me.

Her voice, at times childlike, morphs into a caustically, cutting cadence when she speaks of how her alleged victims have wronged her. When she describes hitting Francis with the jam jar and holding his body under the water she shows no emotion. At times she keeps her tone flat, a matter of fact recounting of something from her childhood, trying to show that she was no more excited by the death than she was about any other incident in her life.

I put my pen down and lean forward across the gap between us.

'How did you feel when you hit Francis?' I ask. I explain that I need to get to the core of her actions. What did she gain from them?

'How did I feel?' she repeats the question glancing around her, seemingly searching in the depths of her mind for an answer, a frown crinkling her brow. 'I don't think I felt anything. It was something that had to be done. Satisfied I suppose. I felt satisfied. He had lied to me. That was unforgiveable.'

I turn the page in my notebook. 'What did you think Christine wanted to tell you?' I'm having trouble working out her relationship with the traveller girl.

'Probably that she was being abused. I wasn't interested. If anyone asked, she would say I'd been at hers that afternoon, but no-one ever did.'

'So she was your alibi? Was what you did to Francis pre-meditated?' I asked.

'If you're asking if I had gone to the quarry to kill him, I'm not sure if I can answer that. I wanted to hurt him; to get him back for lying to me but it was only when I saw him and he laughed at me that I knew I wanted to kill him. It made sense to me to go to Christine's. I doubt if I even knew what an alibi was at that age, but I didn't want anyone to know I'd been with Francis.'

This surprises me. I had expected her to say it was

all part of the plan. 'Clever...'

'Not clever. I'm a killer, not an idiot. As I said. I felt satisfied. I had dealt with the problem. No point in confessing to anyone or turning their suspicions on me. I felt good.'

Chapter 7
TOM'S DIARY

August 14th, 1966
Francis is dead.
~~I don't~~
~~I Can't~~

Tom 2015

That was one of those childhood memories which was burned into his brain, written the night he had discovered his best friend Francis had died. He picked up the evidence bag containing the jam jar. The string tied round its neck was worn, the label missing. He opened the folder which held the results of the investigation. Three pages, one from the path lab listing the cause of death as drowning.

Had any mistakes been made during the investigation? Three dead fish on the ground beside a small fishing net. Why hadn't they looked for the jam jar? Had they never fished for minnows before? Why was the net on the bank? Surely if Francis had fallen in, the net would be in the water too? "Accidental death by drowning" was the conclusion. A quick, easy answer readily accepted by a lazy force.

Ginnie had provided the jar as evidence that she had used it to kill Francis but there was nothing about it that proved it had been a murder weapon. Every home had them, and every child had one they used for fishing for minnows. Later searches of the quarry had found several pieces of broken glass in the water around the edges, a mix of jars, lemonade and beer bottles. Any of the jars could have been the one Francis had been using.

'Tom? Do you want a coffee?' Maria called up the stairs.

'Yes, please.' He stood up, wincing as a bolt of pain shot through his leg. Arthritis had set in, a continual reminder of the day he had been shot. He walked to the top of the stairs.

'Stay there, I'll bring it up.' A few minutes later he heard her climbing the stairs. 'What did Fiona say?' She stopped in the doorway, a tray laden with coffee and biscuits balanced on her hip.

He took it from her. 'She says Ginnie wants to see me. Wants to apologise.'

'That bitch isn't coming here when she gets out. I don't ever want to see her face again.' Maria had lost all affection she had ever had for Ginnie. Time hadn't mellowed her feelings. She would never forgive the woman who had almost wrecked her life. 'Seriously Tom. I don't want you to see her.' The look she gave her husband spoke volumes. Forty years of marriage had taught him that once Maria made up her mind about something there would be no arguing with her. She placed the coffee and a plate of biscuits to the left of the pile of folders on the desk, careful not to move anything out of place. She kissed him, taking the tray from his hands. 'I'm off to Joe's, I'm taking the girls to see *The BFG* so he and Ann can finish packing. Don't sit too long. Remember to take Bert out.'

When she left, he picked up one of the files, absently sipping his coffee as he read. Thoughts of the dog lying in the kitchen soon disappeared from his mind as he immersed himself in the paperwork.

He read the file on Francis's death. Ginnie had admitted killing Francis, had described in detail how she had knocked him unconscious then held him under the water, drowning her best friend. The doctors who had examined Francis's body had double checked their notes and concluded there was no evidence that Francis had been killed deliberately, agreeing with the initial findings from twenty years before. They were positive that Francis had slipped and fallen into the quarry, dislodging rocks and sods on the way. The damage to the back of his skull was consistent with striking against a rock and there was evidence of the bank being disturbed and further stones hitting his prone body.

When the 1986 investigation team had asked for Francis's body to be exhumed and examined, their request had been denied. Neither the church nor the family was interested in dragging up the past and the Procurator Fiscal had agreed. No one believed that Ginnie, a tiny girl, could have killed her friend. They were content to believe the original examiner's findings – Francis had slipped, hitting his head on rocks on the way in and had drowned. A tragic accident. The time had long gone when other evidence could have been found, Tom had to agree with their findings.

He rubbed his knee. A reminder of why Maria was so against what he was doing now.

Chapter 8
GINNIE'S TRANSCRIPT
1966

The night before Francis was to be buried in the cemetery beside the Catholic church they worshipped in, Tom came across the road and asked to see me.

'My mum says you should come and say goodbye now if you're not going tomorrow.' He stood on our doorstep, still in his school uniform, green jacket and grey shorts, grey socks and white shirt. His tie was undone and hung limply round his neck. Francis's body had been brought from the chapel the previous night and the coffin would sit, open in the darkened living room until the hearse came the next day.

I didn't want to go, but Tom insisted, and he dragged me across the road to Francis's house. Every bit of me wanted to run but he held tight to my arm and pushed me forward when Kevin answered the door. 'Hiya Ginnie,' he said turning to Tom, 'Your mum's just away Tom. Mum says to take you through. He's through here.' He led us into the living room. The main light was on, and the curtains drawn. The coffin lid was up revealing the pale, still form of the boy who had been my best friend.

There was a strange smell in the room, sweet, cloying, infiltrating my head even though I tried to breathe through my mouth. Tom approached the coffin and bent to kiss Francis, mumbling some words which I guessed were a prayer. Mrs Hyslop busied herself around the room, tidying cushions, lifting and replacing the vase of flowers which had been sent from the school. They were already wilting in the stifling heat. Her red rimmed eyes were full of tears, but none fell.

'Come closer Ginnie.' She held out her hand, but I kept mine firmly behind my back. I wasn't going to kiss the cold, dead body lying in front of me, surrounded by emerald silk. She saw the stubborn look on my face. 'It's ok. He's with Jesus and Mary now,' her voice caught, and she coughed. 'You don't have to kiss him, just say goodbye.'

I took a step closer. 'Bye-bye Francis.'

I wanted to add, "LIAR" but refrained.

'Are you not sad?'

Tom and I sat on the front steps of Francis's house, pulling our legs in when visitors squeezed past to pay their respects. His face was smeared with dirt where he'd wiped the tears from his eyes.

'Not really. He lied to me and stole from me, and I haven't forgiven him.' I picked at a scab on my knee.

'You have to forgive him so he can go to heaven.' Tears welled in his mismatched eyes. It was the first thing you noticed about Tom, one brown and one blue, they gave him an alien look. He blinked hard, trying to hide how upset he was.

'No such place. He'll just be eaten by worms and rot

in the ground.'

Tom crossed himself and shouted that it wasn't true. Mrs Hyslop came to the door to check on what was happening. She hauled Tom up by his arm and dusted him off, wiping his face on her apron.

'Off you two go. I'll see you tomorrow, Tom. Tell your mum thanks for the casserole.'

As was normal in the close-knit community everyone had stepped up to help after Francis's death. Cooking and baking for the family, offering lifts to the funeral home, the registrar's; anything to help the grieving family. The priest was a regular visitor to the house, everyone intent on keeping Mrs Hyslop busy making endless cups of tea. Anything to distract her from the fact that her youngest child lay dead in the next room, curtains drawn to banish the light.

Chapter 9
FIONA

2015

'Can you imagine how Tom felt?'

'Not really. His Catholic upbringing had indoctrinated him into behaviours that are alien to me. Francis was dead. He couldn't hear me, nothing I could say would bring him back.' Her brow furrows as if the question is ludicrous. 'What was I meant to say to him?' she adds finally.

Until she says something like this I find it difficult to align the woman in front of me with the callous child she purports to have been. Ginnie looks like everyone's favourite aunt, small, delicate with a gentle lilting voice. My opinions of her are changing daily.

'Do you think Tom's beliefs are any less important than yours?' I am trying to elicit some sign of empathy from Ginnie. My question makes her laugh.

'Oh Fiona. Really? What's this? "Lack of empathy – tick". Do you think I'm a sociopath? A psychopath? I'm sure you can tell me the difference.' She opens her eyes wide feigning the look of a mad woman. 'Oh no, I forgot. You're not a psychologist, are you? Do you know the difference? Go on, scribble your notes, don't miss anything. Nice pen by the way. I used to have one like that.'

Chapter 10
GINNIE'S TRANSCRIPT
1966

The next day, while everyone else went to the funeral, I was packed off to Ranald's farm where my father kept his greyhounds. My parents didn't think it was good for a child to attend funerals and I hadn't even been at my gran's one six months previously. I had shown no interest in going and was happier to spend time at the farm. It was a small croft really, with hens and pigs and a half dozen or so Jersey cows dotted in the rough fields round the small white cottage. Ranald was a family friend. He would turn up at the house with a chicken; feathers, feet and all, for my mum to prepare for Christmas or Easter. We also got Jersey milk from the herd. Metal churns of the thick creamy liquid, from which my mum made butter when there was a glut, sat in shining rows in the cool of the byre.

'I'll keep an eye on her,' I heard Ranald tell my father. 'She can help feed the beasts. You get on to the funeral. Poor boy, shame to lose someone so young. Is she missing him?' He nodded towards where I stood in my pink and white floral summer dress. Not really the right attire to wear when feeding hens, but my mum had thought I'd better look decent even if I wasn't going to Francis's funeral. I saw my father shrug. They exchanged some more words, then my parents drove off in the car they had borrowed from Uncle Robert for the day. They were picking up some of the neighbours on the way.

'Come on Toots.' Ranald extended a short, fat arm to me. I refused to take it, his hand looked deformed, a tight metal-strapped watch seemed to cut off the blood supply from his arm and his hand looked swollen and dark.

I hated him calling me Toots.

'It's Ginnie.' I also hated the full name I'd been given. *Virginia*. Named after my grandmother.

I ran into the barn. I knew where the hen food was kept. Filling the galvanised bucket, I struggled with it to the hen run, firmly gripped in both hands, banging the metal edge against my shins. I tipped most of the contents into the round feed bins but kept a few handfuls aside to hand-feed my favourite hens, the Black Rocks, the friendliest or maybe bravest of the flock. They came and sat beside me pecking the corn from my outstretched hand. Ranald watched me. It wasn't only his arms that were short and fat. All of Ranald was short and fat. He wore stained, dark green overalls. I don't think I had ever seen him in any other clothes. And he smelled. A mixture of pig, hen poo and stale sweat.

He came into the hen run, the corpse of one of the white hens swinging in his grip. 'Here, pop that into the kitchen and take it home for your mum.'

I reached out and took the still warm body and ran to the cottage, throwing the bird on to the kitchen table where it lay among piles of newspapers, cups and dirty dishes. Ranald had followed me and, as I turned to leave, he appeared in the doorway. He was stretching the expandable bracelet of his watch and pinging the body back against his arm. He removed the watch and placed it on the mantlepiece.

'Come and help me feed the pigs now.'

I squeezed past him, my tiny body brushing between his stomach and the doorframe; I held my breath, trying not to inhale the sourness of him. 'The swill's over there.' He pointed to another bucket and I struggled to lift it. The mashed- up contents, boiled food waste, threatened to slop over my dress. I took a few steps, the handle gripped firmly in my hands.

'Here, give it here.' Ranald took the bucket from me, swinging it easily in his small pudgy arms. 'The weaners are big now, you'll not recognise them.' He spoke about the piglets which the large white sow had had the last time I'd been at the farm. Now eight months old they looked like adult pigs.

We reached the pigsty. Ranald calling the creatures as he tipped the contents of the bucket into an old sink. The twelve young pigs galloped towards us across the field where they'd been shading from the sun under an old spreading oak tree. They were ugly, big brutes, no longer the cute little creatures they were when born. Their screams rang out across the field, battering against each other and nipping at the heels of the sibling in front in the race to get to the feed trough.

Ranald turned from his task. 'There's some old apples in the shed, bring some and you can feed them. Need to fatten them up, they'll be going for slaughter soon.' He handed me the bucket. His talk of slaughter didn't bother me; I was well aware of the pigs' fate.

The shed was dark and dusty, spiders' webs hung across the corners. I brushed a grey tendril from my face as I reached under the shelf to get to the apples, last year's windfalls stored for pig food. I have no fear of spiders, beetles or any other creepy-crawly creatures except daddy longlegs. I am absolutely terrified of their dangly legs, their bouncing flight causing them to catch in my hair. I peered round the shed but there was no sign of any, so I grabbed a few handfuls of apples, placing them in the bucket and returned to where the pigs had finished the food in the trough. Ranald watched me as I walked towards him, my skirt held high, caught on the handle of the bucket. He lifted me over the fence and into the field.

I held an apple in the flat of my hand and offered it to the nearest pig. Ranald slapped it from my hand. 'No, just throw it on the ground. He'll have your hand off, he's not a pony.' His cackling laugh joined the squeals of the pigs. The scent of the apples exciting the permanently ravenous creatures, I dropped the rest of the apples into the trough and picked out a few to drop on the ground in front of the pigs. They snuffled and grunted, each grabbing a fruit and crunching it, long drools of saliva trailed from their mouths, their teeth making short work of the hard flesh. They moved towards me, biting and pushing each other to get to the trough. 'Watch your toes. You don't want them nipped off,' Ranald shouted from across the fence; I threw the remainder of the apples towards the advancing pigs and ran to him. He lifted me back over the fence, laughing at the fear on my face. He ruffled my hair.

'Come on Toots. Want to help with the ploughing?'

'Yes please. And it's Ginnie. My name's not Toots.' I ran after him as he crossed the farmyard and hefted his short fat body into the cab of the red tractor that sat at the field gate. I clambered in after him. Trying not to breath too deeply, the stench which emanated from his sweating body, almost made me gag. He started up the engine and we swung into the field, recently cleared of the silage crop which now sat in bales at the end of the field. He lifted his left arm and swung round to look behind him, dropping the blade of the plough, cleanly scything through the dry soil.

'Here, do you want to drive?' He indicated the wheel of the tractor. I didn't need to be asked twice and stretched across to grab the small steering wheel. Space was tight in the small cab. 'Here sit on my knee and I'll work the pedals,' he patted his knee. I clambered over the seat and sat between him and the steering wheel. 'Ready? Go.'

I screamed with laughter. I was steering the tractor. Ranald had put his hands in the pockets of his overalls to let me know I was in charge. I could feel his hands rubbing against my bottom. I stared grimly ahead, trying to keep the vehicle on a straight trajectory down the field line. Glimpsing behind me I noticed Ranald had even shut his eyes. As we reached the end of the field, I swung the wheel round sharply to the right and the tractor teetered on two wheels for a second or two. Ranald made a grunting noise. He wriggled in the seat.

'Careful Toots, nearly had us over then.' He slowed the tractor, allowing me to gain control again. We continued, making another sweep of the field until we reached the far fence.

'Well done.' Ranald stared across the newly furrowed rows. 'Some are a bit wavy, but not bad for a first attempt. Come on, let's get some lunch. Your parents will be back soon.' I jumped down from the cab and ran to the cottage. Ranald followed behind, his gait slow and deliberate, wiping his hands on his overalls.

Chapter 11
TOM'S DIARY

August 20th, 1966

I wish Ginnie had been there. She'd have been brave, she's always brave. She'd say something to make me smile, make everything ok, because right now nothing is ok. I watched them as they lowered Francis's coffin into the ground. My best friend, apart from Ginnie, was in a wooden box and was being covered in soil. Ginnie says he'll just rot and be eaten by worms, but I want to believe he'll be in heaven, looking down on us.

When we went to say goodbye to Francis, Ginnie didn't cry, just looked at him and said goodbye. Mum said it was because she was upset, that deep down Ginnie felt the same as me and she was just being brave to make me feel better. I'm not so sure. I've never seen her cry; not when she broke her arm, or when she was bitten by one of the tinker's ponies, or when her gran died. I wish I was like her. Whenever I think about Francis, I get a big lump in my throat. Mum says it's ok to cry but Jim says I'm being a sissy. I try not to, but I can't help it.

I feel guilty because it's my fault he died. If I'd gone fishing with him, he'd still be here. I could have pulled him out of the water or not let him get near the edge. If I hadn't been at my gran's we'd be playing football or cricket this morning, not standing there in that horrible place.

The priest said a prayer as people started throwing soil into the grave. Mum handed some to me but I dropped it on the ground, I didn't want to go near the edge of the grave. What if I heard him knocking on the coffin, what if it started to open? I stood behind Jim, hoping no-one noticed me snivelling.

I wish Ginnie had been there.

Tom 2015

Tom scratched his head, trying to remember the finer details of the day he had written this entry in his diary. Ginnie's reaction to anything which would have any other child in tears was something he took for granted, a part of her make-up. A few years after this, at her mother's funeral, she had sat in front of him in the crematorium, her back straight, her gaze firmly fixed on the trees and gardens which could be seen from the service room. At the wake she had busied herself handing out sandwiches and making endless pots of tea for the people gathered to pay their respects.

He recalled the day she had broken her arm. The three of them, Ginnie, Tom and Francis had been on the roof of the newly-built flats, after squeezing through a tiny gap provided by a loose chain on the door that led to the roof of Morven Court. Francis and Ginnie had scrambled on to the parapet that surrounded the roof, shouting into the wind. Even on calm days there was wind at the top of the flats, it funnelled between the buildings and caused tiny dust devils to skitter across the roof. As they held their arms out, the wind billowed their clothes making them look like two colourful kites fluttering on the edge of a cliff. As one they had yelled, 'JUMP!' and Tom had screamed, until he had realised that they had jumped backwards on to the roof. Ginnie fell awkwardly, her ankle twisting, and she landed in a heap beside him. She sat up, her arm hanging by her side, twisted at an unnatural angle. They had helped her up, but she shrugged them away, cradling her damaged arm with the other. Back home Ginnie had simply bitten her lip and glared through her blonde fringe at her mother when she had wrapped the broken arm in a towel as a makeshift sling to take her to hospital. Not a single tear.

He shuddered when he remembered the next time Ginnie had played that trick on him – on the same parapet, on the same block of flats. He shook his head and returned to the examination of the diary.

Her words about there not being a heaven had shocked him as a child, but he now understood and agreed with Ginnie's stance on religion. Despite Maria still attending church each Sunday, he seldom joined her; too many abused children, dead teenagers and evil bastards had knocked his faith. Maria had tried to get him to go, ensuring that their son was raised in the faith he had been Christened into. She argued that the priest had noticed his absence, so he had gone along with her wishes, but once Joe was older, he stopped attending the weekly mass, passing on various excuses, usually work-related.

He read the diary entry again. Part of him still felt that guilt; he had recurring dreams where Francis appeared, his blue tinged lips calling his name, weed and debris from the quarry matting his hair. If he'd been there that day Francis wouldn't have died. Whatever had happened to his friend, he would have been there to stop it. He would have dragged him from the water or something. At least tried to save him.

He didn't believe that Ginnie had killed Francis. Despite her insistence during interview and in the transcripts Fiona had shown him, he couldn't make himself even consider the possibility.

Something in the tone of her voice when she had spoken in the interview room had chilled him though. She said she had wanted Francis dead. Her reaction to seeing his body in the coffin underlined this. It wasn't that she was afraid of seeing her dead friend, it was that she didn't seem to even care. Neither of these things though were enough to persuade him that he was wrong about the decision he had come to that Ginnie was making up the tales she was telling.

He turned the page of the report, biting the inside of his cheek as he read on.

The bruises on Francis's body, at the time thought to have been caused by falling and hitting the rocks at the side of the quarry, could easily have been the result of Ginnie's version of the story, holding her friend underwater with a branch was feasible. But was it likely?

There had been too much evidence to the contrary. Could a tiny ten-year-old girl hit someone with enough force to render them unconscious? The doctor providing expert witness evidence during the investigation had explained that a lucky strike on just the right part of the head could have knocked Francis out and made him unable to stop himself drowning. In Tom's opinion the chances of that were slim. In his time on the force, he had never seen a case like it, had never seen a child show the behaviours Ginnie was saying she had, the ability to kill with impunity. He had studied the Mary Bell case, but Bell's known aggressive and disturbing behaviours and mannerisms had not been apparent in Ginnie. His childhood memories of Ginnie were of a tough but kind friend, not someone to fear or despise.

He took some notes on his laptop and placed the folder to the right of the pile, straightening the edge as he did so. He returned to his diary.

Was Ginnie brave? Had her behaviour at funerals

and when looking at the body of her dead friend been a sign of bravery or insensitivity? Maria said she was callous, that Ginnie didn't care about anyone but Ginnie, a typical sociopathic response. But he knew that Ginnie did care about some things, some people. Or was that an act? He couldn't believe that someone could put on an act for so long. He had only ever felt affection for, and from, his friend. Surely a sociopath couldn't keep up that pretence for a lifetime?

Looking back at their childhood Tom realised now that Ginnie had freedoms most children weren't afforded. Freedoms or a lack of concern? Had her parents ever shown her love and affection, was that where she had learned not to show emotion? He was amazed at her recall, the detail in her discussions with Fiona, transcribed word for word for the book made him think he was somehow lacking, that his memory was nowhere near as precise as Ginnie's. His diaries helped him, reminding him of his feelings at the time but large parts of Ginnie's tale, even when they involved him, were vague memories to him.

Chapter 12
GINNIE'S TRANSCRIPT
1968

During the summer holidays when I was twelve, just before I was moved up to secondary school, I was sent to stay with my cousins while mum and dad went on holiday to somewhere in the north of Scotland. My aunt said they needed some time alone and that they thought it would be good for me to be with other girls; that I was becoming too much of a tomboy. The two sisters were extremely close, Charlie, a year younger than me and Ada, who was only two months older than me were more like twins than sisters. We spent our time pretending we were various girl singers; I was Lulu mainly because I was short and had a very loud singing voice. Ada was Sandy Shaw and would sing in bare feet, Charlie was Cher. On typically wet summer days we'd perform in their bedroom, singing into hairbrushes while jumping on the bed. When the weather cleared, my aunt would chase us from the house and we'd go play tennis or explore the area.

At night we'd play board games, *Operation* or *Monopoly*. Or, in fine weather, gather in their neighbour's shed with a group of other local girls and tell ghost stories, scaring each other witless with tales of mad men decapitating a girl's boyfriend then banging their victim's head on the roof of the car the unsuspecting girl sat in. Or the one about the old mad man who lived in the woods nearby. He lured girls to his den by making the call of a distressed kitten or puppy then skinned his victims alive. We swore you could hear their screams through the open shed door.

One of our favourite places to visit was an old tunnel which led from one end of Coatbridge to the other, a remnant of the war we guessed, although we never did find out its exact use. We'd walk along the tunnel, sharing a torch and jumping at every noise and shadow which reared from the depths of the concrete dome.

On one of those days, Ada, Charlie and I set off on our own with Lassie, their pet dog. Lassie had a trick, she smiled by showing her bottom teeth when you mentioned the word "biscuit". It looked like she was growling. She was a Heinz 57 mongrel. Heaven knows what her lineage was, but she was black, roughly the size of a collie, but with short wiry hair and a grey beard which made her look like an old man. Why she'd been named after the rough collie on TV I had no idea.

We were dressed in shorts and cotton tops – feet encased in brown plastic sandals and short socks of varying hues. As we approached the tunnel, we noticed a man sitting on the bench on the walkway which led to the entrance. He had on a heavy overcoat, scarf and flat bunnet. At his side was a brown leather shopping bag and he appeared to be sleeping. I pointed to him and whispered, 'He must be boiling.'

'Dare you to go and poke him.' Ada pushed Charlie

towards the bench.

'No way. I'm not going near him. He might be the killer from the woods. Shh. Don't wake him.'

'I'll do it.' I picked up a stick and strode over to where the tramp sat. I thrust the stick at him, he grunted and turned, swatting the annoyance away. I dropped the stick and ran back to where my cousins looked on in awe.

'Quick, he's waking up.' I shoved the two of them towards the tunnel and we ran full pelt into the cool darkness of the doorway. We stopped and checked behind us, giggling. I enjoyed my cousin's company, despite my being a tomboy it was fun to have girls to play with and I fit in easily as their leader. I'm not sure who had the most influence on the other. My mum wanted me to be more feminine, less tomboyish but that wasn't going to happen. If anything, I was making them wilder, more daring than they had been. Once inside the tunnel Charlie took out her torch to guide our way.

'Watch out for rats.' Charlie swung the torch beam onto the floor in front of us. There was a sound behind us, a shuffling and rustling. Ada screamed and we turned to look back the way we had just come but there was no sign of any movement. We clung to each other.

'Let's go back.' Ada started to walk back towards the entrance. 'It's too far to the other end.'

I pulled Lassie closer on the lead. 'Come on then.' I led the way as we began to retrace our steps at a more urgent pace. Ahead there was a dark shadow against the side of the entrance. Charlie played her torch in the direction of the misshapen bundle. It was the tramp. As we got closer the light from the torch picked out his features. He was staring straight at us, but it was what his hands were doing that horrified us. He had his penis out, and he was rubbing it with his left hand, running his hand up and down the length of it. We all screamed then and ran, tripping over each other and the barking dog, in a blind panic to get out of the tunnel and as far as possible from the man. He emitted a low groan as we ran past, it reminded me of the noises Ranald made when we were in the tractor.

The man didn't follow us, but we didn't stop running until we were inside my cousin's front gate. Aunt Meg met us at the door, trying to get some sense from our garbled story.

'I've told you not to go down there.' She glared at the three of us, 'What were you thinking of?'

We all examined our shoes, unable to meet her gaze. 'Sorry Auntie Meg, I made them come with me.' I didn't mind taking the blame.

'Robert,' She yelled into the house and my uncle left what he had been doing and rushed to her side.

'What's up?'

She recounted our story. Uncle Robert clenched his fists. 'I'll get Billy and go and deal with this pervert. You stay here with the girls.'

Aunt Meg ushered us into the kitchen and made a jug of diluting orange for us. 'Here, drink this and sit down. What you saw was a bad man.' She then explained to us that what he had been doing was against the law and evil, using simple words even Charlie could understand. 'Always look for an adult if you ever see anyone doing that again, a policeman or a woman.'

Realisation hit me. Had Ranald been doing the same? I had no idea that old men would get their kicks from touching or looking at us girls, but I remembered Ranald's hands rubbing against my bum. I felt sick.

Half an hour later Uncle Robert returned. 'No sign of him. We dropped into the station on the way back and reported him. They'll send someone round soon to speak to the girls.'

'I'll let Karen and Mark know once the girls have spoken to them. Not that they'll be worried in the slightest,' said Meg.

I overheard what she said. Of course my parents wouldn't be worried. They knew I was tough and could look after myself. I'd never had to rely on them for support before so why would they start now? What the tramp had done was wrong, very wrong. The adults wouldn't be getting the police involved if it wasn't.

Later two police officers arrived at the house. The woman officer came and sat with us in the kitchen, asking us what had happened, her kind eyes and gentle voice aimed at getting the information they needed without scaring us.

'What did he look like?'

'He had black hair,' I ventured.

'No, it was brown,' Ada and Charlie chipped in. 'And it was all tangled and matted,' added Charlie, 'and he had on an old raincoat.'

'Duffle coat,' said Ada.

We argued over the colour of his hair, had he a beard, what was he wearing? Each of us had a slightly different version, there was only one bit we agreed on, obviously the sight of an erect penis had terrified us. We could all describe it in detail much to the amusement of the male officer. PC Davies glared at her colleague.

'OK you all agree he was dark haired, rough looking with a dark coloured coat,' she said and sighed. Our description could be any of the tramps that walked the Airdrie countryside. 'Thank you girls, you've been very helpful.' She folded her notebook into the pocket of a little bag she had round her waist. She rose and, thanking my aunt, pushed her colleague out of the door. I ran to the window as they left. I could hear the laughter of the young officer as he marched down the path.

A week later there was still no news from the police. They had forgotten about us. Not interested in the story a bunch of young girls had told, it was a joke. Even my uncle had stopped looking for the tramp. I overheard him tell Aunt Meg that there was no point, he'd be miles away by now.

But he wasn't. He was in the woods, sheltering in an old fort we had built the previous summer and had abandoned. I had seen him when I had been walking

Lassie. If the adults weren't going to do something, I would.

Chapter 13
GINNIE'S TRANSCRIPT
1968

'Have you taken your pill?' Aunt Meg busied herself getting everyone ready for church. The pills were for a condition which caused me to faint in hot stuffy places. Various tests had come back with no definite results, but our family doctor had prescribed me with phenobarbitone, thinking I had a form of epilepsy. Every day I had to force down one of these foul-tasting pills, terrified that if I didn't, I would black out and collapse as I had done several times during assembly at school.

That Sunday I was tasked with taking Lassie for a walk while my aunt, uncle and cousins went to church. Going was not an option for me. My mother had explained her strong beliefs when it came to church going, or not going, to be more exact. Her father had been a member of the Orange Lodge and she and her mother had attended Orange Walks and Eastern Star meetings, but at the age of eighteen she had seen through the charade and left both the lodge and the Church of Scotland. She raised me with the belief that once I was old enough to understand religion, I could choose to join a church or not. She was not going to indoctrinate me the way she had been. Aunt Meg respected her wishes, and I was never expected to go with the family on the

Sundays I stayed with them.

I set off up the hill past the graveyard while they trooped into the church in their Sunday finery. Aunt Meg had managed to get me into a dress. I wore brown plastic sandals and had been warned to stay on the path and not get dirty. I had other plans. I was heading to the woods to find the tramp. What he had done was bad and he'd have to suffer. My fingers played with the knife I had hidden in the waistband of the dress. Since stealing it from Christine I had carried that knife everywhere with me.

As I approached the clearing where I knew he had set up camp I could smell smoke. He sat in front of a small fire; an empty whisky bottle lay beside him. He was swigging from another half-finished bottle. He looked up when he heard me approach and shuffled round to face me, staggering to his feet.

'What do you want girl?' he slurred. His voice was gruff, and he coughed, spitting green phlegm into the fire.

'Nothing,' I said in barely a whisper.

'Bugger off then.'

'What are you cooking?' I pointed to a black pot hanging over the fire. I needed to get close to him. I stepped closer, pulling Lassie with me, 'Is that tea?'

'Aye.' His lips split in a toothless sneer.

I nodded and moved to within two feet of his stinking, filthy body. He had removed the overcoat and I could see he was clad in a threadbare checked shirt.

Missing buttons caused it to gape open as he swayed in front of me.

'Do you have any biscuits?' I asked. At the word "biscuit" Lassie showed her teeth. The tramp's gaze left me and focussed on the apparently growling dog. I slipped Christine's knife from the waistband of my dress and rushed towards the tramp with it grasped firmly in my hands and plunged it into the centre of his chest where I hoped his heart was, praying that the *Operation* doll was accurate. His eyes bulged as I pulled it back out. Blood spread over his chest, some dropping from the knife on to my dress. He looked into my face, his mouth twitching then he slumped forwards onto the fire. I picked up the whisky bottle and poured the remains of the spirit over his body, jumping back as the flames whooshed high into the air.

I wiped the knife on the grass and placed it in my pocket, then picked up a branch and smacked it hard against my nose causing it to bleed. Black and silver stars swam in front of my face and the blood from my nose mingled with that of the tramp on my dress. As I walked from the clearing the crackle and what I imagined was the scent of burning flesh filled the air.

I arrived back at the church gate to meet my cousins, tears streaming down my face, blood and snot covering my dress.

'How on earth did you do that?' Aunt Meg took me into the toilets and placed a wet handkerchief against my quickly swelling nose, trying to staunch the bleeding.

'I fell,' I wailed, sobs wracking my body. I knew how to cry; I just chose not to. Now was the time to feign upset.

Aunt Meg pulled me close to her and wiped my face with the handkerchief, cleaning off the blood and snot. She whispered into my ear as she worked, soothing, gentle words to calm me. I melted into her arms. I'd never been hugged like that, and it stirred a deeply hidden feeling of belonging in my heart. I let myself be enveloped by her love, then just as suddenly pulled away. 'I'm fine. It's ok.'

She took my hand. 'Come on, it's not ok. It might be broken. Let's get you to the hospital.' She guided me to her car. At A&E I was examined, and my bruised nose patched up.

That night I walked into the hall and heard my aunt on the phone. 'She's in a state. You need to get home now...' She looked up when she saw me. She waved her hand, shooing me from the room. Through the door I heard her continue. 'Get home now. We'll bring her over tomorrow. For God's sake your daughter needs you.' She paused listening to the other side of the conversation that I couldn't hear. 'That's not the point. Just get home now!' I heard her slam the phone down and I ran across the room, not wanting to be caught eavesdropping.

The next day Uncle Robert drove me back to Airdrie.

'She's had a bit of a shock.' He handed me over to my mother, 'Meg says to keep her home for a couple of days and look after her. She'll phone you at the weekend.' His words were abrupt, and he left without sharing any of the normal pleasantries.

My mum took my bag and tipped the contents on to the floor. I had slipped the knife into the pocket of my anorak, which now hung at the front door. I'd collect it later and return it to the drawer. The blood covered dress was placed in the sink with cold, salted water in an attempt to remove the stains. There was a knock on the door.

'Tom's here.' My mum ushered him into the room.

'What happened?' Tom stared at my blackening eyes.

'I fell.'

'No. What happened at your cousins'? My mum says you were interviewed by the police.'

'Nothing much.' I told him about the tramp. Not about what I did to him of course. 'The police weren't interested, they just asked us loads of questions.'

'Must have been dead exciting. Did they take you to the station?'

'No.' It was becoming difficult for me to speak, blood and gunge blocked my nose and bubbled out when I breathed out, so I kept my answers short.

'I'd have been excited. I want to join the police when I leave school. My Uncle Gary's an inspector. He gets to catch murderers and all sorts.'

I pointed to the draughts board which sat beside my bed. 'Want a game?' I snuffled. Speaking was difficult. The clotted blood in my nose made swallowing difficult too. We fell quiet. I watched Tom as he concentrated on the game. This was the first time he had said he had any plans for his future. I had no idea what I wanted to be; never thought that far ahead.

A few weeks later the local paper reported on finding a badly burned corpse in the woods. Reports were that it was the body of a tramp. An unsolved crime that no-one really cared about.

Chapter 14
TOM'S DIARY

July 14th, 1968

Ginnie was interviewed by the police during the holidays. Lucky her – I wish I'd been there. I want to be a policeman when I grow up. I want to wear a uniform and have a truncheon and maybe a police dog. I'd call him Sabre.

Her nose was all bashed and bruised when she came back from her cousin's, but she said it didn't hurt.

We'll soon be starting high school. I have to go to Coatbridge on the bus every day. It'll be after five by the time I get home and then I'll have homework so I'm not going to be seeing Ginnie so much. She says I'll make new friends at St Pat's, that I'll forget about her, but I won't. I won't have Francis there to protect me; they'll notice my eyes. I can't exactly hide them. They'll laugh and say I'm a freak.

Ginnie says I'll have to grow up and look after myself. If I want to join the police, I'll have to get tough. I won't be able to chase criminals if I'm afraid. She's right.

Tom 2015

Throughout his childhood Tom had wished he had been like Ginnie. She had always stood up for him against bullies who teased him about his eyes. She could silence their taunts with a few well-chosen words, but he'd never seen her show any signs of physical violence towards anyone when they were children.

He recalled one particular day, when they'd been walking in the fields where the traveller camp kept their ponies. A group of children were riding the ponies bareback, gripping a handful of mane to keep control of the barely broken beasts.

'Hoy Buffers,' a tall skinny boy had yelled at them. 'What are you doing here? Fuck off back to your scheme.'

Tom had turned to walk away but Ginnie had grabbed his arm. 'Come on Tom.' She'd dragged him towards the group. Tom had been wary, these boys had taunted him the week before, joking about his odd-coloured eyes and pushing him around. On that occasion one of his neighbours had seen them and chased the boys off. He'd told Ginnie what had happened, and she had insisted they come to the camp today to 'sort it out' as she'd put it.

'Want a race?' she'd shouted as she approached a large, dun Highland pony, tickling the creature's nose and putting her head down to its mouth.

'Better watch Buffer, he'll bite you.' The boy had kicked his mount, a white Welsh pony, and manoeuvred it between Tom and Ginnie.

'No, he won't.' Ginnie grabbed a handful of the

horse's mane and sprang up on to its back. 'Come on tinker boy, bet I can beat you.' She kicked the beast's flanks and trotted to the burn which crossed the field. 'Race you to the oak tree and back.'

Tom had stood back, watching as the boy on the white pony had laughed and urged his mount to stand beside Ginnie's. The rest of the group had dismounted and surrounded him, nudging him with their elbows.

'If I win, you leave my pal alone,' Ginnie spoke quietly to the leader of the group.

'Deal.' The boy spat on his hand and held it out to Ginnie. She reached out to return the action when the boy yelled 'Go!' and kicked his pony into a gallop up the hill towards the ancient oak that stood sentinel on the ridge.

She smacked the dun on the neck and urged it in pursuit. The boy reached the oak fifty yards ahead of Ginnie and pulled on the pony's thin leather rein. His mount bucked and pulled, straining against the tug of the rein and swung wide around the tree. Ginnie shifted her weight and turned the dun tightly around the oak, kicking him into a gallop back down the hill towards the waiting group who were all yelling at their leader who was now ten yards behind her. She kept the lead as she jumped the burn and pulled up next to the group. She slid from the pony, patting it on the shoulder.

'Deal?' she shouted at the group's leader.

'Deal.' He jumped from the grey. Tom had expected

him to be angry and to want to fight but the boy just walked off, his band of friends following him.

'What did you say to him?' Tom asked Ginnie as they fed the ponies with carrots Ginnie had brought with her.

'Nothing. We had a bet. I won.' She grinned at her friend. 'They'll not bother you again.'

And they hadn't. The taunting stopped and although he'd never made friends with any of the group, he'd never had cause to be wary of them.

*

In that incident Ginnie had shown negotiating skills he had wished he had. She hadn't threatened the boys, seeming to know instinctively how to gain their respect. He would have just tried to avoid the group but knew now that running away would have encouraged them to continue their bullying behaviour. How could someone with that innate ability to deal with problems resort to the level of violence she said she had?

Tom returned to the diary. As he read his 12-year old's words, he smiled at the comment about wanting to join the police. He never had got the police dog called Sabre but had loved his time on the force. Even on his worst days when he'd failed to talk down a jumper on the Avon Bridge, or when his team had found the decomposed body of a child in the Bluebell Woods (such an innocent name for a place of death) he had never regretted joining up. After he had been injured Maria had tried to persuade him to retire on health grounds. They could live on his pension from the force and her teaching salary, he could start up a security firm. Her arguments were sensible but the thought of not being a detective was the stuff of nightmares for Tom. However, despite undertaking gruelling physiotherapy he had been tied to a desk job for the second half of his career.

When Ginnie had related her version of the tramp's death Tom, listening in the next room, had been incredulous. Could she really have stabbed an adult then watched him burn? There had been no sign of a stab wound in the pathologist's report although the body had been badly decomposed when found. Insects, birds and rats had eaten much of the flesh and soft organs. Had they even looked for a stab wound? He tried to remember the details of the report, searching through the files he found it. It had said it was accidental death by burning, presumably exacerbated by excessive alcohol consumption. The man had never been identified, no family had ever come forward to claim his body. He had been known to drink heavily, often being found unconscious by a member of the public.

Again, no direct evidence had been found linking Ginnie to the death of the tramp. The knife found in her drawer was spotless. Not a single trace of blood or tissue. He had a vague recollection of Ginnie whittling a piece of wood at some point in their past, but didn't all kids have penknives in those days? No-one thought there was anything wrong with children carrying knives when he was a child, the fact that she had kept one in a drawer as an adult was accepted by the officers who had investigated her confessions as just a child's collection, a box of memories. There was no suggestion that it was memorabilia with a more sinister meaning.

Chapter 15
FIONA
2015

'What did you think about being sent off to stay with relatives while your parents went on holiday?'

Ginnie looks across the table at me, one eyebrow raised. 'What has that got to do with anything? I didn't think about it. They often went away without me, it was normal.'

I wondered how often she'd been abandoned, fobbed off on babysitters or family. Worse still, left on her own. The fact she didn't think this was unusual spoke volumes.

'Do you still keep in touch with Charlie and Ada?'

'No. My aunt and mother had an argument, and I wasn't allowed to visit them anymore. My Aunt Meg was annoyed that my parents hadn't wanted to come home when she'd called them, despite my having a bloody nose. They said there wasn't anything they could do that Aunt Meg couldn't, but she was angry at their response.'

'And how did you feel about that? About your parents not rushing to your side.'

'I don't think it bothered me. I could look after myself.'

'And losing touch with your cousins? Did you miss

them?'

'Not really. They were ok but I preferred Tom's company and being at home.' She picks at her nails as she speaks. I wonder if this was a way of keeping focussed, a way of ensuring she didn't wander out of character. Her description of being with her cousins hinted at the friendship between them. She had said she had fun in their company but now she is insisting that she didn't care about them. 'I never really liked girls. Those at school were bullies and bitches. They liked their wee cliques, didn't they Fiona? Don't you remember what it was like at school?'

She sits back slightly, with a look that burrows into me. 'My memories of school have nothing to do with our task Ginnie, but it's not how I recall the Academy.'

'That's because you were one of the clique.' Her mouth twists into a sneer.

Chapter 16
GINNIE'S TRANSCRIPT
1968

'Are you excited?' Tom swung his legs gently, scraping the toes of his shoes on the ground beneath the wooden seat.

I viewed him upside down, I was hanging from the top crossbar of the swings, my knees draped over the rough metal pipe.

'About what?' I couldn't think of anything to be excited about.

'Big school.' He looked worried.

I swung down from my perch and stood on the swing next to his, pushing the seat from side to side. Tom had become even quieter since Francis had died. He hadn't made any new friends in the two years since the accident, no-one would be there to watch his back if the senior boys picked on him. We were going to separate secondary schools.

'It's just another day at school. Are you worried?' I asked.

'A bit. What if no-one likes me? What if the teachers don't like me either? Jim says some of them are evil. They like belting the first years. Says it's to make us behave.'

'You'll be fine.' He was obviously becoming quite panicked. 'The first days will be the worst.' I tried to calm him. 'Don't worry. Tell you what – do you want to go fishing after school?' I spent a lot of time at the quarry, catching perch and collecting newts and frogs to keep in an old aquarium I had in the garden. Tom never came with me anymore. We had been banned from going anywhere near the water, but I just told my parents I was going to Christine's. They never checked. I kept a fishing rod, hooks and weights under an old tree root at the edge of the quarry. I liked my own company and was happy to sit for hours but it would have been nice to have Tom there with me.

'No. I've got football.' He always had an excuse not to go. He had told me he had nightmares about Francis's body floating in the water.

'OK.' I jumped from the swing. 'There's your bus.' I ran off, not looking back. I didn't want him to think that I cared that he seemed to be growing apart from me already, avoiding meeting up.

I don't remember any more about my first day at secondary school. At the school gate I watched as some parents dropped their children off. I don't think mum or dad ever walked with me to school. I'm sure they did when I was very young, but I'd have been mortified if they'd accompanied me to the secondary school. Friends now say they can recall every detail of that day. Some have good memories, others were traumatised. To me it's just a blank. I do remember what happened after school though.

The late August sun was still warm at 4pm. I threw

my uniform onto the bed and changed into shorts and a light top. Grabbing a jam sandwich, I yelled that I'd be back soon and ran off before my mum could question where I was going. As if she would.

I needed to get to the farm before Ranald finished feeding the pigs. They were fed twice a day. If I ran, I'd get there before five.

'Hiya Toots.' Ranald was crossing the yard when I rushed in. 'Long time no see. What are you after?'

'Can I feed the pigs?' I skipped along beside him as he waddled to the feed store.

'Of course. Go and get the bucket. You remember where it is?' I could feel his eyes on me as I reached up to lift the galvanised bucket off its hook. I had started to develop breasts which stretched at the fabric of the light cotton top I wore. He squeezed into the shed beside me and lifted another bucket. 'I'll get the water.'

I filled the bucket with feed and carried it into the field to the trough. Ranald followed. I was sure he was walking behind me to get a view of my backside. Until I had seen the tramp masturbate, I hadn't considered that that was what Ranald had been doing in the tractor. Dirty little shit. I had been back to the farm a few times but always with my dad, walking the greyhounds or cleaning the kennels. Since the day of the funeral, I'd never been alone with Ranald. My mind screamed at the thought of what else he may have done to me if he'd had another chance. Sitting me on his knee and whatever perverted thrill that gave him was obviously just the start. I had an innate sense of self-preservation; I hadn't given him a second chance to abuse me even though I hadn't realised what he had been doing at the time. Now it was my turn to be the abuser.

I poured half of the feed into the wooden trough and pretended to be engrossed in the pigs as he filled his bucket from the water butt by the sty. As he struggled to the water trough I walked behind him, swinging my bucket back and forth. As he bent over the trough, I swung it really hard, catching him on the side of the head. He crumpled to the ground, his hands slipping in the mud around the water trough.

'You're a dirty, dirty man. Dirty outside and inside,' I screamed at him.

He pushed himself up on to his hands and knees. Once again, I swung the heavy metal bucket at his head before he could move to protect himself. This time it caught him on the point of his jaw, and he fell unconscious, blood pouring from the wound on his scalp caused by the first blow. The pigs rushed up, looking for more food. I poured the rest of their feed onto Ranald's still, blood-soaked head. I washed the bucket in the water butt then lay it beside his prone body which was now surrounded by hungry pigs. The sounds of them slurping and crunching their meal nauseated me slightly. Then one rushed away from the group, its prize of a jaw bone clasped firmly between its teeth. They were doing their job.

I walked off, the sound of their squeals echoing behind me.

Chapter 17
GINNIE'S TRANSCRIPT
1968

My mum turned off the potatoes which were beginning to turn into mush. 'Ginnie. Take a run up to the farm and see what's happened to your father. He should have been home an hour ago. His dinner will be ruined.' Like many homes in the sixties, we didn't have a phone so there was no way to ring the farm.

My dad stopped off at Ranald's every evening to feed and walk his greyhounds who were kennelled in one of the outhouses on the steading. I knew what would be keeping him. He would have found Ranald's body or what was left of it. A thought struck me. Would the pigs have eaten all of the small fat man? Would there be anything left for my dad to find? I grabbed my bike and pedalled as quickly as I could up the country lane towards the small farm cottage. There was a police car and an ambulance blocking the gateway. I dismounted and squeezed past, a thrill of excitement ran through me when I saw Ranald's body being worked on by the ambulance man. No-one noticed me approach and I got close enough to see the scarlet, mashed mess of my abuser's body. The ambulance man stood up, shaking his head. He spoke to my dad when he saw me, and I was grabbed and lifted into the air and taken back to the farmhouse.

'Don't look Virginia. Ranald's had an accident.' Dad carried me into the farmhouse and sat me at the kitchen table, fetching a glass and pouring some of the thick, creamy Jersey milk into it. 'You sit here while I speak to the policeman.'

'Have the pigs been fed?' I saw him wince. 'And the hens?'

'The pigs are fine. Go and feed the hens and shut them in.' This would keep me away from the pigsty.

'OK, once I've finished my milk.' Dad left and I gulped the milk down and went to the shelf where Ranald always left his watch. I slipped it over my hand. It was much too big, but I liked the feel of the metal on my skin. I put it into my pocket then ran from the kitchen towards the hen run. I knew Ranald was dead. The look on the ambulance man's face and the amount of blood I had glimpsed testified to that. I was disappointed the pigs hadn't eaten more of him. The hens clustered round me as I spread their corn on the ground outside their coop.

When dad came back to pick me up, I giggled, as I held my hands out for the birds to take food from my palm. 'They're tickling me.' I said, using the action of the birds to disguise the reason for my grin.

'Come on Virginia. Let's get you home. Your mum will be burning the dinner.'

He walked between me and the pig pen, trying to protect me from the horror scene that was being lifted into the ambulance, Ranald's mashed head was covered by a green blanket, but I knew what lay beneath.

Back home I was given my meal on a tray and told to watch the TV. This was something that never happened. We always ate at the kitchen table, but my dad had shaken his head when my mum had begun to serve the meal.

I could hear him telling her what had happened. He sat slumped in a kitchen chair, his head in his hands. I could hear the sound of my dad sobbing, and when I peeked through the kitchen hatch, I could see my mum with her arms around his shoulders comforting him.

I caught snatches of the conversation.

'No, she didn't see anything...They think he had a heart attack...Collapsed in the pig run...Horrible...Eaten...'

I tucked into my dinner. Neither of them spoke about it again.

Chapter 18
FIONA
2015

'You're not a real psychiatrist, are you?'

Ginnie is trying to distract me. I have been asking her to tell me about the abuse she had suffered at the farmer's hands, but she deflects my questions with one of her own. I note this, she has used the same technique several times. Whether she's hoping I'll forget my line of questioning or whether it's her way of blocking out unwanted memories I'm not sure yet. I go along with her this time.

'No, I'm a writer but I've studied psychiatric books and have friends who help my research. Obviously, you have spoken to many in that profession over the years. I need to know as much about you and your motives as you're willing to share to enable me to write your story. My knowledge of psychiatry is that of the interested writer. If I want my books to ring true, I need to understand what motivates my protagonists. If you're uncomfortable talking about it just say so.'

She sits back in her chair. We are sitting opposite each other in the visiting room at Cornton Vale, Scotland's biggest women's prison, set on the outskirts of Stirling. I'm Ginnie's only visitor. She has refused to allow Tom to visit, a fact that his wife is glad of. Maria finds it difficult to understand why Tom would want to see Ginnie, but her continual refusal to allow him to visit has prevented a clash between the couple. After each meeting I write up my draft of the book, letting Ginnie read it before we continue the next chapter.

'I thought you'd have a better job, been a lawyer or doctor. You were one of the school's shining lights, weren't you?' She stares at me with a look of disdain. 'I remember you had the Head Girl's braid on your blazer. It was obvious that you'd be chosen. The Academy loved girls like you, posh, popular. No way was I going to be rewarded.'

I wonder where we're going with this. She's right, I had been Head Girl but why would that bother her? I had no intention of sharing my past with her. She didn't need to know I'd dropped out of Uni in third year, unable to cope with the stress of academic life. 'If I remember correctly Ginnie, you were dux in sixth year.' I'd done a bit of research and had looked up the school records from 1974. 'Wasn't that reward enough for you?'

'I never collected it. No-one cared that I had the best results.' She stops at this point. Changes the subject. 'Ranald was just a dirty old man. He got his rocks off touching young girls, I doubt if I was the only one. The tramp was the same. They think they have a right to use girls for their own pleasure.'

I go along with her changing the subject. 'Don't you think you should have told the authorities of your accusations? Did you even mention it to your parents?'

'That went well with the tramp, didn't it? All they did was laugh. I was quite capable of dealing with it myself. And anyway, they wouldn't have listened to me, would they?' She leans back in her chair and folds her arms. The shrug of her shoulders challenges me to disagree. 'Ranald was their friend. They cared about him.'

I couldn't argue. With no physical evidence of abuse, it was highly unlikely that she would have been believed. I tried a different tack.

'Did you plan to kill Ranald?'

'If you mean, did I know exactly what I would do when I went to the farm then no, I didn't. If you mean, did I know I wanted to kill him then yes, I did. I knew I could get close to him, close enough to hurt him, knew he wouldn't be suspicious. He would never have thought a wee thing like me could harm him. He thought wrong, didn't he? Using the bucket to knock him out was the obvious way to incapacitate him and the pigs did the rest.'

'Do you think he was still alive when you left him?' If she had really intended to kill Ranald surely just knocking him out was a risky method. What if he had lived? He would have been able to identify his attacker. Had she not thought it through? Or as a child had she been so confident of her plan to kill him that she hadn't imagined failure? Or had it happened at all? Had Ranald simply had a heart attack and died in the pig run as the medics at the time had concluded? I watch carefully as she answers.

'If the pigs hadn't started eating him, I would have gone back and finished him off. A couple more whacks with the bucket would have been enough. As it was I didn't need to.'

I decide to stop there. She's relishing telling me this. I can't feed in to that.

Chapter 19
TOM'S DIARY

26th August 1968

Mr Queen's friend was eaten by his pigs. Everybody's talking about it. Ginnie said she saw the body. His face was all mashed up and she said she could see his brains.

I nearly threw up. She laughed; said I'd turned green.

I'm never going to eat bacon again. God knows what they feed them on.

Mum says I've not to spread rumours when I told her what Ginnie said. She says the man had had a heart attack and that the pigs were just nearby but how could Ginnie describe what she saw if he hadn't been eaten. How could a heart attack leave his brains oozing from his head? Ginnie knows how to paint a really realistic picture. I've never seen a brain before, she said it was grey and looked like boiled cauliflower.

Tom 2015

He picked up the plastic bag which held the watch which Joe had found so many years later. This had been the main piece of physical evidence which could be linked to a death Ginnie admitted to. No-one could explain how she could have the watch if it had not been taken from the body of the farmer. Would she have had the presence of mind to stop and remove it? She had been twelve. He couldn't imagine children in the sixties having the nous that kids have nowadays. He thought about Carrie, his granddaughter. She had argued that she was too old to go and see *The BFG* with Maria and Jess and had thrown a bit of a hissy fit. The promise of a veggie burger afterwards had gone some way to change her mind. He thought her knowledge of environmental issues was way beyond her years, but she insisted that all her friends discussed them. At twelve, he and Ginnie had football and ponies on their minds, not how to save the planet. Were they both as innocent as he remembered?

Tom read through the medical file detailing the farmer's death. Ginnie had said she had hit him with the water bucket and, when questioned about there being no blood on the weapon, had said she had washed it in the water trough. Was it possible for a twelve-year-old girl, especially one of Ginnie's build, to swing a galvanised zinc bucket hard enough to knock out an adult? He remembered the gasps from the investigating officers when she had described what she had done. Hardened cops stunned by what the woman across the table from them was saying. He Googled a similar bucket and checked the spec of the item. There was no mention of the weight. Did he still have an old one in the shed?

He hobbled to the garden, searching among the piles of rubbish in the shed finding the bucket at the back. He hefted it in his hand. It was heavy even when empty. No way could a child have swung it hard enough to render someone unconscious.

He had always thought that Ginnie was really strong as a child; he pictured her climbing up rope swings, rattling serves at him on the tennis courts but she was tiny, even now. Was she strong enough at twelve to kill someone? Back at his desk he checked the height of the dead man – 5 foot 6 inches. She had described how she had hit him when he had been bent over the water trough, how she had covered him in feed to get the pigs started. What she had described wasn't an impulsive act. The washing of the bucket suggested she knew that what she had done was wrong and the cold-blooded removal of her victim's watch had all pointed to pre-meditated murder. If she had been telling the truth that was.

When he was questioned, Ginnie's dad had said that Ranald never wore the watch when he was working; that it had been a gift from his deceased parents for his twenty-first birthday. He only wore it when he was away from the farm. Could Ginnie just have stolen it from the mantlepiece? The officer's report from the scene said he remembered the child running around the farmyard, trying to catch glimpses of the body. He had remembered the girl's father chasing her away but couldn't recall if he'd seen her going into the farmhouse. Had she just been witness to the aftermath of Ranald's death and woven a horror story round the circumstances?

The original report on the farmer's death had concluded that he had suffered a heart attack and had collapsed in the pig run, banging his head against the feed troughs as he had fallen. The damage done was not unusual according to other farmers who had been questioned at the time; there were several apocryphal tales of the fate of individuals who had fallen in pig pens. With no evidence to counteract the idea that his death was anything but an accident and natural causes, Tom pondered the idea. What had come first? The heart attack or being eaten by hungry pigs? He shook his head. His heart told him Ranald's death had nothing to do with Ginnie. It wasn't physically possible for her to have had any part in it. Anything else was impossible to comprehend. The Procurator Fiscal had agreed, and no charges had been brought.

He was pulled back into the present by the noise of his granddaughters running up the stairs. 'Hi Grandpa.' Carrie tumbled into the room. 'Can we take Bert out?'

Tom felt a pang of guilt when he realised he hadn't even thought about the dog while Maria had been out. He would be desperate for a walk. 'OK, come on.' He followed her downstairs to the kitchen. 'Grab his lead. What about you wee yin?' he called to Jess who was happily drinking a glass of juice at the kitchen table.

'You coming too?'

'On you go,' Maria shooed her husband and elder granddaughter out of the back door. 'Jess and I have a jigsaw to finish.' She knew Tom loved chatting to Carrie, and Jess wouldn't be able to keep up with the two of them.

They walked to the woods which surrounded the estate, the local walking group had built walkways and bridges across the streams which criss-crossed the area. Carrie told him all about the film, which she had obviously enjoyed despite her earlier misgivings. She waxed lyrical about the veggie burger she'd had at Mrs Brown's café. 'Grandma had a bacon butty. I wish she wouldn't eat meat, Grandpa. Can't you make her stop?'

'I don't think I can make your grandma do anything love. But it would have been a happy pig.'

'It wouldn't be happy when they killed and cooked it.' She ran off, throwing a stick for Bert who bounded along beside her.

He watched her as she ran among the trees with the dog. He couldn't imagine her harming anyone, never mind having the presence of mind to kill someone then hide the evidence as Ginnie had said she had done at the same age.

Chapter 20
GINNIE'S TRANSCRIPT
1968

'Where are we going?' I asked for the third time in about five miles. I gazed out the window as we passed Luggiebank.

'It was going to be a surprise but if it gives me peace, I'll tell you.' Dad was concentrating on the road. He'd borrowed his friend's car and we had been packed off for the day while mum met up with some old school friends. 'We're going to Stirling to Billy's stables. You can see the horses while Billy and I discuss some business.' I knew that would be *dog* business. Billy was another racing greyhound man, but he also owned a trotting stable. I'd never been to a racing stable before. This was my parent's way to try and help me forget the horror of Ranald. I didn't tell them I didn't need to recover, but the doctor they had taken me to had said I was suppressing my memories and needed to face the issues. I had no idea what they wanted from me. I had said I didn't think about Ranald and no I wasn't having nightmares, but the experts said otherwise. This day out was a part of my recovery. Dad and I had already been to the zoo and seaside in the past few weeks; places we'd never been before. Mum never came with us; she'd say she had a headache and let us go off together. I don't recall her ever going out with me and the treats were short-lived.

An hour later we drove into the yard of what looked like a big farm. There was a long stable block, and I could spot a variety of colours of horses, their heads nodding over the half stable doors. A small, dapper man walked towards us as we climbed out of the car.

He greeted my Dad then said, 'I'll get one of the boys to take Ginnie around. Colin,' he called across to a younger man who was trundling a large wheelbarrow laden with straw and dung across the yard. The man waved and beckoned me over. 'On you go Ginnie, your dad and I will be in the office.' He handed me a packet of polo mints, 'Here, the horses will love you for these.'

I ran across the yard and tagged behind the young man Billy had called Colin. He had an Irish accent which I liked. 'Come on, I'll introduce you to our horses.' He was kind, answering all my questions about the type of racing they did. Trotting was nothing like normal horse racing. He let me sit on a sulky, the little cart which the jockeys sat in during the races. We walked along the rows of stalls, each horse receiving a polo mint and a hug from me. I was in my element. These were nothing like the ponies I'd ridden when I was younger. Their long limbs and muscular bodies revealing the athletes they were. Behind the stable block was a running circuit where I could see more horses being exercised. Some walked the circuit, others trotted gently. 'They're not allowed to break into a canter, if they do that in a race they have to drop back and can be disqualified,' explained Colin. Some horses were harnessed into the sulkies and were doing circuits of the track. The power in their taught bodies was evident as they sped past.

'Can I have a go?' I asked Colin. He laughed.

'No chance Ginnie, it's not as easy as it looks.' He patted the nose of the bay that pulled up beside us. 'Even this old boy would pull your arms off.' He looked at my crestfallen face. 'OK you can sit in the sulky, but Danny will lead Frith.' He gestured to the jockey who had stopped the bay beside us. Danny stepped out of the carriage and showed me how to sit on the tiny, curved seat and hold the reins. He walked to the front of the horse and spoke to him gently. 'Walk on Frith.' He clicked his tongue and we walked forward. The sulky felt fragile and light under me. I wriggled in the seat, finding the best way to place my feet to keep my balance, only just reaching the board. As we walked round the ring, I grew bored. I lifted the whip from the holder in the side of the sulky and flicked it at Danny's ear. He jumped and dropped the reins in surprise. I slapped Frith on the rump, gathering up the reins, shouting encouragement at the horse to move and we were off. I turned to see Danny running off in the opposite direction, heading across the track to meet us on the other side. Frith trotted steadily round the bend then picked up speed on the straight, his gait high, hooves thudding into the ground. On the next bend I could feel the sulky rising on one side so shifted my weight to get the wheel back on the ground. It was just like riding a bogie. The wind in my hair was exhilarating, the speed of the horse exciting, much faster than the tinker ponies. I pulled gently on the reins as we reached Danny and Colin, and Frith slowed to a walk.

'Fuck's sake Danny, you'll get us sacked.' Colin aimed a slap at Danny's head. The jockey grabbed the reins, and Colin dragged me from the sulky. 'Don't you mention this to anyone.' He glared at me, his kind face distorted into a mix of fear and anger. I thought for a moment he was going to slap me too, but Danny stepped between us.

'Calm down Boss. She's fine. She's a natural; did you see how she righted herself on that corner?' Danny was finding it hard not to grin. 'You're ok lass, aren't you?'

'Great, thanks. That was brilliant.'

'Take him in.' Colin turned to me and held my arm, squeezing it a bit too tightly. 'Come on, you can help with the mucking out now. Less trouble.' He marched me to the stable block where he handed me a fork and a wheelbarrow, rubbing his face as if in disbelief at what he'd just seen.

'Ok,' I grabbed the fork and started shovelling the straw and dung into the barrow. 'Thanks for that. I promise I won't tell dad or Billy.'

I'd had a fabulous time, the thrill of the speed of the horse and the precarious balance of the sulky had set my pulse racing. It was the nearest I'd come to that rush of excitement when I'd killed someone.

Chapter 21
GINNIE'S TRANSCRIPT
1970

My fears that Tom and I were growing apart were unfounded. He always made sure I was included in parties and days out. We still went for long walks in the countryside, although we seldom went near the quarry. We both discovered we had a love for tennis and played on a regular basis at the club near the town centre.

It was during one of these tennis games that he first introduced me to Maria; more importantly it was during this game that I discovered I didn't need the drug I had been prescribed for years.

It was a hot summer's day. Strange how I seldom remember any wet, miserable days from when I was young. Summers seemed to stretch out into weeks of sunshine.

'Come on Ginnie,' Tom yelled from the gate where he balanced on his bike, 'Court's booked for nine.' I grabbed my bag and ran down the steps to join him. We met two of his classmates at the court. A tall slim girl with long, black hair which she had tied back in a swooping ponytail and a short, skinny boy with terminal acne were hitting balls across the net.

'Ginnie, this is Maria and Philip.' Tom walked across to join Maria at her side of the net. It was obvious I was going to be partnered up with Philip.

I looked at my doubles partner. He smiled, revealing crooked, discoloured teeth. I nodded my head to acknowledge him but didn't speak. Tom and Maria were standing close to each other. I couldn't hear what they were saying but Maria laughed, a tinkling, infectious giggle and she touched Tom gently on the arm. She wore a gold chain bracelet which caught the sun.

The game began. We played three hard sets. Despite his stature Philip was nimble and accurate with his shots and made a great doubles partner. We won two sets to one. Philip tried to hug me when I played the winning volley, but I ducked away from his embrace, and he did a little dance trying to hide his embarrassment.

'Well played Ginnie.' Tom placed his racquet into his zippered bag, popping the two tennis balls we had used into a side flap. He always used his own equipment; said he didn't like to touch anything someone else had used. The rest of us returned our hired racquets to the hut at the side of the court. 'I told you she was brilliant Philip.' He removed the balls from the bag, turning them in his hands before replacing them and smoothing the flap down over them.

We walked to the café on the bandstand, Maria and Tom held hands, but I resisted Philip's attempts to get closer to me. I flopped onto the bench, wiping the sweat from my brow, my hair plastered into my head and my tee-shirt sticking to my damp skin. I looked at

Philip. Black circles stained his armpits. Maria, however, looked cool and collected, unaffected by the searing heat of the sun.

She had a strange accent and when Philip asked where she was from, she explained that she had been brought up on Gozo, but had moved to Coatbridge with her Scottish father earlier that year.

'Where's that?' asked Philip.

'It's the next town along from here,' she said, straight faced then she laughed, and Tom joined her.

'Huh. I mean where's Gozo?' Philip blushed.

'Sorry Philip, I couldn't resist that. Gozo is Malta's second island. It's between Africa and Italy in the Med.'

'Oh. Why did you move over here?' Philip was asking all the questions I should have, but I didn't want to show any interest in Maria.

'Dad's Scottish and he's had to move here for work. They thought I'd get a better education in Scotland so here we are.'

Tom had started seeing Maria at the end of second year. She was in his year at St Pat's, and she seemed to like him for himself and not because he had eyes like David Bowie. At least the older kids had stopped teasing him about them; Bowie's look was one that a lot of the kids envied, and Tom had a head start on them. He had started growing his hair longer over the summer holidays and had taken to wearing flowery shirts and jeans. He was still Tom though.

We held the cold coke bottles against our wrists

and foreheads to cool us after the game and slurped the sweet, sharp liquid.

'What do you want to do when you leave school Ginnie?' Maria tried to draw me into the conversation.

I hadn't considered it. I loved sciences and wanted to do chemistry and biology O Grades but beyond that I hadn't thought. 'Don't know. I'll think about it.'

'Don't you know what you want to be?'

The thought had never struck me. I never made plans, taking each day as it came. I was clever enough for university, but I had never discussed the future with anyone. Mum and Dad weren't interested, they barely looked at my report cards.

'Maybe I'll be a jockey.'

'Aye, right,' Tom said.

'Aye. It is right. The guys at the stable said I was a natural.' Tom's double negative annoyed me.

Maria continued, 'I'm doing languages. Aren't you going to uni?' She looked at me with an incredulous expression on her face. As if it was strange that I didn't have fixed plans.

'Don't know. That's years away.'

'But you need to start thinking now – we need to choose next year's subjects soon. Do you prefer languages or sciences?' Maria clearly couldn't understand that the future was something I paid no heed to. I'd worry about it when it came.

'Sciences I suppose. That's what I'm good at.' I had won a beautiful fountain pen for being top in second year and I found most subjects easy. Except history. It wasn't so much that I dropped history as it dropped me.

Philip joined in. 'I'm hoping to study engineering at Strathclyde. If I get the results that is.'

Tom prodded him. 'If? You'll walk it. You're forever studying, and you always get straight As in all your exams. You and Ginnie would be rivals for the dux prize if she was at St Pat's. Some of us have to work really hard, you two have it easy.'

Philip blushed, his acne scarred skin burning crimson.

Tom was right. I had always been bright, winning prizes each year through primary school and top pupil at secondary. What he didn't know was that I did work. I read voraciously. Mum never checked that I'd put my light out so I could sit up until 2am, learning as much as I could about all manner of subjects.

'Talking of studying, I'd better get home.' Maria stood, gathering the empty bottles to return to the counter.

Tom jumped up. 'I'll walk with you.'

'What about your bike?' I reminded him we had cycled into town.

''I'll just push it.'

I was a bit put out that he wouldn't be coming home with me but could see he was besotted by Maria. I was happy for him. She was his first girlfriend, and she was ok. She wore her looks with an easy charm and would be good for his confidence.

Philip looked eagerly at me, but I ignored him. 'See you later,' I called as I cycled off. In my pocket I had tucked the bracelet which had slipped from Maria's arm during the game. I had spotted it glinting on the court and had picked it up, unseen by any of the others. Maria had Tom's heart, I had her bracelet.

Back home I ran into the kitchen to get a glass of water. On the worktop sat my phenobarbitone pill. I had been extremely hot, but I hadn't fainted or fitted. If I had known I hadn't taken it, would I have reacted differently? Did I need to take what was essentially a barbiturate? Had my doctor lied and mis-prescribed them for years? I had read up on them and knew what effects they could have on your body. I had missed out on so much, I couldn't take swimming lessons in case I had a fit in the water, I had never been allowed to go on school trips.

Why hadn't my parents questioned the diagnosis? They had put their trust in a decrepit old woman; someone who probably hadn't looked at a medical book since she'd graduated. I had to check that it wasn't a one-off. I had often fainted during Friday morning assembly in the hot, airless hall. We had to stand for the thirty minute meeting and I'd usually feel my breathing quicken, a strange taste would appear in my mouth and black spots danced in my vision. The next thing I'd be aware of was a group of stupid faces standing over me while the teachers tried to bring me round. Seemingly I would fit during these episodes, my body stiffening and twitching.

The next three Fridays I didn't take my pill before heading to school. Not once did I faint or fit.

From then on I stopped taking the phenobarbitone and never had a recurrence of the symptoms. I placed the bottle, which still contained about twenty tablets, in my dressing table drawer. Each month I added another bottle, I didn't tell my parents I had stopped taking them and picked up the repeat prescription as normal. Tucked into the back of the drawer was a box into which I placed the bracelet, alongside Ranald's watch, Christine's knife and a few other things I had picked up over the years.

I examined each of the items in turn before closing the drawer. I never knew when I may need them.

Chapter 22
TOM'S DIARY

June 6th, 1970

Maria said she'd go out with me. Oh God she's gorgeous. We met Ginnie and Philip for a game of tennis today. Ginnie won, as usual but Maria didn't mind. She's not like Ginnie, she doesn't have to win everything or be best at everything. She let me walk her home and she kissed me goodbye. SHE KISSED ME!!!!!!!!!!!

Thank you, David Bowie. If it wasn't for you, I'd still be the weirdo. The guy with the funny eyes. Now everybody likes me cos Bowie has the same eyes. It's cool to be my pal. I don't believe any of them. Except Maria. She really does like me. I hope.

Oh God, maybe she's the same as the others. Maybe it's just cos I look like David Bowie. I'm stupid. Of course that's what it is. Someone like her would never like me for me. Oh God. I'm an idiot.

Bugger

Tom 2015

Tom smiled. Maria still had the same effect on him. He'd never looked at anyone else, never been tempted to stray. What a wee softie he had been. No wonder his brothers had laughed at him when they read his diary. Maria had been his first and only love. Even when they were married, he caught himself watching her and wondering what on earth she saw in him. She could still elicit a thrill of excitement in him with just a touch of her hand. Ginnie had seemed to like her too at first. Or had she just put up with her for his sake? Maria had always been so sure of what she wanted from life, knew what university course she needed to become a languages teacher. She was the exact opposite of Ginnie who wandered through life, not making plans, falling into jobs as and when it suited her. Immediately after giving birth Maria had returned to her studies, catching up quickly with course work and graduating with honours.

They had both retired at the same time, she from her role as Head Teacher in St Pat's, the same school they had both attended as teenagers, he as Assistant Chief Constable. He had never wanted to get any higher in the ranks. He could have retired early following the injury he had received at the hands of Ginnie but had had preferred to stay on in a non-physical role. He had never intended to be desk-bound but if the choice was that or not being in the force, he was happy to do what was required. He had worked at Tulliallan, Scotland's police school, training the theoretical side of policing to new recruits. He had loved his job, knowing that he was filling a demanding and important role and that although the injury had prevented him doing the job he loved, he had paid back to the service in a satisfying way. Maria just couldn't understand why Tom was still loyal to Ginnie. How could he forgive someone who had hurt him, and more importantly, who had threatened their child? He sometimes wondered this himself. Time was a great healer; Joe had been unharmed and had never seemed to have been affected by the incident. Maria's argument was one of, "What if...". She imagined the worst-case scenario; imagined losing Joe. He understood but he couldn't agree.

Chapter 23
GINNIE'S TRANSCRIPT
1970

I watched as my hair fell around me, shocked that my mum was taking such drastic action. She wielded the scissors like pruning shears, until I was left with a short bob of curls. I had nits. Head lice.

'It'll have been that Christine. Dirty tinkers. You need to stay away from her.' I watched her in the mirror, saying nothing in reply. She'd changed her mind about being glad I had a female friend when she had noticed me scratching my head.

I knew where I'd caught the lice, Christine did what she could to keep clean but every few weeks she'd appear at school her hair plastered in an oily lotion. The 'nit nurse' had been round to check us all for infestation and the killing shampoo was the sign that someone had lice. I had been doing my homework, absently scratching my head as I worked on some maths problems. Mum had grabbed me and started checking my hair, the small white eggs of the insects, evidence of the presence of the adults. She had tried to comb them from my hair, but the tight curls made it difficult, so she decided to cut my hair short to make it easier to control.

I'd always hated my hair. I wished I had mum's thick, dark waves or even dad's dead straight black and silver, but I had blond, tight curls. Brushing it was painful and it always looked messy, but this was ten times worse.

Everyone in my class had laughed when they saw the rough job she'd done, it was obvious why I had been shorn. One girl had been particularly cruel. 'Don't come near me,' she'd screamed when I walked into the geography class. 'Keep your bugs to yourself.' She shifted forward in her seat, leaning away from my desk as if the lice could leap on to her.

'They're not fleas,' I spoke quietly. 'They can't jump.'

She wrapped her long black hair round her hand and secured it in a high bun. 'They can crawl across the desk, my mum told me,' she said, loud enough for everyone to hear. The rest of the class laughed.

'In your seats everyone.' Mr Johnston the geography teacher put an end to the taunts. I glared at the back of my taunter's head. Bitch.

Her name was *Fiona*.

On Saturday afternoon Tom, Maria and I went to the pictures to see *Butch Cassidy and The Sundance Kid*. It never occurred to me that they would want to be alone in the cinema. They held hands as we walked back out into the bright sunlight.

'That was brilliant; who was your favourite?' asked Maria.

'Butch.' I had no doubt. Most girls swooned over Robert Redford, but Paul Newman was my favourite. I had felt pangs of jealousy when Katherine Ross had been riding on the handlebars of his bike. This was a new sensation. The intense feeling of dislike for someone I didn't know, someone in a film, felt unnatural. I had to control it. The actress reminded me of Fiona from school, the same long black hair, pinned on the top of her head. Another bitch.

'Sundance is cuter.' Maria glanced at Tom who removed his hand from her grip and stuck it in his pocket. 'C'mere,' she laughed. 'Not as cute as you.' She grabbed his arm and held him close, kissing him on the cheek. He blushed, his neck and face flushed bright red. Was this what she was like when they were alone? I walked on ahead, pretending to be embarrassed by their behaviour.

'Come on you two,' I called over my shoulder, 'We'll miss the bus.'

*

When I saw Fiona at school on the Monday the creeping fingers of jealousy filled me, making me feel sick. I'd never felt like that before. Was it because she looked like Butch's love interest in the film that clawed at my throat, or was I still thinking about Tom and Maria? Tom was my best friend. The presence of Maria would never change that, no matter how much he loved her. I wasn't interested in Tom in any romantic way but the hormones rushing through my body were having I strange effect on my mind. I had never felt jealousy before. Why would I be jealous of anyone?

As I sat behind Fiona, noticing that she still leaned forward in her seat, keeping her hair away from my desk an idea formed in my mind.

I walked to the back of the room and sat down beside Christine. 'Do you want to come for tea tonight? We could do our homework and fix each other's hair and listen to my records. I've got the new Jackson 5 single.'

She looked at me from under her long fringe. 'Can't. I need to get home and make dad's dinner. You could come to the caravan. He won't be in until half five.'

I could make that work, so said yes.

*

'Sit down for a minute. I want to style your hair.' I sat on the bench seat, pulling my feet onto the cushion and patting the space beside me. Christine had said she had to get the potatoes peeled but I needed to get her to relax and sit beside me. 'Just for a minute.'

She sat beside me, and I turned her so her back was facing me. I took my hairbrush from my bag and began brushing her long, straight hair. 'Need to get the tangles out first then I'll show you how to pin it up.' I didn't really know how to pin it correctly, that wasn't really part of my plan. She had something I needed.

As I pulled the brush through the tangle of her hair, tugging at the knots to loosen them she told me about her dad and brother.

'They love me. They keep telling me that. Since mum died, I've been the woman of the house. Dad says I'm a good girl. Just sometimes he gets angry. He doesn't like me playing with you Buffer lackins. Says I'll get ideas from you about boys.'

'We whats?' I mumbled through a mouthful of Kirby grips. I'd heard the word Buffer used about us from the camp boys but lackins was new.

'Buffer lackins,' she repeated. 'Non tinker girls.' She continued to chat, telling me about her brother. I'd never seen him at school. I don't think he ever went, her dad made him work with him, selling and buying scrap round the doors.

'He hits me sometimes. They both do,' she faced the wall, I think she found that easier than speaking to my face, seeing my reaction. 'Sometimes they do more...' she tailed off, turning slightly towards me to see if I got her meaning.

'What else?' I knew she wanted to tell me.

'It's because mum's not here. It was dad first, then Jake did it too.' She was crying.

'Why don't you stop them?'

'How? No-one will believe me, and I haven't anywhere else to go.'

'No, I mean stop, stop them. Kill them.' The answer to the abuse was clear to me. 'Stab them when they're sleeping or when they're drunk.'

'Don't be daft. I can't do that.' She pulled her long

jumper round her.

'OK. But if you want them to stop you need to stand up for yourself.'

She shook her head. 'Forget I even mentioned it,' she said, a look of abject misery on her face.

'Sit still. Nearly done.' If she didn't want to speak about it, I wasn't going to push her.

Once I had untangled Christine's hair, I removed the tiny bone comb from my pocket and pulled it through her tresses. Each stroke caught at least one adult louse which I placed in a tissue on my knee. Once I'd gathered a dozen or so, I coiled Christine's hair round my hand the way I'd seen Fiona do it and pinned it in place on the top of her head with the kirbies. I folded the tissue and comb together and hid them in my pocket.

'There you go. Lovely.' I pushed her towards the mirror.

She stared at her reflection, tugging the oversized jumper she wore over her hips and stomach. She did look much better even though I'm not the world's best hairdresser. She glanced at the clock on the caravan wall.

'Shit. You'll have to go.' She pulled the pins from her hair and threw them at me. 'They'll be home in a minute, and I've not started the dinner yet. I'll get battered.' She ushered me out of the door and down the wooden steps.

I wasn't bothered about being rushed out.

I had what I had come for.

Chapter 24
TOM'S DIARY

June 10th, 1970

Maria does like me. I told Ginnie I thought that she was just using me because of the David Bowie thing and Ginnie asked her! Just went up and asked her! And she says Maria really, really likes me.

We went to the pictures, and she let me hold her hand when I walked her home. I didn't try to kiss her in the pictures, Ginnie was there, and it didn't feel like the right time. But she kissed me when we got to her door. I'm going to ask her to go to the pictures next week. Without Ginnie.

Tom 2015

He hadn't read his old diaries for years. Writing them had been his way of making sense of what was happening, a method of control when things seemed to spiral away from him. Maria had never commented on his habit, just accepted it as being part of his makeup. Now he was glad he had kept them. They dragged long forgotten memories from his brain, taking him back to his childhood and life with the two women who meant so much to him. He knew later entries in his diary would be more difficult to read. Life hadn't always run smoothly. It was good to read about his early times with Maria. He still couldn't believe his luck. His wife was as beautiful now as she had been as a teenager. He remembered the times he'd pinched himself in those early days, amazed that such a gorgeous girl could like him. He had fallen in love the first time he had seen her, his stomach lurching when she spoke to him.

She still had that effect on him.

He had almost lost her after he had been shot. His continued support for Ginnie was beyond Maria's comprehension. He had had to promise never to contact Ginnie and he had been able to keep that promise but only because Ginnie had refused to let him visit her in prison. He was grateful that Joe hadn't been affected by what had happened. He and Maria had agreed to not discuss the issue in front of their son, the boy seemingly believing that it was all a big adventure.

Now all the bad memories had come flooding back. Maria hadn't wanted anything to do with Fiona's project and it had taken all of Tom's persuasive skills to make her understand that he needed to help.

Something Fiona had asked him had him thinking. Did he think Ginnie had been in love with him? Had she been jealous of Maria? He had never given it a thought when they were growing up. Ginnie had never shown any obvious signs of jealousy and had never shown anything beyond close friendship to him. They were more like brother and sister than boyfriend and girlfriend so when he had started dating Maria he had never considered Ginnie's feelings. Would his behaviour have been any different if he had thought Ginnie fancied him? He pushed the thought from his mind – there had never been anything like that between him and Ginnie. Surely he would have noticed?

Chapter 25
GINNIE'S TRANSCRIPT
1970

The geography teacher wittered on about ox-bow lakes. No-one was really paying attention, too excited by the prospect of the holidays to come. I slipped the envelope containing the lice and nits from my pocket. Leaning forward I tipped the contents on to Fiona's hair, which cascaded down her back and on to the front of my desk. I had imagined her having her mane chopped; she'd look so normal without her crowning glory. The insects didn't move. I had expected them to scurry into her hair, but they lay there, like dust motes, dead. I dug my nails into the palm of my hand. The bitch had won.

It was the last day of the Christmas term. There was a party for years one to three in the afternoon, but I sneaked out of the hall, feigning sickness. I didn't want to mix with my year group or the younger kids. Some of the girls taunted me because I wore old-fashioned clothes, or didn't wear make-up, or didn't conform to their idea of a 'normal' girl. I was never a part of their cliques, never wanted to be. I was given permission to go home but instead I walked to the tinker encampment. Christine hadn't come to class that morning and I wanted to see her. She probably didn't want to go to the party either.

The area where their caravan had sat was empty, bare ground described a rectangle where it had been, and piles of rubbish lay scattered around. One of the women saw me and shouted across that they had gone. 'Back to Ireland with that whore of a lackin,' she yelled. 'Good riddance, don't want their type round here.'

'What do you mean?' Christine wasn't a whore. How dare she say that.

'Gone to find a home for her bastard child. The nuns will take it.' She glared at me, relishing the look of disbelief that must have flooded across my face. How on earth had I not noticed Christine was pregnant? Her clothes had been getting baggier and she always kept her coat on, even inside class. How had she kept such an enormous secret?

'Bugger off Buffer. There's nothing here for you now.' The woman slammed the door of her van closed.

I wandered home. My mind filled with thoughts of Christine. I knew she had been raped by her father and brother but had never given a thought to the consequences. She was only fourteen and was pregnant. What would it be like giving birth with just nuns around her? They'd probably hate her, no blame on the father of course, she'd be the one at fault. She'd have saved herself a lot of trouble if she'd just done what I suggested. People like her father and brother didn't deserve to live. I obviously couldn't have done anything to help her, they'd never done me any wrong. Why couldn't folk just take control of their own lives. Christine had let others use her. I'd never be that stupid.

Chapter 26
FIONA
2015

'Don't you remember me Fiona? Don't you remember taunting me and being a bitch? Don't worry, we can change your name in the book. No-one needs to know that I knew you as a child. That you were a bully and you and your friends made my life a misery.'

I had let Ginnie tell her version of her childhood memory although mine was totally different. I had long hair until I went to university, only cutting it then because I was in the rowing team and it became a pain to dry every day. I may have been in the same geography class as Ginnie in first and second year, but I don't remember the incident she mentioned.

Was this just Ginnie reacting to the jealousy she felt for her better-off classmates?

'I don't even remember being in the same classes as you Ginnie. Are you sure you're not mistaking me for someone else?'

She's watching me closely as I write notes. I put my pen down.

'Positive. Maybe I wasn't important enough for you to remember me, Fiona. But I definitely remember you.'

'We were the first of the comprehensive schooling process. There must have been two hundred pupils in first year. It's not surprising that I don't remember you.

I have a copy of our sixth year class photo and you're there, but I don't think we ever crossed paths. I certainly never bullied you, nor anyone else. Let's move on.' If she was lying about this though, what else was she lying about? What else had she imagined? 'Can we talk about your friend Christine now? You suggested to Christine that she should murder her family as they slept. What did you think when she dismissed your idea out of hand?'

'I thought she was an idiot. She could have stopped what they were doing. I told her what to do.'

'Did you offer to help?'

Her lip curls slightly, 'No, why would I do that?'

'Because you could? You'd done it before so why not for your friend?' If Ginnie was such a cold, calculating killer, I had to understand why she hadn't helped a fellow victim.

'They'd never touched me. It was Christine's job to deal with them. Not just trot off to Ireland at their whim. As I said in my transcript, why would I harm someone who had never wronged me?' She crosses her arms. Conversation ended.

Later, back in my office, I will transcribe her recordings on to my computer. If she was right, what level of 'wrongdoing' deserved death? For anyone else the perceived threat to her was more akin to a childish prank. To Ginnie it means the perpetrator deserves to die. I had never been a bully, but if she had thought that I was, or if I just annoyed her because I reminded her of an actress in a film, what had prevented her harming me more seriously, even killing me? I shivered, as if someone had walked over my grave.

Had I just been lucky?

Chapter 27
GINNIE'S TRANSCRIPT

1971

At the end of the Christmas term in fourth year, I trudged home through sleet and snow and as I rounded the end of our street, I spotted our GP's little red mini parked outside the gate. When I'd left in the morning mum had been complaining about a headache. She had suffered from migraines for years, what she described as rainbow zig zags heralding the onset of a headache which would render her bedbound for two or three days. As I had poured some cornflakes into a bowl for breakfast, she had said she was going to lie down.

'Never had one this bad before,' she said. She leaned against the stair handrail, one hand on the side of her head. Her face was ashen.

'Are you sure you don't want me to stay home in case you need something?' I poured her a cup of tea and followed her to her room. I always enjoyed a day off, but they were few and far between. My parents would send me to school no matter how ill I felt.

'I'll be fine, just need a wee sleep. Your dad's coming home at lunch time. You get off or you'll be late.'

I rushed up the steps, slamming the door behind me. The doctor was coming down the stairs from mum's bedroom. She ushered me into the living room where my dad sat on the couch, fear etched in his face.

'I've given her some painkillers,' said Dr Stannier. She was a short, middle-aged woman who had taken over the GP practice from her father. 'She has a condition called trigeminal neuralgia. It will ease over time, just keep her warm and give her these four times a day.' She handed him a bottle of pills. I stared at the large black mole on her chin, three long hairs sprouted from it, and they waved up and down as she spoke. 'Now where's that cup of coffee you promised me, Mr Queen?'

Dad turned to me, the worried look on his face easing as the doctor explained what was wrong with my mother. 'Ginnie get the doctor a cup of coffee, and tea for me and your mum. And some of the biscuits, the chocolate ones.'

The doctor settled on to the couch, making herself at home. 'Thank you Ginnie. Nice and strong with milk and three sugars please.'

I scurried into the kitchen and made the drinks. I grabbed one of the chocolate biscuits and hid it in my pocket. Placing the tray on the table I took mum's cup upstairs.

She lay on the bed, curled into a foetal position, her body shaking as pain wracked her head. She whimpered as I sat beside her.

'I've brought you some tea. Do you want anything else?'

'No. Just make the pain go away.' She lifted her hand

to her face. As I watched, her arm spasmed and her eyes rolled back in her head. I screamed and ran back downstairs, yelling for the doctor to come up.

Dr Stannier waved me away. 'She's ok Ginnie. It's a severe nerve pain but it will go.'

'But she's shaking and looks weird.' I pulled at her arm to get her to come upstairs and see what was happening.

'No, she's not.' The doctor finished her biscuit and rose, picking up the small leather satchel she carried everywhere. 'Make sure she takes her pills. She'll be fine in a couple of days.' With that she left, and I rushed back to mum's side. Dad's voice calling after me.

'Trust Dr Stannier, Ginnie. She knows what's best.' Dad was of the old school. You never argued with professional people. It would be disrespectful.

Over the next hour I watched as mum's hand spasms continued. I knew there was something very wrong. When her legs began to draw up into her chest and her body shook in a full convulsion, I ran downstairs and yelled at Dad, 'I'm calling an ambulance, she's having a fit.' He looked at me, frozen to the spot when he saw how serious and scared I was. I ran straight across the road to Mrs Hyslop's. We didn't have a phone, but she kindly let us use hers for emergencies. I dialled 999 and explained mum's symptoms. There was no hesitation, an ambulance was dispatched, arriving at our house ten minutes later. The ambulance men rushed up the stairs returning soon after with my mum on a stretcher.

'When did she start fitting? Having the seizures?' the taller one asked, a look of concern on his face.

I told them what I knew and what the doctor had said. He shook his head and mumbled something that sounded like 'Bloody Stannier'. They loaded mum into the ambulance. Dad climbed in beside her and told me to feed the dogs then join him at the hospital.

I threw the dogs' food into their bowls. Typical that they were the first thing on his mind. Tom appeared at the door of the kennel.

'I saw the ambulance. What happened?' he asked.

'Mum's really ill. They've taken her to hospital.'

'Why aren't you with her?' He had a look of concern mixed with confusion on his face.

'Because the bloody dogs need their dinner.' I dropped the dishes onto the floor and the greyhounds wolfed down the food. I slammed the kennel door shut and ushered Tom out in front of me. 'I need to get to Monklands now. She looked terrible.'

'Do you want me to come with you?'

I grabbed my bike. 'No, I'll be fine.' I jumped on and started to pedal away. 'Thanks Tom,' I called over my shoulder. I hadn't meant to be so brusque with him.

An hour later I ran into the A&E reception just as someone was helping dad into a waiting room. Mum had died. A subarachnoid haemorrhage, they said, a massive stroke. How had that stupid doctor not recognised the symptoms? Why didn't she call an ambulance?

'Do you want to go in to see her, to say goodbye?' the nurse who had been sitting with my dad asked gently.

'No.' I shook my head. 'I don't want to see her. She won't be able to hear me so what's the point in saying goodbye?'

'It can help you grieve, sweetheart,' the nurse continued. 'Are you sure?'

'Perfectly sure,' I said. There was only one thing on my mind. I sat in silence as dad sobbed. Dr Stannier. She was the reason why my mum was dead. Her inability to diagnose a massive stroke had been the reason I was now left without a mother. This was the same woman who had put me on barbiturates; who had robbed me of many of the pleasures of childhood because she thought it would be unsafe for me to do many of the things my friends did.

Incompetent bitch.

Chapter 28
GINNIE'S TRANSCRIPT
1971

On the day of the funeral Dr Stannier appeared at the house to offer her condolences. Mum's friends and various members of our family had come back to the house for sandwiches and cake. I busied myself serving copious pots of tea, trying to avoid the banalities: "So brave", "It'll hit her soon" and other such idiotic phrases. They were concerned that I hadn't cried during the service.

Aunt Meg was in the kitchen, spreading butter on slices of bread, slicing the sandwiches into triangles.

'I'll get the teas and coffees,' I offered, and stood on the opposite side of the kitchen table, my back to her and the door to the living room. I tipped twenty phenobarbitone tablets into a bowl and ground them to a powder with the back of a spoon, added a large teaspoonful of coffee and placed the mix into a cup of boiling water with three sugars and milk, I placed a slice of the gingerbread I had baked on a small rose-covered plate, extra ginger and nutmeg and the sweet icing on top would disguise the taste of the drug in the coffee.

Dr Stannier sat on the couch and sipped the whisky dad had offered her. I handed her the cake and coffee and stepped back. She grimaced when she sipped the drink, tipping some of the whisky from her glass into the cup before taking another one. The strong spirit must have disguised the bitterness of the drug. I kept an eye on her, offering another slice of cake to ensure she finished the coffee.

Back in the kitchen I took the empty medicine bottle, scraped off the label and placed it in the pocket of my cardigan. Grabbing a half empty whisky bottle, I slipped out of the back door, knowing nobody would notice that I was missing. Everyone was too busy gossiping and checking out the dust on the fireplace. It wouldn't be long before one or other of the spinster neighbours would be dropping in to help dad out; a bit of cleaning here, some shopping and cooking there. Dr Stannier's car was unlocked. No-one ever locked their doors. I took the empty pill bottle and put it in the door pocket of the little red mini and placed the whisky on the floor of the car just under the driver's seat.

I went back inside and continued topping up the drinks in the mourner's glasses, pouring extra in Doctor Stannier's glass. Rumour had it that she had a drink problem and the way she downed the whisky confirmed this. She had finished the cake and coffee too, so I removed the plate and cup and washed them thoroughly, leaving them to drip by the sink.

Half an hour later she staggered slightly as she rose from the couch, and I could hear tuts from my aunts. It was unusual to see a drunken woman, especially during the day and moreover she was a doctor. I could hear their hushed comments as Dad took Dr Stannier's arm and led her to her car. No one cared that she was unfit to drive, the roads were quiet but more importantly no-one was going to argue with a doctor. I watched from the front door as the mini wove its way down the street and out of the estate.

*

"Esteemed doctor found dead in car in garage" was how *The Advertiser* announced the death of Dr Stannier. "Suicide…Pills and Drink…Depression…" All the causes were outlined in the report in the Friday edition of the local paper. I smiled as I read the details of how the doctor's housekeeper had found her on the Saturday morning, the day after the funeral. Worried that her employer wasn't at home when she arrived for work at 7am, the hapless helper had searched the house and garden, only checking the car in the open garage as a last resort. She had found the doctor slumped in the driver's seat, a half empty bottle of whisky and a pill bottle in her lap. I laughed. Stanier must have spotted the bottles. I could imagine her wondering how they had got there as she had slipped into unconsciousness. I wonder if she knew what was happening to her. I hoped so.

I ripped out the page out of the newspaper, placing the rest into the coal bucket and hiding the folded sheet in the back of my drawer, tucking it under the knife and watch. It would be good to be able to read it now and then. I removed the bottles of phenobarbitone that I'd accumulated over the months. The next day I'd throw them into a bin in the next street. I didn't have a use for them anymore.

Chapter 29
FIONA
2015

This is one of the hardest of Ginnie's stories to understand. Firstly, I am amazed that any professional would misdiagnose the symptoms of a stroke for those of trigeminal neuralgia. Perhaps Ginnie had mixed up two different episodes of her mother's illness in her mind. Secondly how would a child know to keep such a potent drug as phenobarbitone; what would draw her to do such a strange thing? How would she know what effect the drug would have if an overdose was taken? That knowledge wasn't available to a layperson back in the early 70s – no Medical Information Sheets were provided to patients at that time. During a break from our meeting, I Google phenobarbitone. One of the rarer side effects was increased violent behaviour. Could this explain Ginnie's alleged offences as a child? I'm clutching at straws. If Ginnie's tale was true then her behaviours worsened as she got older, taking the drug in childhood wouldn't explain what she had done in her twenties.

I had discussed the death of Dr Stannier with a friend who is a retired doctor. He remembered the GP well. They had been at university at the same time. Stannier had wanted to be a teacher. Her father, also a GP, had insisted that she study medicine, pulling strings at

Glasgow to get her a place. The woman had acquiesced, never one to disobey her father. She had hated the job and had suffered bouts of depression throughout her studies and during her practice as a GP. It had been no surprise to her friends when her suicide had been announced.

According to Tom there was no hint in any of the reports that Ginnie had anything to do with the doctor's death. Her account of the time leading up to the death is specific and detailed. Did the experts miss something?

We pause to take a break.

I say little during our meetings, I want to hear Ginnie's version of what happened. The court appointed psychiatrist deemed her fit to stand trial and as a result she has been locked up now for almost thirty years. Long years of behaving like the perfect prisoner, apart from the incidents which extended her term, gaining the trust of the warders and governor, running the prison library, ensuring her fellow inmates had suitable reading material. Now she's due for release, no longer deemed a hazard to society. Every member of staff I have spoken to in the prison has had only good things to say about Ginnie and the governor sees her as a success story in rehabilitation.

As her story unfolds, and I discuss my thoughts with Tom, I wonder if she is a sociopath. She shows many of the traits but her relationship with Tom belies this. Is this the story of a poor, innocent, abused child resorting to the only way she can protect herself or is she a psychopath, incapable of feeling remorse, a continued threat to anyone who wrongs her? I take copious notes, pausing occasionally to speak into the recording equipment. The Tascam is intended to blend in, to be invisible, allowing Ginnie to relax and tell her whole story without need to censor the tale. It sits on a side table, not quite out of sight but not intrusive. I have asked Ginnie to recount everything she remembers, and I'll edit it into a cohesive account. Her attention to detail astounds me. Is this because she has gone over the stories in her mind countless times? Has she rehearsed these tales until she can recount them verbatim? Or is she just one of those people who have a photographic memory, who can see scenes from her past as clearly as if they had just occurred?

Ginnie smiles, tipping her head to one side. 'Can I see horror in your eyes Fiona? You look uncomfortable. Wait until I get to the bad bits. There's much worse to come.'

'This is my job Ginnie, I doubt if anything you tell me is something I haven't heard before. Please don't hold back on my behalf, the readers will want to know every detail.' I don't want Ginnie to feel she has the upper hand in these interviews. I don't want her to withhold anything but neither do I want her to embellish her story for the sake of sensationalism. I wonder what horrendous crime she is alluding to. Is killing someone not bad enough? I'm finding it hard to believe she would have the strength or ability to kill in the way she has described so far. The sheer strength of mind it must take seems beyond anything a child could do.

'You've said before that you only killed people who harmed you? Why change this habit with the doctor you say killed your mother?' I think I've discovered a mistake in her story. She's contradicting what she has insisted on previously. Her answer chills me.

'I didn't kill her for what she did to Mum. She had me on barbiturates for years. Have you any idea the effect that had on me? When the whole first year went on a cruise to Norway I was left behind. They didn't want to take the chance that I would have a fit and have to be shipped home. I was never allowed to swim. Everyone else went to classes in first year PE lessons but I had to sit at the side with the lazy ones, the girls on their period, the ones who were called remedial back then. I wasn't like them, but I was lumped into that group. Even after I stopped taking the pills I couldn't go out of my depth in the pool. I was scared, Fiona. I'd never been scared of anything, but Dr Stannier had destroyed my confidence. Do you know the exhilaration I felt when I first swam in the sea on Gozo? The first time I went out in a kayak? I missed out on all of that because of that woman.'

I said nothing. She was mixing up timelines. Surely it would have taken time to develop the hatred for the doctor to the extent that she would want to kill her, but Dr Stannier had died in 1971, the same year as Ginnie's mother. I made a brief note. This was something I'd have to look for in the rest of her statement.

Chapter 30
TOM'S DIARY

23rd December 1971
Poor Ginnie. This is the first funeral she's been at and it's nothing like the ones I've been to before. I could see her from the back of the crematorium. She sat at the front of the room, her head held high and back straight. Her dad was in bits, I could hear his sobs throughout the service. Although it wasn't really a service. There was no prayers or hymns, no priest or minister comforting the family. It must be really strange for her. Even when the coffin slid behind some curtains she didn't appear to be crying. Gran says that it's a mortal sin, burning the body. That Ginnie's mum will go to hell, that her body cannot be raised again if she's been burned. Mum says Gran's talking nonsense although she did look worried and crossed herself when the coffin disappeared.

Ginnie lined up with her dad outside the Crematorium. Everyone said it was a shame and that it would hit her soon. She winked at me as I went past. I think she'll be fine.

Tom 2015

Reading what he'd written, it was obvious that Ginnie had a strange relationship with death. The look would suggest that she didn't care that she'd just lost her mum. What she had told the officers had happened next was incredulous.

Drugging a doctor by lacing her drink with barbiturates had been dismissed as impossible by the medical experts they had consulted. The pills had a specifically bitter taste. That number in a drink would have been noticed by the intended victim. It had been well-known that Dr Stannier had been a heavy drinker and had been undergoing treatment for depression. Her overdose hadn't come as a surprise to her colleagues or her own doctor. The pills Ginnie had been prescribed may have been similar to the ones that the doctor had ingested at her time of death, but they were commonly used and had been readily available to any GP.

He wouldn't have blamed Ginnie if she had taken revenge on the GP. If she had diagnosed the stroke earlier Ginnie's mum might have been saved, although it was described as a massive bleed it was impossible to second guess the outcome. He was surprised when Fiona told him about the barbiturates; he had never known his friend had been epileptic. He had checked the newspaper archives and discovered that several cases had been raised pointing to the GP's incompetence. Many grieving families had blamed her for the untimely deaths of family members, but no charges had been raised. This was in the days before the blame culture had crossed the Atlantic from the US. People trusted doctors and were reticent to say anything against them. He doubted that anything would have been done even if they had been taken seriously.

It made perfect sense that the doctor's suicide would have pleased Ginnie, and she had imagined that she could have played a role in the death. Maybe it had served to give her some form of control over what had happened, given her some kind of closure. He had serious doubts that any part of her story was true.

Chapter 31
GINNIE'S TRANSCRIPT
1972

I sat the heavy medical tome on the dining table after spending the evening reading about sub arachnoid haemorrhages. I needed to know what caused them and whether or not I was at risk. Dad looked up from his paper.

'Where did you get that?' He pointed to the book.

'Library.' What I didn't say was that I had stolen it from the reference section. The librarian hadn't noticed when I had slipped it into my schoolbag. She was used to me wandering the shelves, dipping into crime, natural history, psychology. I was a voracious reader. She never noticed the books I slipped into my bag and my parents never questioned me as to why my bookshelves filled with reference books and novels. If they asked me, I would say I'd been given them by a teacher for hard work or as a prize at the end of term. This was the excuse I'd used for the collection of pens, pencils and crayons I'd amassed at primary school. They never mentioned the over-stuffed jam jar on my desk. I think they thought it easier just to believe me and to think their daughter was top of the class and had been rewarded for her schoolwork.

'What are you studying?'

I told him. 'I want to know if I'll die like mum. I

read that some diseases run in families.'

'You don't need to worry about that.' He pulled the book from my hands and slammed it shut. I could see tears forming in his eyes. 'You'll never be like her.'

'Why not?' I knew I didn't look like my mum but how did he know I wouldn't suffer as she had? 'Some conditions are genetic according to what I've been reading.' I tried to take the medical book back from him, but he held it firmly. 'What makes you the expert?' I spat the words at him. 'I might have weak blood vessels in my head, I might have high blood pressure. You wouldn't know. I don't want to die young because of something she's passed on to me.'

He closed his eyes, hesitating before answering.

'Sit here.' He patted the bed beside him. 'We should have told you long before now.' He took a deep, harsh breath, coughing into his handkerchief. 'You'll not suffer the same disease she did.' He spoke quickly, as if he had to get it out before he changed his mind. 'We should have had this talk years ago. You were adopted Ginnie. I'm sorry, I know we were wrong not to tell you, but it was easier for you not to know. There has never been the right time. It was something we discussed at lot but thought you were too young to understand.'

I stared at him, unable to form any of the words I wanted to say. They had lied to me. They had never been overly emotional or loving towards me but that worked both ways. I wasn't a cuddly child and thought that it was normal to be slightly distant from your parents. I knew my cousins were closer to my aunt and uncle, but I just thought they were soft. Now I wondered if my parents had ever loved me.

'How could you not tell me? You know I'm not stupid, of course I would understand. How could you let me believe I was yours all this time? When did you adopt me? Who are my parents?' The words tumbled in a rush, so many questions, so much I needed to know. I looked at the man in front of me, he had aged perceptibly after the funeral. He seldom washed and his clothes had the dirty, worn look of things dropped on the bedroom floor and worn again day after day. His smoking had become worse, and he seemed to have a constant, hacking cough.

'We got you as a two year-old. It was easier to get an older child than a new-born although that brought its own problems. Your real mum was too young to keep you, she gave you up as a baby and your foster family decided that they didn't want to go through with an adoption.'

'What do you mean "problems"? I was a baby. How many problems could I give you?'

His shoulders dropped, and he looked at me, his brown eyes welled with tears although I doubted if they were for me. He had a look of abject misery.

'You were a difficult child. You never slept, we were run ragged trying to sooth you but nothing ever worked, Eventually we'd just let you cry. You never bonded with us, but we didn't give up. We had chosen you, so we decided to keep you, to make sure you had a good life.'

'Keep me? You decided to keep me? I'm not a dog that you got from the kennels.'

'That's not what I meant. We could have taken you back to the home, but your mum said she'd promised your birth mother that we'd take care of you. She was just a child; no-one knows who your real father was, and her family wouldn't support her.'

I stood over him. 'You bastard. You lied to me.' I picked up the book and threw it at him, slamming the door as I ran from the room.

I still had hundreds of questions I needed answered but I couldn't face him. I ran to the quarry. I needed to be on my own and the cold, dark water beckoned me. I sat on the ledge Francis had fallen from, throwing stones into the depths, watching the ripples dissipate over the inky surface.

'Ginnie.'

I turned to see Tom running towards me. He sat beside me on the edge of the water. 'Your dad told me that you'd run off. I thought you'd be here.'

'He lied Tom. They both did. He said I was adopted. He's not my dad. Who the hell am I?' I refused to look him in the eye.

'Adopted?' A look of surprise flitted over his eyes as he gathered his thoughts. 'But you're still you. It doesn't make any difference, does it? They probably thought they were doing the right thing.'

I stood up. 'Don't take his side. He lied,' I screamed.

'I'm not taking sides and if I did, it would be yours. You know that. Come on. Come home with me. Mum's making dinner, you can stay with me until you calm down.' The sun had set as we sat on the water's edge, and the quarry looked ominous in the darkness. I imagined Francis's blue, bloated body crawling from the water, bugs dropping from his outstretched arm. Tom reached for my hand. I'd never held his hand, never shown him any affection but this simple gesture calmed me, dragged me from the imagined horror. The fact he had come to the quarry when it held so many fears for him showed how much he cared for me. I followed him across the fields to his home in silence.

'You go in. I'll tell your dad you're ok, you're with me.' He ran across to our house and left me at his door. I waited until he returned, not wanting to face his mother on my own. If she asked me any questions, what could I say? I had no answers.

I needn't have worried. Mrs O'Brien asked nothing, just spoke to me in gentle tones and fed me soup. Did she know already? Did everyone know? We had been neighbours forever; the first families to move into the new estate in 1958.

'Did you know I was adopted?' I had to ask.

'I remember when you came to them, Ginnie. It was just after they moved in. They were so pleased to have finally been given a child. You were their dream child. Your mum couldn't have children, she was so proud of you.'

'That's not what my dad says. He says I was difficult. Unlovable.'

She came over to me and wrapped me in a warm embrace. 'You were a baby. You had a difficult start, but she loved you so much. Believe me. Your parents loved you.'

'But he said...'

There was a flash of anger in her eyes. 'He's just grieving. He doesn't know what he's saying. Give him time, love. Here, finish your soup and I'll make some pancakes.' She bustled over to the cupboard, pulling flour and sugar onto the worktop, and mixing the batter with a vigour that seemed unnecessary. I couldn't decide if she was angry at my father or at me for being a difficult child.

Chapter 32
TOM'S DIARY

3/1/72

Ginnie's adopted. I should have guessed. She's nothing like either of her parents. Her mum was tall and dark and her dad's at least six foot tall. She's not even like her cousins.

Mum says they adopted her when she was a baby. She says they should have told her long before now. I think it's dead exciting. I wonder who her real parents were? She says she's going to find them. She wants to know why they gave her up. Mum says they probably weren't married or were too young.

Maybe they're really rich or foreign.

Maria let me touch her breast at the school dance. She's lovely.

Tom 2015

Much had been made of Ginnie's past during the trial and the later investigation. Had her upbringing played some part in making her the way she was? He recalled how he had always been jealous of the freedom she had been afforded as a child. No set bedtimes, no-one stopping her spending hours at the quarry while he and

Francis were under strict rules to be home by a certain time. The fact she had a house key and was often left on her own in the evenings when her parents were out had not seemed odd to him as a child. As an adult, and especially as a parent, he recognised the obvious signs of neglect. He would never have left a ten-year-old Joe at home alone. It had made Ginnie self-sufficient, she had never had to answer to anyone and had developed a strong sense of her own worth. It had also led her to have little empathy with others. If a child isn't given love and care, could they develop those feelings for others?

Ginnie had seemed to be in love with Mike, but apart from her friendship with himself, Tom couldn't recall her being close to anyone else, even her late husband. He had discussed this with Maria the previous night.

'Ginnie care about anyone? Are you kidding? She was a self-centred bitch. I don't know why you kept in touch with her for so long.' He had obviously touched a raw nerve in his wife. 'Remember how she had reacted when we asked her to be Joe's Godparent? It was obvious then that she didn't care what I thought, nor you. What would it have cost her to be there for us, for our child? No Tom. Ginnie didn't give a shit about anyone else.'

Maria never swore. He had been shocked by the vehemence in her words. Why had he never realised before now that his wife had hated his best friend even as teenagers? He understood why Maria had no time for Ginnie now, but she had hidden her feelings throughout their early lives together? When he had asked her why she'd never said anything she had glared at him over the rim of her spectacles.

'Seriously? You thought I was OK with your friendship. You would never have dropped Ginnie, no matter what I said. You had already lost one of your best friends as a child, I wasn't going to ask you to lose another. You're lucky I knew you loved me and that there was nothing physical between the two of you.'

He had pulled her into his arms then and held her tight. He knew how lucky he was. Maria was his life.

'I never knew you felt that way. I love you...'

She had placed a finger over his lips. They were fine. No apologies needed.

Chapter 33
GINNIE'S TRANSCRIPT
1972

'Tell me.' I sat opposite my dad, the dining table between us. 'I'm fourteen, I'm old enough to understand.' He refused to meet my gaze, but I remained steadfast, if I could see his eyes I'd know if he was lying. 'Look at me and tell me.'

He met my gaze. His dark brown eyes, rheumy and full of sadness. Eyes nothing like my pale blue ones, no resemblance at all. How could I have been so blind? Was this why I hadn't been allowed to go to my gran's funeral? Were they scared that someone would slip up and mention that she wasn't really my gran?

'We couldn't have children. Your mum had always wanted a family and when she found out she couldn't conceive she started looking for ways to adopt. The church would have been the easiest way, but she refused to join. You know what she was like about religion, she had never believed and wanted nothing to do with them. Our other choice was a private adoption or to use an agency. Jamieson's was always after money; their collection tins and envelopes were everywhere so she contacted them. She told them the child didn't need to be a baby and they were delighted to help.'

'You keep saying "she". Did you not want me? Was it her decision to adopt a baby?'

His face confirmed my thought. 'I just wanted her to be happy. All I wanted was for the two of us to get on with our lives and I'd have done anything for her.'

'Go on.'

'It didn't take long for them to find us a child. Your natural mother was fifteen and her family refused to help her keep her baby. You'd been placed in foster care when you were less than a week old. You were a tetchy baby and a disruptive toddler. The terrible twos they called it. They said you'd grow out of it soon. The temper tantrums and hours of crying, they said they'd stop once you were a little older. They didn't. If anything, you got worse. It was easiest to let you get what you wanted. Everyone said we were spoiling you, but it made our life easier.'

I thought about the Christmas and birthday presents I'd been given. Always what I'd asked for. Nothing was too expensive or unsuitable. Was it really just easier to get me what I wanted?

What about the times they'd go out together leaving me at home on my own? I'd read or watch TV until they arrived back after 10pm. I had never considered this to be anything strange although I knew Tom and Francis had never been left alone in their houses, I had just thought I was lucky. That my parents allowed me free rein. Was it freedom or neglect?

My mind whirled, his words forming sentences I struggled to process. Who were my parents? Not this man and his wife. Was it someone like Christine? Pregnant too young, no husband, no chance.

'Who were they? Where are my real parents?' I stood directly in front of him, arms folded instinctively across my chest.

'They were nobodies. They don't matter. You are our child. We raised you. We gave you everything we could.'

'It's not about what you gave me. It's about what you didn't give. You kept the truth from me. You must have some paperwork, you must know how I can find them,' I screamed.

'If we had anything it will have been thrown out years ago. We didn't keep anything.'

I couldn't believe what he was saying. 'Why would you not want to remember who your child's parents were. Didn't you think it might be important to me in the future? Or did you just think about yourselves. What I might want wouldn't matter.' I picked up a vase, the nearest thing at hand and threw it at him. He stood up and grabbed my arms, pining them to my sides so I couldn't move.

'What we did was for the best. She gave you away, didn't want you. Why would you care about her?'

I screamed through clenched teeth and pulled away from him. I needed to be alone to process what I'd learned. I ran upstairs and threw myself on my bed. I'd write to Jamieson's. They'd surely have some form of records. I took out my notepad and began a list of things I needed to do.

Chapter 34
GINNIE'S TRANSCRIPT

1972

I climbed the wall behind the offices, dropping on to the tarmacked surface. Forcing open the sash and case window which opened into the back room of the adoption agency was easier than I had imagined. A few twists of the screwdriver had loosened the catch; no-one ever fully closed them and staff were lax with security. I climbed in and began searching among the rows of filing cabinets in the storeroom.

My letter to Jamieson's had gone unanswered and despite several more attempts they continued to ignore my requests for information. I had gone to the offices and demanded to speak to someone in charge. The elderly woman who spoke to me explained in a sugary sweet voice that there were few records from the 50s, but even if they had them, they couldn't be released until I was eighteen and, even then, my parents would have to give consent. She tried to pat my hand as she spoke, but I pulled away. I didn't want sympathy. I wanted answers. My raised voice brought others from the inner offices to the reception area and eventually I was escorted out of the building. So, I had taken matters into my own hands. I didn't want to wait years only to be told that my birth mother didn't want to speak to me. If I could find her, I could confront her face to face.

She wouldn't be able to ignore me then.

After an hour of searching through their files, some records were in date order, others in name, I finally found a folder with my parents' names on the front. I grabbed the file and retraced my steps back through the window. I needed time to scour the file for as much information as possible. No-one would notice it was missing.

*

I lay the documents out on my bed. In a manilla envelope was a buff-coloured document, my original birth certificate. Mother's name – Caroline McGeachie. Father unknown. Mother's age 15. Place of birth – Shotts. I stared at the document. She had been pregnant and given birth to me when barely out of childhood. The name McGeachie would be useful. Fairly uncommon. Shotts was a small village, maybe someone would remember her. Maybe she still lived there.

I barely slept that night. Different scenarios played through my dreams and waking moments. Would she be like me? What was she doing now? Did I have siblings? I had to find out. And I had to find out now.

Chapter 35
GINNIE'S TRANSCRIPT
1972

By 8am the next day, I was on the bus heading to the tiny mining village in the Lanarkshire hills. I'd never been to Shotts, and I was shocked by the depressive sight which unfolded as the bus drove through the hills and into the main street. Rows of dirty grey houses and shops with boarded up windows dulled my excitement. Where would I start? On the corner of the main street sat a pub, its tired façade barely brightened by a poster announcing a quiz night. In the car park two young boys kicked a ball around, a small black dog nipped at their heels, trying to grab the football. It was just after 9am, the boys should have been at school but were showing no inclination for heading to the grey sandstone building further along the street.

Opposite the pub was a paper shop. The woman behind the counter looked up as I entered. 'What can I get you love?' Her eyes crinkled when she spoke.

I picked up a bar of chocolate and handed her a pound note. 'I wonder if you could help me?' I smiled, fixing her with a pleading look. 'I'm looking for a Caroline McGeachie. That might not be her surname now, I don't know if she's married.'

A fleeting look of suspicion crossed those previously friendly eyes.

'She was a friend of my mum and I want to let her know my mum died. Thought she'd want to know.' I let a tear slip from my eye. The woman's demeanour changed immediately.

'You poor thing. Come away in.' She gestured round the back of the counter and ushered me into the back room of the shop. 'Sit, sit.' She pulled out a chair beside a Formica topped table. 'Would you like a cuppa?'

I shook my head. 'No thanks.' I sniffed. 'I just hoped that you might know her.' She handed me a tissue.

'McGeachie. McGeachie.' She let the name roll round her mouth. 'There's a Billy McGeachie in North Street. Might be related. I've only been here a couple of years and don't know everyone. I'd try there first of all. Are you sure I can't get you something?'

I shook my head. 'Which way is North Street? Do you think he'll be in?'

'Aye he'll be in. Nae work up here for young men.' She drew a map of the village on the back of a paper bag, putting a cross where Billy McGeachie lived. 'Hoose wi' the blue door. Ye cannae miss it.'

I thanked her and made my way to the north end of the village. Only one house had a blue door, the rest were in council house green. I battered the door knocker. The man who answered the door gasped when he saw me. 'Aye?' His single word welcome made me feel anything but.

I explained who I was looking for.

'Aye, ah can see who you're looking for. She'll be at

the pub.' He made to shut the door in my face. I stepped forward and placed my hand on the handle. 'She cleans there three times a week. Jist knock and she'll let you in. You'll know who she is when you see her.' With that he turned and disappeared into the depth of the dark hallway.

I raced back to the pub I'd passed earlier and banged on the front door.

'We're no' open yet,' a female voice yelled from inside.

'I don't want a drink. I'm looking for Caroline McGeachie. Her brother said she'd be here.' There was a rattle of a snib being unbolted and the door swung open. An older version of my face stared back at me; a cigarette attached to her lower lip. Now I knew what her brother meant and why he'd gasped when he saw me.

'Oh my god.' She dropped the duster she had held, her hand shooting to her mouth. We stood and stared for what felt like minutes. The resemblance was obvious although her hair was dyed, and her face covered in the fine lines of the long-term smoker.

'Caroline?' I asked. The woman in front of me nodded. 'I think you're my mum. Can we talk?' I moved into the room, closing the door behind me, not giving her the chance to bar my way.

She looked flustered, her eyes darted between me and the floor. 'How did you find me? They said I couldn't have contact again.' She dropped into the chair opposite me, hands scrabbling to extract a packet of cigarettes from her apron pocket. She struck a match, her hands shaking as she lit another cigarette and took a sharp draw of the acrid smoke.

I told her how my mum had died and how I'd only just found out about her.

'I'm nearly finished here. Do you want to come home with me? You can meet your half-sister; she'll be home at dinner time frae the school. Oh my God. I can't believe it's you. I never thought I'd see you again.'

We went back to her tiny council flat, and she made tea then sat down opposite me in the sparse but clean kitchen. 'I've told you all I know. I was adopted at two years and according to my dad they decided to keep me even though I was "difficult".'

'I thought I was doing the right thing. Everyone told me I couldn't keep you, that it was for the best. I had no money, no job, no husband. I was a wean.' I could see the hurt in her eyes, tears threatened to spill over. 'I wanted to keep you, but my mum and dad took over and arranged everything.'

'If by best you mean, was I fed and looked after, then they were right. But I was never loved. I don't remember mum ever cuddling me.' I sipped the hot liquid, not letting my gaze leave the woman who'd given birth to me at the age of fifteen. 'Your turn. Tell me everything. Who's my dad? Are you still with him?'

Her hands shook, spilling her tea as she explained how she'd been raped at fourteen and how her parents wanted nothing to do with her or her child. Social Workers had become involved and had taken me away immediately after she'd given birth. 'They wouldn't even let me see you or hold you. I only knew you were a girl because the midwife said so when you were born.'

'So, my mum didn't promise you she'd look after me?' I remembered what my dad had said when he'd confessed that I was adopted.

'No, I never met her. I'm so sorry. I should have fought harder to keep you.'

Yes, you should have I thought. I felt the knife in my pocket. She was standing at the cooker putting two pies on a tray into the old but sparkling clean oven.

I grabbed her hair from behind and pulled her head back, slicing through her throat in one clean sweep. Crimson blood sprayed over the worktop, splashing on the walls in front of her. I held her close to my body until I felt her arms drop as her life ebbed from her.

'Sugar and milk?'

I was dragged from my daydream. 'Just milk please.'

I tried to imagine what she'd been through. I had thought I would be angry when I met her but all I felt was her grief. She had done no wrong. I was nearly the same age as she'd been when she'd had me. There was no way I could cope with a baby. But was she lying about not having met my mum? Either she was lying or dad was.

There was a commotion at the door and a red-haired child flew past the kitchen door and into the living room opposite. 'What's for dinner, ma?' she yelled throwing herself on to the couch and grabbing the large, black cat which had been snoozing there. 'Come on Harry. Move over puss.'

Caroline stepped into the doorway. 'Caitlin. Come and meet Ginnie.'

The child came through to the kitchen still clutching the struggling cat.

'Put Harry down and say hello to your big sister.'

She glared at me through her fringe, and I could see the likeness in her eyes. She had the same wariness of people as I had.

'Hello Caitlin. I'm Ginnie.' I held my hand out.

She stared at it but didn't take it. 'You're my sister? How come I've never seen you before?'

I laughed. She was as forthright as me. I might have liked this child as my wee sister.

'Leave this one with me.' Caroline glanced at me as she took the pie from the oven and slid it on to a small plate. She placed it in front of the child, piling beans on top of the steaming crust. 'Eat your dinner and I'll tell you all about Ginnie in a minute.'

The child dismissed me, more intent on her food than a stranger. At Caroline's bidding I went through to the living room, leaving her to explain to her daughter who the stranger was. A few minutes later Caitlin appeared at the doorway. 'Do you want to see my room?' she asked, holding out her hand.

'OK? I'd love to.' I stood and took the proffered hand

and she dragged me upstairs. Her bedroom walls were festooned with posters of Canada, a maple leaf flag was draped across her bed. 'I take it you like Canada?' I asked.

'Yes. We're going next month. Mum says I'll make new friends and I can have a dog. We can take Harry too.' She pointed to the calendar on the wall where a large red cross marked a day as MOVING DAY. Caroline hadn't mentioned this. I went back downstairs and joined my mother in the kitchen.

'I hear you're emigrating.'

'Yes. My husband's part Canadian. There's more work prospects there for both of us. Caitlin's so excited. It's such a shame that I've just found you. I would really love to get to know you more, but we won't have a lot of time before we go. Give me your address and I'll write, maybe you could join us one day?'

'That would be good.' I had to get out of there. I'd only just found her, and she was abandoning me again. I checked my watch. 'I'll need to get going. There's a bus at one, then none 'til four. Thanks for talking to me Caroline. I'm really glad I met you.'

'Hang on. I've got something you might want.' She left me in the tiny kitchen, returning a few minutes later clutching something in her hand. It was a tiny white band with 'Baby McGeachie' written on it. 'It's the one thing they let me keep of you. I think one of the younger nurses felt sorry for me.'

I took the band. 'Thanks Caroline, I'll keep it forever.'

And I did, it's in my memento drawer.

'Will you come back another day? Spend some time with us?'

'I don't think so. You'll be too busy packing. I was just curious about you but there's nothing we share so I don't think it's a good idea. I would have been a good sister for Caitlin, but you never gave me a chance.'

She looked hurt at this and stepped towards me, reaching out to touch me. I stepped away and took the knife from my pocket.

Chapter 36
FIONA
2015

'Tell me how you felt when you were told you were adopted Ginnie. Had you had any inkling as a child that the people you thought were your parents weren't really?' Having seen photographs of Ginnie and her parents I found it hard to believe that such a bright, clever girl had never questioned her parenthood.

'I felt let down. I couldn't believe that those who were supposed to be closest to me could live a lie for so long. I knew my parents weren't like Tom's or Francis's, there had always been a distance between us, but I just accepted it as their way. They weren't overly demonstrative, they seldom if ever hugged me, in fact I don't remember mum ever showing me any sign of affection. Even when I was ill I was put to bed and given disprin. I don't remember them even telling me a bedtime story, or us going anywhere as a family group. Dad took me out with the dogs sometimes but that was it,' she says this with a dismissive shrug, a look of nonchalance on her face. Is she really not bothered?

'Did you feel that your parents were simply ensuring you had material things but that they couldn't show you real affection?'

Ginnie settled her piercing gaze on me again. 'I had what I wanted, could do what I wished. They never interfered with me, I mean interfered with the things I did or plans I made. They never abused me but neither did they show me any real love. It suited me.'

She didn't realise that their lack of input into her behaviours was, in itself, a form of abuse. She insists her reaction to finding out about her birth mother was more one of anger that they had lied to her.

Her confession years before said that she had killed her birth mother and sister. That she had left them in a pool of blood. This had been dismissed when the pair had been tracked to Canada, alive and well. I noticed that she didn't actually say she had killed them in her account of this period of her life.

'When you first confessed you said you killed your birth mother and half-sister. Is that not true?'

Ginnie seemed unfazed by my direct questioning. 'I thought I had. Maybe their injuries weren't as bad as I thought. They must have recovered from my attack and for some reason didn't report it to the police. I definitely intended to kill them.'

This was a totally different account from the one in the original notes according to Tom. She had said that she had slit the throats of the woman and girl, that she had made her daydream come true, hardly a minor injury. This was the first time Ginnie had been caught out in a definite lie. Her blustering suggestion that perhaps the injuries weren't as bad as she had thought didn't ring true. According to Tom, Carol and her daughter told the authorities in Canada that there had been no attack when they'd met Ginnie. Would there be any reason for them to lie?

Chapter 37
TOM'S DIARY

10th January 1972

Ginnie found her real mother. Says she has a sister. I asked if she'd stay in touch with them, but she said she has no further need for them. I think that's a strange way to describe meeting your real family for the first time. She can be really cold and uncaring at times. When I asked if that was what her real mother wanted, she said she didn't care. It wasn't her choice.

Tom 2015

During her interrogation Ginnie had said she had killed her birth mother and sister, had slit their throats and left them to bleed to death on the kitchen floor. Tom searched the police statements. They had done a thorough search of birth and death records to try to identify the victim. There had been no record of a Caroline and Caitlin McGeachie being murdered in 1971 nor for any year either side of the alleged incident. Why on earth would you admit to such a heinous crime when none had been committed?

Further searches had revealed that Caroline had married a James Morrison in 1970 and had emigrated with him and her daughter to Canada two years later. The Canadian police had interviewed the two but neither had any recollection of Ginnie being in any way violent towards them when she had visited them. Caitlin had no memory at all, she'd only met Ginnie that one time and the encounter had been unremarkable. Caroline said she had tried to keep in touch, but letters and phone calls had gone unanswered, and she had eventually given in, deciding that Ginnie didn't want anything to do with them. When prompted she had remembered giving Ginnie the birth band which had been found among Ginnie's collection.

This one was the absolute decision maker. Not only had there been no evidence that Ginnie had been involved despite her confession, but there was also no evidence of the crime having been perpetrated at all.

Chapter 38
GINNIE'S TRANSCRIPT
1972

'OK I'll go out with him.' Tom and Maria had been nagging me for days. Their friend Philip, my one-time tennis partner, wanted to go out with me and they had organised a double date at a bowling alley. I wasn't interested in dating anyone, but if it would get them off my back I'd have to agree. Philip had seemingly been lusting after me since we had first met two years previously but with no self-confidence he'd never approached me. It's not like it was a date date, and Philip was ok. Like me he was shorter than his classmates and his pasty white skin and hair made him a bit of a loner, other girls weren't interested in him, and he spent more time studying than seeing friends. I think they thought we could save each other from eternal loneliness.

'Great.' It was obvious it was Maria's idea. I think she thought she'd get more time alone with Tom if I was seeing someone else. Tom often dragged me along to the cinema or a football game if Maria didn't fancy going with him. He'd told me that she had been complaining about it. This was obviously her chance to get me out of the way.

We met the next night and took the train into Glasgow and walked the short distance to the bowling alley.

I'd never played before. Philip put his arm around me to show me how to hold the bowling ball. I let it slip from my grasp and dropped it on his foot.

'Oops, sorry Philip, are you ok?' I stooped to pick up the bowl again, I could see Tom shaking his head. 'What?' I mouthed at him. He answered with a raised eyebrow, and I laughed. 'Got it now. It's heavier than it looks.' I stepped up to the line and swung the ball, again it slipped from my fingers, narrowly missing Philip's foot again as it bounced behind me. Maria screeched with laughter.

'Maybe you should use the pink one.' Philip collected the blue ball I'd dropped and placed it in the machine. 'It's the lightest.'

I lifted a pink ball, glared at Maria who was still in hysterics, swung again and this time the bowl flew down the lane, scattering the pins for a strike.

'Yayy,' Philip yelled. 'That's better. Your fingers are so tiny you need the wee one.'

Maria went next, scoring a measly two. By the end of the night Philip and I were miles ahead of the other two. On the way home we stopped off for burgers and cokes then headed back to the train station. Tom and Maria dawdled behind us. Philip tried to take my hand, but I stuck both fists into my jacket pockets and strode on through the dark Glasgow streets. On the train he sat beside me but didn't impose on my space. The boy could take a hint.

As we walked home from the station Philip told me

all about the course he was going to take at university and how much it meant to him. He seemed worried that he wouldn't get the grades he needed.

'I thought Tom said you always got A grades? What are you worried about?' I tried to make small talk.

'I only get As because I work so hard. This is a rare night off. I'm only here because Maria said you wanted to go out with me.'

'Did she now?' I glanced over my shoulder at the happy couple behind us. 'How about we go out again? Maybe once a week so you can study the other nights.'

Philip was innocuous. Having a 'boyfriend' might stop the taunts I got at school. I had heard whispered comments about "Virginia the Virgin" and, although I didn't care what they said, it was a pain. The clique were still at it. They were the most popular girls, each one as pretty as the other with Fiona as their leader.

'Really?' Philip's pale eyes lit up and his skin blushed pink. 'How about the pictures on Friday?' He was getting in quick before I changed my mind. I agreed to meet him as we parted ways at the end of my street. Tom and Maria had caught up, their grinning faces revealing that they had heard us making the date.

'Night, Ginnie,' they called as they headed across the road. I could hear Maria's laugh as I walked away.

Chapter 39
TOM'S DIARY

November 10th, 1972

Ginnie's going out with Philip. Maria's delighted. Says we'll get more time to ourselves, that sounds interesting. I hope she means what I think she means.

We've got our prelims in January, so mum says I'm only allowed to go out on Friday and Saturday. I want to see Maria as much as I can. I really love her. Maybe I should tell her.

Tom 2015

He remembered that night with Ginnie and Philip. Maria had been delighted that her plan had worked. She had thought they made a perfect pair, looking more like brother and sister than boyfriend and girlfriend, two lonely people, pushed together by Maria playing Cupid. He vaguely recalled that they had gone out all through November and December but had split up before Christmas. Ginnie had never told him why they'd broken up, not that he had asked. He remembered what had happened to Philip. Such a sad affair.

As usual he had been too wrapped up in Maria. They had slept together for the first time after a Christmas party. Neither had planned it but they'd gone back to a friend's house and had slipped upstairs and had got carried away. How stupid had they been? He recalled that first time. Neither of them had any experience and the whole thing had been a bit of a disaster but he hadn't cared. They were in love.

Chapter 40
GINNIE'S TRANSCRIPT
1972

Philip and I dated throughout November and December. On our first night out, we went to the cinema. He sat with his arm along the chair behind my back, his hand slowly slipping to rest on my breast. I grabbed it and forced his arm down between us where it stayed throughout the film. At my gate we kissed fleetingly then I stepped back and ran up the steps to my front door. I turned at the top and saw he was still standing at the gate, watching me.

On our second date, we sat on a park bench, and I kissed him. I took his hand and placed it on my chest, stopping him when he tried to slip his fingers inside my blouse. 'It's too cold,' I said fastening my jacket round me. I continued in this way for three weeks. I wanted to be in control. If I was going to have sex it would be on my terms. He had invited me to the St Pat's Christmas party, and I had bought a really short, black dress, the hem barely skimming my bum. I wanted him to be desperate for me by then, his teenage hormones running rampant. On each date we went a little further, by the week before the party I had let him touch my breast under my top, scared by the feelings this elicited in me. I realised that I probably wanted sex as much as he did.

The day before the end of term I overheard some

girls in the changing rooms after PE. They were giggling and one said, 'So Virginia the Virgin isn't any more.' I recognised my taunter's voice. Once again Fiona was taking pleasure in hurting me. Throughout my school days she had always been ready with a snide comment, a bump in the corridor causing me to drop my books. I had lost my fountain pen earlier that year. The last time I had seen it was when we were getting changed for PE and the last person to come into the gym that day had been Fiona. Not only a bully, but a thief as well.

Her friends screeched with laughter. 'According to my brother, Philip says she's a real goer, he has her soaking her knickers every time he sees her. Who knew wee Philip had it in him?'

I ran from the room, grabbing my shoes and jacket. I didn't want them to see me.

When Philip phoned me that night, I told him we were finished. I had to think about what I wanted to do about him. How dare he say such things. How could he lie about me to his mates?

The night of the dance I spent at home, planning. Tom phoned me the next day wondering why I hadn't been at the party. He sounded excited.

'We split up.' I sniffed.

'Oh, I'm sorry Ginnie. I thought you two were getting on so well,' he said. He sounded genuinely upset. It was obvious he hadn't heard the gossip, I supposed Philip wouldn't dare say anything to my best friend.

'So did I, but he wanted to go too far. It's ok, I'll be

fine.' I changed the subject. 'When are you going to Jim's?' His older brother had married, and the family were going to the newlywed's house for Christmas.

'We're leaving tomorrow morning. Maria's coming over on Christmas day and we'll be there until New Year.'

'Have a great time. I'm just going to spend my time studying, dad won't be interested in doing anything Christmassy, so I'll get peace. I'll see you when you get back.' It was easy to fool Tom. We hung up. I was going to be busy over the next fortnight, but he didn't need to know that.

Christmas was as I'd expected. The house went undecorated, and we didn't cook a special meal nor exchange presents. Dad had given up any pretence at us being a family. On Boxing Day, I called Philip and asked to meet him that night. I told him I had missed him and was sorry. He seemed delighted that I was making the first move. When we met up later, I kissed him, slipping my tongue into his mouth.

'Come on, I know somewhere we can be alone.' I took his hand and led him to the flats at the top of the hill. We took the lift to the top floor, and I showed him how to slip through the gap held only partly closed by the chain and padlock that had been on the Morven Court roof access since the flats had been built. He was slightly built and could easily slide through. I took him on to the roof where we sat on a ledge and looked up at the stars above us. That night we kissed for hours, and I let him slide his hands into my knickers.

'Can I see you again tomorrow?' I asked as we kissed on the way back home.

'I need to study Gin. If I don't do well in my prelims, I might not get the place I want at Uni.'

I rubbed against him, and he groaned. 'Please? You've got plenty of time to study.' I ran my fingers down his jacket and bit my lip. Where was this coming from, when did I become a flirt? I tried not to laugh.

We agreed to meet the next night and every night after that. We spent our time either on the roof or on the stairwell if it was wet. Each time I let him go a bit further. By the time we returned to school after the holidays we were spending hours together. Philip forgot about studying, his hormones a more potent urge than the need to get good grades.

We began sleeping together, every chance we had to be together was spent having sex. It was no surprise that he failed his prelims. No surprise to me that is. According to Tom his teachers were shocked that Philip had done so badly. What they didn't know was that we had been up the whole night before. We had sneaked into my bedroom, dad not even noticing we were there. Too unbothered to check.

The day he received his results we agreed to meet up. He was upset. He had failed his maths prelim. He tried to talk about it but I shushed him. It would be our last date, not that he knew that. We walked to the flats and headed to the rooftop. I undid his tie, slowly slipping it from his neck and loosening his shirt. 'Come on, follow me,' I stood on the parapet, his tie blowing like a banner in my hand. He hesitated. 'Come on Philip, let yourself go, live dangerously for once.'

He climbed on to the edge and took my hand. 'You are mad,' he yelled against the noise of the wind.

'You better believe it.' I jumped back on to the roof, turned quickly and pushed.

Chapter 41
TOM'S DIARY

January 22nd, 1973

Philip committed suicide. He failed his prelims and teachers had warned him that if he didn't improve, he wouldn't get into Strathclyde. He was really upset when I saw him. All he'd ever wanted was to be an engineer.

I didn't think he was that upset enough to kill himself though.

I should have told him that he'd be able to catch up before the finals. I should have stayed with him. I should have just been there for him and not with Maria.

I'm a crap pal.

Tom 2015

During Tom's police training he had learned that it was almost impossible to stop someone who really wanted to kill themselves. Throwing yourself off the roof of an eight-storey flat was a serious method to commit suicide and he consoled himself that there had been nothing he could have done differently when he was seventeen.

When Ginnie said that she had thrown the boy

off the roof, Tom's colleagues had told him that they thought she had lost it completely. There had been no doubt in the investigating officers' minds in January 1973 that Philip had killed himself. How could Ginnie have physically done what she was admitting to? They had found a St Pat's tie in her drawer, but Philip's family had said that the night he died he wasn't wearing uniform. They concluded that Ginnie could have taken the tie from him at any time.

A fleeting memory of Ginnie and Joe on the edge of the same roof caused Tom to shiver. He shook his head, pushing the thought from his mind.

Maria appeared at the door. 'Someone walking on your grave?' She handed him a mug of coffee.

'Just a thought. Do you remember Philip and Ginnie going out? Can you mind how they were together?'

Maria sat on the bed. 'Didn't they finish quite quickly? I don't think it was ever going to last. Philip was too serious, poor boy had always been a sensitive soul. Why do you ask?'

'Do you think she could have killed him?'

'I think your Ginnie could kill anyone. She was always callous. Remember when I asked her about her friend Christine?'

He remembered it well. They had both been shocked by Ginnie's reaction. They had been talking about sex. Ginnie had guessed that they had started sleeping together and had been joking with them that they'd need to be careful as their parents would know what they were up to. 'It's dead obvious,' she had laughed. 'The pair of you can't keep the grins off your faces when you're together. Maria's dad'll kill you, Tom if he finds out.'

'I know,' Maria had blushed, 'Don't you dare say anything. Anyway, what about you and Philip? I've heard you two aren't exactly innocent.'

'Says who?' Ginnie had sounded furious.

Maria had glanced towards Tom, obviously looking for support. 'Philip's sister says he told her that you were a couple. I just thought he'd meant – you know – that you had done it.'

'No way.' Ginnie had looked offended by the question. 'I'm not taking the chance that I'll end up like Christine.'

'Christine? Your pal in third year? What happened to her?' Maria had asked, concern in her voice.

'Silly cow got pregnant. Had to go back to Ireland.'

'Oh my goodness,' Maria had gasped, 'I had wondered where she'd gone. I thought they'd just gone travelling again. Who was the father?'

'Her dad, or her brother, she wasn't sure which of the two it was,' Ginnie said, absently chewing on her nail.

'What?' Maria cried out, 'She had sex with her dad? Seriously? Don't kid about something like that Ginnie.'

'I'm not kidding. She said they had raped her. Not my problem. By the way, Philip was a liar, I never slept with him.'

Maria had rushed out, a look of horror on her face. Tom ran after her. He caught up with her in the bathroom, tears flooding down her face. 'How can she be like that, Tom? She doesn't care that her friend was raped. Worse than that, raped by her dad or brother. That's not normal.' Her words had been punctuated with sobs. All he could do was hold her.

She was right, Ginnie hadn't seemed bothered that her friend had been raped. She didn't care that her boyfriend had killed himself. She had seemed more concerned that Philip had lied about her. Maria had always been empathetic towards others, and he knew she found it hard to understand how anyone could be otherwise.

It occurred to him that his memory of Ginnie finding out people were talking about her, and Philip was different from Ginnie's version. He had forgotten the conversation about sex completely until his memory had been jolted by his diary entry. Another inconsistency in her tale that he would have to mention to Fiona.

Tom considered Philip's suicide. He knew fine well how depression could lead to such an act. In his diary he had thought that Philip wasn't upset enough to kill himself but who knew what was in the boy's head? He must have believed that he had no future, that his life was over. There's no reasoning with the black dog when it digs into your psyche. What appears trivial to others could have been overwhelming in Philip's head. Tom had talked several people down from would-be suicide events in his career. He was good at it; knew first-hand how they had felt – although he had never explained this to his bosses who had chosen him as a negotiator. They just thought he was empathetic and had a gentle way with words that resonated with the person attempting suicide. He had spoken to Philip's parents, years after the death. They had admitted their son had mental health issues, something Tom had never been aware of while at school.

Chapter 42
FIONA
2015

'Are you telling me you killed Philip? That he didn't commit suicide?'

'Got it in one, Fiona. I shoved that lying toad off the roof. Actually, the landing killed him, not the fall.'

According to Tom, Philip was a bright child who had never had difficulties with exams in the past, his seven O Grades proved this. Even failing prelims wouldn't finish his chances of getting a place at university based on his expected Higher results, so why would he be so depressed by failing these practice exams? There had been no suicide note, the family had kept quiet about Philip suffering from depression. But there was no doubting the fact that somehow the boy had died, plunging to his death from Morven Court.

Ginnie's alternative story that she had thrown him off the parapet was preposterous. Had it been a game that had gone wrong resulting in the boy's death? Had Ginnie been with him when he fell and had she twisted it to take the blame? Now that I'm getting to know her, I have doubts that she would care what anyone thought of her. Other people's feelings seem to register low on Ginnie's empathy scale.

I go back to something else she had said. 'Are you sure the girls you overheard were talking about you?'

She answers my question with a look that speaks volumes. I try again.

'You say that I was part of the group, but I didn't know Philip at school, how would I be aware of the gossip from Saint Pat's? Wouldn't it have been easier just to ask Tom to have a word with Philip if he was spreading lies about you?'

'Why would I do that? I've always dealt with things myself. I didn't need anyone's help. It wasn't Tom's problem. And anyway, I wasn't bothered about what others thought of me. Why should I?'

'So why go to the extreme of killing someone who you obviously liked? Why not just deny his accusations? After all, Tom believed you, and he's the only person whose opinion you seem to cherish.'

'Because he lied!' She slapped the table. This was one of the few times I had seen any extreme physical reaction from Ginnie. 'The bastard lied. Not acceptable.' She shook her blond curls and sat back in her chair. I recognise this as her closing stance.

Once again, she had referred to me in her story. I didn't know Philip, and I definitely wasn't the instigator in any bullying. I had never stolen anything in my life. Was she doing this to unnerve me? Was she trying to get under my skin, make me feel threatened? If I had wronged her in the past, why had she never targeted me? Or was she trying to make me think I might be a possible future victim?

Chapter 43
GINNIE'S TRANSCRIPT
1974

'What do you mean you're not going to uni?' Maria sat up. We'd been lying on Tom's bed listening to *Tubular Bells*.

Tom looked up from the book he was reading. 'Are you kidding?'

I had gained five straight A Highers, was sitting sixth year studies chemistry and maths, and had an unconditional acceptance from Glasgow University to do pure sciences. The school guidance staff had insisted I apply to university. I think they hoped that I would change my mind when all my friends got places. Didn't they notice I didn't have 'friends' at school?

'I think I want to work in a hospital lab, I don't need a degree for that, they'll train me up. I need to earn some money. The grant won't be enough to pay the bills.' Dad had stopped working after mum died. At eighteen I had started working in a local bar to help out. We survived on benefits and my bar tips but there was no extra money. Going to university was out of the question. 'I've applied to a couple of hospitals.'

'But that's a waste of your brain...'

Tom stopped Maria mid-sentence.

'You'll never get her to change her mind, Maria. Once Ginnie sets on something there's no arguing with her.' He turned to me. 'Are you sure it's what you want to do? Is it just the money?' He looked worried, but he knew we had been struggling recently. His mum often sent pots of soup or a cake over with him. There was always a story about it being extra or needing to be eaten but I knew it was her way of helping.

'Of course it is.' I wanted to change the topic. 'Flip the album over, I want to hear side two.' The music was haunting, not like anything any of us had heard before.

'Will you not get a grant? What does your dad say?"

'He doesn't give a shit. As long as he has money coming in for booze and fags and the dogs then he doesn't care. Even a full grant won't be enough. I'd need to work full time and study, so I'd rather work at something I want to do. I'll get paid while I'm studying on the job.'

'Are you giving up the hotel?' Maria asked. I had been working as a waitress at weekends, covering weddings and functions at the local hotel.

'I'll keep it on for a while. The tips are good.' The pay at the Highland was rubbish but drunken guests at weddings were generous with their tips, especially if you flirted a bit with the men when their wives weren't looking. The short kilts we wore helped.

'Ginnie!' My dad's voice rang out across the road. What now? 'Get over here now. The dogs need walking.'

The two greyhounds were kennelled in our shed; he'd stopped using Ranald's farm after he died. 'Why can't you walk your own bloody dogs?' I muttered under my breath as I stomped down Tom's stairs. Dad always managed to walk when he was at the dog track but feigned back problems at home.

I slipped on their leads and strode over the fields where I'd played with Francis and Tom as a child. At the top of the hill, I let them off and they raced off quartering the field in search of rabbits. A scurrying noise and a yelp indicated they'd been successful, and I watched as they disappeared into the distance. 'Shit. Paddy, Cage!' I yelled knowing there was no point, the dogs wouldn't return until they'd either caught and killed the rabbit or lost it down a burrow. I ran after them, catching the odd glimpse of their brindle backs in the long grass. There was a squeal, they'd caught it. I reached them as they finished the creature, their muzzles smeared in blood, tongues lolling, exhausted by the chase. I walked them back home but there was something wrong with Paddy. His breathing was heavy, and he stumbled as we neared home. At our garden gate he collapsed. My dad appeared at the door and ran down the steps to the stricken dog, his bad back forgotten. He lifted the dog. 'Take Cage into the kennel. I'll deal with Paddy.'

He carried Paddy to the garden tap and began playing water over his body. I'd seen him doing this to a dog which had overheated after a race, years before. He cradled the greyhound's head on his knee, showing the dog more affection than he'd ever shown me. Paddy staggered to his feet; he was ok.

'Get out of the way.' Dad shoved me aside and led

the dog into the shed. A few minutes later he came into the house. I was making tea in the kitchen. He walked towards me and slapped me hard as I turned to ask how Paddy was. 'Never, ever do that again.' He stormed through the house, leaving me holding my cheek. I'd never been hit before.

Chapter 44
TOM'S DIARY

June 30th, 1974

Ginnie came over last night. She had an enormous bruise on her cheek. Said it had been her dad. She was very quiet. Just said she had to get out of the house.

Tom 2015

This was the first time he had ever heard Ginnie mention abuse. He recalled that she hadn't seemed too bothered about the fact that her dad had hit her. She had shrugged off his concern when he had asked about the bruises.

When her mother was alive, Ginnie's parents had been a quiet couple.

At the time he had wondered what had caused her dad to snap, to slap her. He was drinking a lot, Tom had often seen him staggering home from the pub. He had lost his wife, it was as if the man had given up on life. As a couple they had seemed to spend all their spare time together; he couldn't recall ever seeing one without the other except when Mr Queen had been at work. He remembered his mum had once commented on them being like Siamese twins. He couldn't recall Ginnie ever being part of their closeness. His own childhood had been very different. Family days out, picnicking, seaside jaunts, he and his brothers had always been included. He had never been left at home alone until he was a teenager and, even then, his older brother who had moved into a nearby flat, had been charged with keeping an eye on him.

He had been jealous of Ginnie then. Had wished for her freedom. Now he realised that her adoptive parents had never really cared for her. Never shown any love or tenderness. They had fed and clothed her, but she had been starved of affection. He recognised now that she had been mistreated in a more insidious way. The times they had gone out together, leaving Ginnie home alone, the freedom they allowed her to run wild from morning until night, although it was not physical abuse it was neglectful in the extreme. What effect had that had on the person she had grown into? He had only once seen Ginnie show any sign of love for another human being. She hadn't loved her husband George but Mike, her first real boyfriend had seemed to be the love of her life. He shuddered when he recalled how that had ended.

Chapter 45
GINNIE'S TRANSCRIPT
1974

I weaved among the wedding guests, balancing the tray of beers and dry martinis in one hand.

'Sorry!' One of the dancing guests bumped into me, causing me to spill some of the drinks.

'Arse.' I glared at him. I'd have to go back to the bar to get the lagers topped up, but my curse was wasted as he swung his partner across the room and disappeared among the crowd.

I placed the tray on the bar. 'Top these up Jimmy.' I had to shout over the noise of the ceilidh band.

I felt a warm hand on my shoulder. 'Sorry again. I'll pay for these.' I looked up at the man who'd knocked into me.

'It's ok. No charge.' I looked up into his face and noticed his startling green eyes. The corners crinkled when he smiled.

'I'll walk you to your table then. Stop any other ee-jits battering into you.' He walked beside me; his arms outstretched. 'Make way, make way.' He shouted at the other dancers who were now engrossed in a Strip The Willow.

'I'm ok. I'll manage.' I ducked under his arm, placing the tray on the table of revellers.

'Would you like to dance?' he asked.

I nodded towards the next table who were clamouring for more drink.

'I'm busy. Or haven't you noticed?' I pushed past him, but he followed me.

'Aw go on. You can take a break for a dance with a visitor to this lovely area.' Airdrie could be described in many ways but 'lovely' wasn't one of them.

'Later.' I liked this stranger's voice, he wasn't local, his sing-song lilt and burring 'r's intriguing.

'Michael E Murphy at your service. Mike to you.' He waited for me to return the offer.

'Ginnie Queen.' There was something endearing about his old-fashioned curtesy.

'See you later then Ginnie Queen. What time do you finish?'

'Once we get rid of this lot.' I indicated the wedding group. Last orders would be at 11pm. 'I'll be done by midnight.' If he was willing to wait, he might be worth getting to know.

*

He wrapped his arms around me, engulfing me in warmth. We had walked from the hotel to my house. Strolling slowly on the way, in no rush to finish our journey. Dancing down the main street, his kilt swinging as he twirled me round until I felt dizzy. Holding hands and laughing like old friends. For the first time I felt completely at ease with a stranger.

'Can I see you again?' He looked down at me, holding my gaze.

'That would be great. Better make it soon though.' He had told me he was in Airdrie for his brother's wedding returning home to Nairn in the next day or two. I had no idea where Nairn was, but his Highland accent gave me a clue.

'Tomorrow? What are you doing during the day?'

'I'm free. See you at ten? We could go for a coffee.' I wasn't going to waste any time. I had never connected with anyone in this way before.

He reached down and kissed me.

'See you tomorrow. I'll pick you up.'

The next day he appeared in a bright red Mini, unfolding himself from the car when he stepped out to meet me. I had been watching for him from the doorway and rushed out to join him. He wrapped his arms around me and kissed me passionately. Dad didn't bother to ask where I was going, he barely spoke to me most days.

'Meet Daisy.' Mike patted the car's bonnet. He opened the passenger door and I slid in, noticing that the driver's seat was pushed back in line with the back seat. I understood why when he folded himself behind the wheel. His long legs touched the steering wheel despite the seat being pushed back as far as it could go. 'Where to?'

'Ayr.' I didn't hesitate. 'Let's go to the beach.' I wanted to get away from home. Dad had kept me awake the night before with incessant coughing. The bedroom walls were thin, and his constant hacking had woken me every half hour. We'd had an argument about his smoking over breakfast. After mum had died, he had gone from a pack a day to two or sometimes three. I needed the freshness of ozone assaulting my nose, wanted the wind to blow away the staleness of home.

Within an hour we were walking along the beach, talking easily, sharing our lives. I took off my shoes and socks and ran into the freezing water, kicking through the waves. 'Come on. Come and join me.' I stood just outside his reach, hand outstretched and beckoning. He kicked off his trainers and rolled up his jeans and waded in after me. He started singing. An old song I'd never heard before, 'Ginnie Come Lately.' I laughed at the soppy words. They described how the singer had just met someone, but they were the one they wanted forever.

'I mean it Ginnie. I really like you. I've never felt like this before. Come to Nairn. You'll get work there and we'll be able to be together. I want to get to know you properly.'

I didn't need time to consider his offer. I wanted to get away from dad, away from Airdrie. The fact that I didn't know anything about this man didn't cross my mind. 'OK. Let's go.' He looked at me, his eyes trying to decide if I was serious. 'Come on. Take me home to pack. We can go tonight.'

He swung me round, grinning, 'You're as mad as I

am. Really? You'd just pack up and go on the whim of a stranger?'

'No, not just any stranger. You're something else Michael E Murphy. You might be just what I need.'

Tom had Maria. I hated my father. There was nothing and no-one else there for me. The chance to get away, make a new start, was too much to miss.

Chapter 46
FIONA
2015

I think Ginnie has just given away something she has never addressed before. 'How did you really feel about Tom? Were you in love with him?' I wonder if she was more hurt by his relationship with Maria than she admitted.

'Don't be daft. I was never "in love" with Tom.' She looks at me as if I'd just suggested that pigs could fly.

'Do you think Maria took Tom's affection away from you? Bear with me here. This was a boy, a man, who had always been there for you, always been a constant in your life. Did you fear that their love would drive a wedge between you?'

She leans forward in her seat. 'Let's get this clear Fiona. Tom and Maria had been an item for four years by the time I left. If I'd been bothered about their relationship, don't you think I'd have done something before then? Remember, I deal with people who wrong me. Do you think Maria would have survived if I had seen her as a threat?'

'I'm not saying she wronged you, although she took Tom away from you. Could that not be construed as theft?' I know I'm playing with fire. I shouldn't put ideas in her head.

'She didn't take the Tom I wanted in my life away.

She fulfilled a part of his life that I was unwilling to give. I didn't want a relationship with Tom. At least not that kind of relationship, we're best friends, that's it. I wanted to get away from home for me. To get away from the bullies at school.' She raises an eyebrow when she says this. 'Away from my dad, from everything about Airdrie that depressed me. This was the ideal chance. There was something special about Mike. I knew that immediately. So don't try to play the shrink with me and suggest scenarios that fit in with your agenda of the poor wee girl running away from a broken heart. There wasn't one.'

'OK,' I say. 'Tell me more about Mike. What happened next?'

Chapter 47
GINNIE'S TRANSCRIPT
1974

Three hours later we were driving up the A9, passing Stirling. I'd never been this far from home before. I had left a note for Tom and one for my dad who'd still been in bed when I got home, sleeping off a heavy session from the night before. Tom's note said I'd call him, dad's just said goodbye. I had packed a small bag and emptied my collection drawer into a box, adding the pencil jar, the one I'd used to kill Francis. These things were the only bit of my previous life I wanted to take with me. I didn't need any other memories of my past.

Mike described his hometown, a small fishing port that was expanding quickly because of the oil boom. He was an electrician working on the fabrication site in Ardersier and lived at home with his parents and sister. 'Inverness has a big hospital, you should be able to get work there, I know the head lab tech, I'll have a word.' I hadn't told him much about my life but shared my plan to work as a hospital lab technician, agreeing that being paid to study for a career you wanted was a good idea.

He had phoned a friend who had a flat in Inverness and arranged accommodation for me. 'Inverness is better if you want work. I can drive out to see you every night and weekends. Taff is a good guy, and he works offshore two weeks on two weeks off. You'd have the place to yourself when he was away.'

'Sounds like a plan. As long as I can see you every night. I think this can work.'

He kept glancing across at me. 'I can't believe this.' He shook his head, trying to make sense of the speed our relationship was developing. 'Are you always this decisive?'

'Yup. No point wasting time, do what you want, when you want; that's my mantra.'

We drove on through the rugged Highland scenery, stopping off in Pitlochry for a break. We spent miles in silence, comfortable in each other's company, singing along to the radio when we could get a signal. At 10pm we pulled up outside a Victorian terrace in the Highland capital of Inverness. Mike pulled my bag from the boot of the mini and, holding tightly to my hand, pulled me up the steps to the front door. His knock was answered by a large, friendly-looking man with a red beard and ready smile. 'Ginnie, Taff – Taff, Ginnie,' Mike introduced us with a wave of his arm.

'Nice to meet you Ginnie. Never thought Spud would come back from Airdrie with a girlfriend.'

'Spud?'

Mike laughed. 'Cos my surname's Murphy. Taff is Irish and he's an idiot who loves tatties. He started it at school and now everyone up here calls me that.' Mike didn't deny the girlfriend comment.

'You don't sound Irish.' I looked up at the big ruddy

faced man, 'And is Taff not a Welsh name?'

'My mum's Welsh, blame her, it's my middle name. My first name's Hamish. Would you no' want to be called something else?'

'True.' I laughed, 'Anyway, thanks for giving me a room Taff. Saves me having to weed out the weirdos in the To Let columns.' I had never lived away from home, and I worried about living with someone apart from my parents. I had hoped that I'd be staying at Mike's until I'd discovered he still shared with his family. I'd wanted to be somewhere we could be alone. 'You always hear stories about mad axe murderers and rapists enticing girls into their flats.'

'You'll be fine with Taff. You're not his type.' Mike laughed. He winked at Taff, and I realised what he was hinting at. I'd never met anyone who was gay, or if I had I hadn't noticed. Some of the kids at school had taunted one boy in sixth year but he had always denied that he was homosexual. It was still illegal in Scotland in the early 70s so it's understandable that people were reticent to come out, 'Just don't tell him any secrets. Biggest gossip in the Highlands. If you want folk to know something, just tell Taff – better than the *Press* and *Journal*.'

Taff tutted. 'News, not gossip Spud, news I tell ye'.' He flounced off exaggerating the swing of his hips. 'Your room is the one on the right at the top of the stairs, Ginnie. Don't believe a word he says, he's just jealous that I've got loads of pals.'

'I'll remember that.' I laughed, picking up my bag. 'OK Spud, come and help me unpack.' I led him up the short flight of stairs to my room. He pulled me towards him. The warmth of his touch reminding me of the feeling I had when Aunt Meg hugged me. This time I didn't want it to end. I felt safe and wanted in his arms. It was a feeling I'd never had before but I knew I wanted more.

*

The next few weeks went past in a blur. True to his word Mike got me an interview at the local hospital, and I was offered a trainee lab technician's job. It would involve night classes and home study but like any other thing I had done I picked up the information quickly. I have a photographic memory, every book or document I read stayed lodged in my brain and I could recall every memory of every day in startling clarity.

One evening the phone rang. It was Tom. We hadn't spoken in weeks and his voice was cold.

'Mum has asked me to let you know your dad's not well. He was taken into Monklands on Friday. It's his heart she thinks. He's back home now. He told her not to tell you, but she thinks you should know.'

I wasn't sure how to respond. I felt nothing.

'Thanks for letting me know.' There was an extended pause from both of us. Tom spoke first.

'Thought you'd disappeared. A quick call would

have been nice.' The sarcasm dripped from the handset.

'I've been busy.' I told him all about the job and Mike. Tom hardly said a word as I recounted what had happened since I had arrived in Inverness. I heard Tom take a deep breath.

'Better tell you my news then.' I hadn't even thought to ask how he was. 'Maria's pregnant...' He paused to let this sink in, 'We're getting married as soon as we can.'

'Oh my god. What about Uni?' I hoped he wasn't giving up his place.

'Maria's mum is going to look after the baby, she's moving in for a while until we can make other arrangements. We can still go. We'll get jobs as well, we'll manage.'

I hadn't asked about Maria. I wasn't interested in her career but was pleased that Tom hadn't given up his dream.

'Could you just join the police now? Work your way up?'

'I could but going in as a graduate recruit fast tracks you to promotion. We'll see how it goes. It's always an option.' Tom had never swayed from the dream he had as a boy. He wanted to be a Detective Inspector and knew the best way to achieve this. 'Anyway. Can you come back down for the wedding? It'll be small, but I'd like you to be there. And you can see your dad at the same time.'

'Of course I will.' I gave him my address to send the invite and promised I'd be there. Why would he think I wouldn't be there? Not for my dad, for him. I slammed the handset down. Taff looked up from the book he was reading.

'Problem, honey?'

'Bloody friend, Tom's got his girlfriend pregnant and they're getting married. They've only just started Uni. Says her mum will look after the kid, but I can't see that working.'

'Don't let it bother you – it's their lives. Never got that need for a kid myself.' Taff patted the couch beside him, and I sat, tucking my legs under me and leaning on his shoulder.

'Me neither. At least you've got the perfect excuse.' He dunted my arm. We never talked about his sexuality but there was a silent agreement that I knew. 'I can't believe they've been so stupid. Probably Maria wouldn't use a condom and isn't on the pill; devout Catholic girl and all that.'

'Tom is as much at fault you know. Doesn't he know they call people who use the withdrawal method parents? He put it in there.'

I laughed. The anger I had felt following the phone call was lifting. I liked Taff. He was easy to talk to and felt like a brother, none of the alpha male posturing I'd seen in most young men. We had a similar sense of humour and if I needed to know anything about Mike I just had to ask. The warning had been right, he was an inveterate gossip.

Chapter 48
TOM'S DIARY

July 13th, 1974

Ginnie has left home. I haven't seen her around for a few weeks, but I had other things on my mind. Maria's pregnant. I'm going to be a dad. I'm trying to hold everything together for her sake, but I haven't slept since she told me. Everyone thinks we'll be fine, that we can still study and raise a child. Everyone is offering help. I'm worried that the offers will dry up as soon as the baby gets older. What the fuck am I going to do?

The wedding's booked for September, it'll be a quiet affair, just family - and Ginnie of course. It'll be good to see her again - we can't chat normally on the phone.

Maria's getting bigger by the minute. She wants to get married before the birth. God knows what the gossips in the church will be saying - there'll be much wringing of gums.

Don't care.

I'm marrying Maria.

Tom 2015

They had managed. Maria's mum moved in for the first few weeks to help them out, baby-sitting to allow her daughter to continue her studies. She had then found a flat nearby so she could still support her daughter without being on top of the two of them.

He shivered when he thought of how he had reacted when the baby was born and how much he owed Ginnie. If she hadn't been there for him his son's life would have been very different.

Should he have spent more time talking to Ginnie? Running off to the Highlands on a whim with a man she barely knew, what kind of friend was he who had just accepted her going? He had been right though, organising the wedding, getting ready for a new-born while trying to study for a degree he knew was the key to a good future for him and his unexpected family had swamped him. The birth of his son had almost overwhelmed him completely. He shut the thought from his mind. He could barely recall any of his student days, had fitted study time around night-time feeds, sat exams with barely four hours sleep and miraculously he had passed, not the first-class Honours that had been expected but a 2:1 which was enough to get him fast tracked into his police career.

Once he had met Mike and saw how Ginnie behaved when she was with him, he had relaxed, thinking that his friend had eventually settled down, hoping that Mike would be someone who would show her the love she had never been given. Even now he was sure that Mike had been the only person Ginnie had ever loved. Or at least thought she did.

He opened the file relating to the next case she had admitted to. He had never heard of such an attack on someone. If she had been telling the truth he would have been unable to fathom the depths of hatred that could cause someone to do such a thing. If she had really loved Mike, could she have done what she did to him?

Chapter 49
GINNIE'S TRANSCRIPT
1974

Every minute I spent with Mike is etched in my mind. Every look, touch, word of those few weeks is as clear in my head as the day they happened.

We spent hours just sitting with each other, content in just being together. We walked for miles along Nairn beach scanning the water for dolphins, spotting seals on the rocks, always hand in hand, unable to be near each other without physical contact. The Hermitage was a hotel on the outskirts of Nairn. We'd spend time there, talking, listening to songs on the jukebox; he played me the original version of 'Ginnie Come Lately' and I'd laugh at the words.

Our love making was tender but passionate. I had been a virgin when we met, the taunts of Virginia the Virgin of my school mates had been accurate. I had never been close to anyone before, had never had anyone who could be described as a boyfriend. Philip couldn't really be counted as a boyfriend; I only went out with him to get Maria and Tom off my back.

When I caught Mike looking at me as I sat reading a book or heard his exhalation of breath when he held me the thrill was physical and overwhelming. When he wrapped his arms around me and held me close, I recalled the feeling I'd had at Aunt Meg's. That was the first time I had ever been loved. I was in no doubt, Mike loved me.

We would talk for hours, he sharing his childhood stories, tales from work, travelling around Europe with Taff, I speaking only of Tom.

'Why do you never talk about anything in your past apart from your friend?' We were lying in bed, wrapped in each other's arms, satiated. 'I want to know everything about you. I love you Ginnie, let me in.'

'There's nothing much to tell. I've not done anything, been anywhere. I was adopted, we didn't go on holidays or have any family adventures. All I've ever done is go to school and spend time with Tom. Pretty boring really.'

'What about work? What are your workmates like?'

'Gregor the boss is ok, but I don't spend any time with the others. Checking smear test slides is hardly a riveting conversation. I'm happy just to listen to you.' I meant that. I loved his voice. The soft burr thrilled me. I loved everything about Inverness and Nairn. The landscape, the town, the slower way of life, the fact that it wasn't Airdrie. But most of all I loved Mike, I found it hard to admit this, even to myself. 'Go on say "butter"' I loved the way he rolled the consonants in certain words. Butter was my favourite.

'Tell me about Tom then? How are he and Maria coping? You hardly mention her.' He was determined to get me to talk about myself.

'We're not close, if she wasn't with Tom, we

wouldn't know each other. I've known Tom forever, he's like a brother. We've always been there for each other. He used to be bullied as a child, but Francis and I looked after him.'

'You've never mentioned Francis before. Have you lost touch with him?' He ran his hand down my cheek as we talked.

'Francis died. When we were ten.' I buried my face in his chest. 'I don't like to talk about it.'

He turned my face towards his. He looked distraught and held me closer, 'Oh no. I'm so sorry Ginnie, I didn't mean to drag up bad things from your past that are painful. I can wait, tell me things when you want to. We've got all our lives to get to really know each other.'

I kissed him. He whispered again that he loved me, but I didn't reply.

Chapter 50
FIONA
2015

'You say you'd never felt loved before. Do you think your parents didn't love you?' I wanted Ginnie to open up about her relationships. This is the first time she has ever mentioned love. Her face reflects a vulnerability I haven't seen previously when she talks about Mike.

Ginnie sits for several minutes before she replies. 'I've never thought about it. Maybe because I was adopted, they didn't need to love me. Just take care of me, feed me, whatever it takes to raise a child. No, I don't think they loved me. No-one had ever told me they loved me before Mike did.'

'Did you love him?'

'Yes.' She doesn't expand on this. She is biting the skin round her nails then notices I am watching her and folds her arms in front of her chest.

'Why didn't you tell him?'

'Didn't want to give him control? Is that the theoretical reason Fiona? If I had told him how I felt would he have too much power over me? To tell the truth it was never a phrase that I'd uttered. Until then I'd never been told I was loved, nor had I said it to anyone. Maybe I was scared.' She looks at me with those big, open, trusting eyes, daring me to question her. I decide to leave it there.

'You say you were a virgin when you met but what about Philip? Did you not say you'd slept with him?'

'What Philip and I did is irrelevant. Childish fumblings. What I had with Mike was different, special.'

That wasn't what I'd asked. Has she slipped up? 'So you didn't have sex with Philip?'

'We messed around a lot but no, we didn't have full sex. I was a virgin when I met Mike. You must have misheard me. I led Philip on so I could do what I wanted to do. He lied about sleeping with me to his pals, maybe that's where you're getting confused.'

She's turning this so that I will doubt what I've written. I'll check on that later. I try a different tack, tapping my pen on my notepad, 'Tell me what you feel for Tom.'

'He's my friend.' Her gaze is on my notepad, refusing to look me in the eye.

'Do you love him, have you ever been in love with him?'

She frowns. 'Not like that. Not like Mike. Tom's just always been there. We've looked out for each other all our lives. I've never thought of him in a romantic way, he always had Maria.'

'What do you think would have happened if he hadn't met Maria? Would you two have become a couple?' I asked, trying to draw more from her.

'I've never given it a thought. I suppose we could have. Maybe everything would have been different. Maybe we wouldn't be sitting here now. But he did meet Maria and she stole his heart, there was never anyone else for Tom. Anyway, everyone says we're like brother and sister but I've never had a sibling and he hardly speaks to his so I don't think we can be described that way. Why should there be unconditional love between family members? You don't get to choose them so what happens if you don't feel love for them?' She changes the subject again, is she uncomfortable talking about her feelings for her lifelong friend? Have I triggered something in her?

'Did you tell anyone that your father was ill? I've noticed you don't mention it again.'

'I didn't care. His health was his problem. He smoked and drank. Didn't look after himself after mum died. What should I have done? Run home to nurse him?'

'Most people would.' This slipped out before I had thought it through.

'I'm not "most people" Fiona. I thought you'd realise that by now.'

She leans back. I now know that means she's had enough, doesn't want to continue the conversation so I pick up my notes and switch off the recorder. 'Let's have a break. Would you like a coffee?' I need to step out for a few minutes to let what she has told me sink in. Her inability to admit love for someone who means so much to her speaks volumes about Ginnie's psyche.

She straightens up in her chair, pointing to the recorder. 'No. let's carry on. Switch it on again.'

I sit back down and do as she asks, wondering what will be next.

Chapter 51
GINNIE'S TRANSCRIPT
1974

'When did you have your last period?' Dr Braithwaite peered over the top of her glasses, tapping her short stubby finger on the clipboard in front of her.

'June, I think.' I've never had heavy periods, took my pills regularly and dealt with the odd cramp with a couple of aspirin. The first I thought something was wrong was when I went off booze completely. Couldn't finish a cider, then I started throwing up for no reason.

'Didn't you think you might be pregnant when you missed the first one? I'd guess you're about eight weeks, a scan will tell us more accurately.'

I fixed her with a solid stare. 'I don't need a scan. I want an abortion.' I was not going to be talked out of this. The last thing I wanted in my life was a child. I must have got pregnant the first time Mike and I had slept together. 'And I want it as soon as possible.'

'What does the father think?'

'He's not in my life. He was a one-night stand. I haven't seen him for months,' I lied. I didn't want the complication of involving Mike in my decision.

She looked at me again, breathing deeply, suppressing a sigh. It didn't matter whether she believed me or not, I was not telling Mike. And I was not having this baby.

'I want you to take a few days and think this over. Discuss it with your parents. You will have to have an interview with another doctor, and they will go over your options.'

'What bit of what I said don't you understand?' I glared at her, sitting forward in the chair. 'I don't need to think it over. I don't have parents to talk it over with. I know what I want, so if you don't mind, what do I do now?'

She moved her chair back slightly, the scraping of the legs on the linoleum floor breaking the silence which drew between us.

'OK Ginnie, if you're a hundred percent sure. I'll arrange an appointment at the maternity unit as soon as I can, you need a second doctor to sign off on the operation. Remember you can change your mind at any point.'

'That won't happen doctor. And can you arrange for a coil to be fitted at the same time please? Thank you.' I stood up and strode towards the door. I could hear her shuffling her papers as I left.

Taff was waiting at the door for me. He had driven me to the surgery. 'Well?'

'Positive.' I walked past him towards the car. He caught up with me, grabbing my arm and turning me towards him, enveloping me in a bear hug.

'What are you going to do? What has Mike said?'

'He doesn't know. Nothing to do with Mike, I'm

getting rid of it.' I pulled away from him and flopped into the car, propping my feet on the dashboard. He rushed round to the driver's door, ducking into the driver's seat.

'What do you mean it's nothing to do with Mike. He's the dad. He'll be delighted. Unlike me, the daft bugger always wanted to have children.'

'Don't you dare tell him. What he doesn't know won't hurt him. I'm not having a baby and that's that. Take me home please.' I knew that Taff didn't agree with me but hoped I could trust him to keep quiet. He had been the one who had persuaded me that I might be pregnant so I couldn't have hidden it from him.

'It's your choice Gin. I don't agree with it, but I'll support you.' He started the car and turned the radio on to cover the silence between us.

Ten days later I walked out of the hospital, a sense of overwhelming relief lifting me. Once again Taff was with me. He really was a good friend to me at that time. I could have managed it all on my own, but it felt good to have someone there. I would have preferred it to be Tom, but Taff was a half decent substitute. He hugged me when I got to the car, driving me home in silence.

Chapter 52
GINNIE'S TRANSCRIPT

1974

'Will you marry me?' Mike gazed into my eyes, he had knelt so he was level with me. At six foot three he towered over my five-foot two frame but on his knees, we were roughly the same height. I felt as if I'd been punched in the stomach. What had Taff said? Had he told him? Did he think I was still pregnant?

'Don't be daft. I'm only eighteen. Got years before I want to think about settling down. Why on earth would you want to get married?' I searched his eyes for any sign that he knew I had been pregnant.

'I'm twenty-two. I just want to get married and have children before I get old.'

He was serious. 'Has Taff said anything to you?' I had to make sure my flatmate had kept his promise.

'Taff? What's Taff got to do with it?'

'Nothing.' I cuddled in close to him, head buried in his chest to hide my cheeks which I could feel flushing with blood. I had never been able to lie.

He sat up and turned towards me. 'Tom's getting married. He's the same age as you and you haven't said anything about him not being ready.'

'But that's Tom, not me. He's a good Catholic boy and Maria's pregnant.' I had suggested a termination to Tom, and he'd been aghast. Neither of them had considered it an option. I pulled on Mike's shirt, trying to get him to face me. 'Come on Spud.' I used his pet name trying to cajole him. 'Let's just have some fun.'

'I don't want just fun. I'm serious. You're the one who said you should do what you want, no point wasting time. "Do what you want when you want" –isn't that what you said? I don't want to wait for years before you make up your mind. What if you decide we shouldn't be together? I want to have a family while we're young. My parents had me when they were both forty. It's not good to have children when you're older, better when you've got the energy and stamina to deal with them. Don't you want a family?'

He could read the answer to this on my face. I didn't want children, ever. I sat back, taking my hand from his arm, releasing him. 'I'm sorry Mike. I can't promise you anything. I don't know how I'll feel next week never mind twenty years in the future. All I know is that I'm happy with you here and now. I don't want to marry, and I definitely don't want children. Ever. Come on, let's just go on as we are. Don't spoil things.'

'I think it's too late for that. I want you, I want to father our children. If you can't see that in our future, I don't think we can go on.'

He got up and walked off, his shoulders slumped, ignoring my calls to come back and talk about it. Was that it? Was that the end of our relationship? I watched him until he disappeared round the corner, willing him to turn around, to laugh and say he was joking but he didn't.

I returned to the flat and told Taff what had happened.

'He's always been like that Gin. Even at school his future plans included a family. Always been a strange biddy. Are you sure you know what you want? I think the only way you'll keep him is to say yes.'

'I can't do that Taff. I'm not ready to settle down and kids are definitely off the table. We're miles apart on this subject.'

'Could be the end then. He's a typical Cancer man. Soft and sentimental and family-oriented. He has no control over it – he was born that way.'

'Do you really believe that shite?' I dug him in the ribs.

'Absolutely. You, for instance, are a perfect Aquarian. You can be cold and aloof. You don't seem to care about anyone apart from the odd one or two. You're concerned about Tom but don't seem in the slightest worried about Maria.'

'That's cos she's not my friend. If she wasn't with Tom, I'd not be in contact with her at all.'

'That's what I mean. Have you any female friends?'

'Apart from you, you mean?' I tried to deflect from the subject. His words struck home. He was right; I didn't have any friends, hadn't formed any lasting relationships with anyone apart from Tom.

'That's what I mean. Mike could be what you need. Don't spoil it.'

'I think I love Mike. Just not enough to settle down right now.'

'I don't know if that'll be enough for hm. I know what he's like. He's not going to change, and neither are you. Here, give me a hug.' His big arms held me tight.

I wanted Mike's arms round me, but I couldn't lie to him just to keep him.

Chapter 53
GINNIE'S TRANSCRIPT
1974

A fortnight later Mike appeared at my door. I had called him several times, but he hadn't been returning my calls. When I saw him at the door my face couldn't hide my pleasure that he had come round. My elation was short lived.

'Is it true? Did you have an abortion?' I had never seen him so angry. I stepped back and waved him into the flat. 'I take it from your silence that it is true. How could you do that? How could you not tell me you were pregnant?'

'Sit down Mike. Calm down.' I wracked my brain to find a way to explain what I'd done. 'Did Taff tell you?'

'Taff? Taff knew? For fuck's sake. Am I the only person who didn't know?'

I reached for his hand, but he drew it away abruptly.

'How did you find out then?' I was concerned that I couldn't trust Taff with a secret.

'Someone I know works at the hospital. She saw you there.'

'And this "someone" just thought she had to tell you? Who the fuck is it? I want her sacked.'

'Oh no no. You don't get to deflect this on to someone else. You knew I wanted a family, and you deliberately didn't tell me you were pregnant. Didn't give me a chance to have a say in my baby's future. My baby! You really are a selfish bitch.' He stood up. 'I just wanted to see your face when I told you I knew. You don't give a shit about anyone but yourself. I was coming round to thinking I could give you time to think about marriage, but I'll never forgive this Ginnie. I don't ever want to see you again.' He strode out of the room, slamming the door behind him.

I had thought about arguing that I didn't know he wanted children when I had had the abortion, but decided that there was nothing I could say that would change his mind. He hated me.

Chapter 54
FIONA
2015

'Can you understand why he was so angry? Why do you think you didn't tell him you were pregnant?' I find this a difficult subject. I've never been able to have children and it is my biggest regret and the cause of my divorce. I can't give any hint of my feelings on the matter to Ginnie though. I must remain impassive during my interviews with my biographees so I don't influence their stories. It's a trick I picked up from my psychologist friends and usually it works. Although I wonder if in this case it would make a difference. Some people feed off the response of others, using their revulsion to fulfil their needs. I now don't think Ginnie fits this category. She gives the impression that her behaviour and actions are perfectly acceptable. Her lack of empathy extends to me.

'It wasn't anything to do with him. He was just the sperm donor. He wouldn't be the one left to bring it up, the one who'd have to give up work. No way was I going to have a child. I had hoped he'd never find out. Pity Inverness is such a gossip minefield. I should have sued the hospital. They had no right to disclose my medical history. But I got my revenge eventually.'

I dread to think what she means by this.

'But you say you loved him. Did that not have an effect on your choice to have an abortion?'

'Nope. I had to make a quick decision. I was several weeks pregnant before I realised. I didn't have time for arguments. He would have tried to persuade me to keep the child but that wasn't an option. I thought it easier that he didn't know anything about it then he wouldn't feel guilty that he wouldn't be able to change my mind.'

I'm not getting anywhere with my questions. Ginnie believes she had the absolute right to exclude Mike from her decision and although I sympathise with the man, I can't argue with her. Having a child at eighteen would have changed her life completely. Only she had the right to decide.

I look over my notes. Something doesn't ring true and is niggling at my brain. Something from an earlier part of her story.

Chapter 55
GINNIE'S TRANSCRIPT
1974

Mike avoided me for the rest of the summer. He didn't answer my calls, I wrote to him, but he never replied to my letters.

In September Taff gave me notice to quit the flat. He felt a sense of loyalty to his old friend and although he apologised, he explained that by avoiding me, Mike had also cut him out of his life, and he didn't want that. He valued Mike as a friend and missed him. I understood. I liked Taff and didn't want to stand between him and his relationship with his friend. Besides that, if he and Mike stayed in contact, I'd get any news about Mike from Taff. I wanted to know what he was doing. Had he moved on or was there still a chance he'd come back to me?

I moved into a new flat in the old part of Inverness and buried myself in studying. Each time the phone rang I hoped it was Mike, I had left my new number with Taff in case Mike ever changed his mind, but no call ever came.

'What's he up to?' I had met Taff for a coffee and after the usual preliminaries I got straight to the point of the meeting.

'Nice to see you too Ginnie,' he said. 'Not a lot. He's working away as usual and doesn't come out much. I think he's seeing someone.'

'Who?' I almost jumped down his throat.

'Just a girl we were at school with. Jean something or other.' Taff could never lie. He concentrated on adding sugar to his coffee and stirred the drink until the movement became irritating.

'Taff. Look at me. Is it serious? This Jean woman. Jean...Ginnie. Must make it easy to remember her name.' I couldn't understand the strength of feeling I was experiencing. This was pure and utter jealousy. I didn't even know this woman and I hated her.

'Don't shoot the messenger Gin. You wanted to know.'

'Sorry Taff. It's just a bit obvious that she's got him on the rebound.'

'But you're the one who turned him down. You know that he wants to settle down and have children, maybe this Jean is willing to do that.' He was right. 'I know that you think you love him but he'll never forgive you for having the abortion. You need to get over it Ginnie. Time you found someone else.'

Taff knew me. Knew that being straight with me was the best way to deal with me. Maybe that's what I needed. Time to find someone else. But there was no-one else I was even vaguely interested in. Besides, I still hoped Mike would come back to me, would see my point of view and be willing to try again. The thought had tormented me for months.

'What's she like?' I needed to know more about this

Jean woman.

Taff raised both eyebrows. 'She's short, brown hair, a nurse, I think. According to Mike's sister Jean's always had a crush on him, knew him at school. Anyway it doesn't matter what she's like. Come on. Let's go to the pub. You need a gin, Gin.'

I agreed despite how I was feeling about Mike with someone else. It wasn't Taff's fault. 'OK, just one though. I've a paper to finish for Monday.' Something Taff had said struck me. 'She's a nurse? That nurse? The nurse who told Mike I'd had an abortion?'

'Behave. You don't know that,. Chances are it was nothing to do with Jean. There's loads of nurses at Raigmore. Come on, let's get that drink.'

I followed him from the café. I wasn't so sure that this Jean hadn't been the one to tell Mike that I'd had an abortion. The one who'd ruined my life.

Chapter 56
FIONA
2015

I wonder if Ginnie has ever known what she wanted. She contradicts herself, suddenly blaming Jean for ruining her life. She had the chance to be with Mike forever but had turned down his proposal. She had obviously not wanted to marry at eighteen.

'Did you think Mike should have just waited? Should he have just hung on until you decided it was time to settle down?' I ask her.

'I don't know. He didn't waste any time finding someone new when he left me. I think Jean realised he was vulnerable and used this to get him to start a relationship with her. According to Taff she had been hanging around for years, just waiting to get her grip on Mike.'

'Is that what Taff said?'

'It's what he meant. She waited until I'd dumped him then told him I'd had an abortion so he would hate me. She knew exactly what she was doing.'

I note that she is now saying she was the one who finished the relationship when it was perfectly clear that Mike had left her. She seems to be twisting the truth to suit her own needs.

'Do you wish you'd said yes? How do you feel about Mike now?'

'I'll answer that later. Let's get on with the story.' She leans forward in her chair and points to the recording machine.

Chapter 57
GINNIE'S TRANSCRIPT
1974

I went to Tom's wedding on my own, congratulating the happy couple and trying to ignore the growing lump under the bride's dress. Maria's cousin George grabbed my attention, he sat beside me during the meal, listening to my tales of the Highlands, keeping my wine glass topped up. He was the exact opposite of Mike physically, short and swarthy with the dark curly hair and black eyes of the typical Maltese man. It made me feel good to receive some male attention and I flirted outrageously with him, much to the obvious disgust of Violet, Maria's chief bridesmaid, who had her eyes on him. When he leaned in to kiss me at the end of the night I pushed him away, propelling him into the arms of the hapless bridesmaid. She could have him. Flirting was fun but I wasn't in the mood for anything else. I slipped him my number to get rid of him and joined the bride and groom in their taxi home. The wedding was a fairly quiet affair, parents, some family, Violet as witness come bridesmaid, and me.

'I see you've got rid of Cousin George.' Tom leaned forward in the cab. 'We didn't have a lot of choice in his being there – it's a Maltese family thing, Maria's mum insisted he should come. Best keep away from him though. He's bad news.'

I looked across at Maria. She had been annoyed when Tom suggested I share their taxi and sat silently looking out of the window as we drove back to their flat. She took a deep breath and rested her head on Tom's shoulder. Obviously she had accepted the fact that Tom and I would always be close.

'Tom's right Ginnie. You don't want to get involved with George.'

I had had no intention of getting involved with Cousin George up to that point, but their comments intrigued me. How bad was this man?

I didn't think it odd that I had been invited back to the happy couple's home. It wasn't as if they'd need to consummate the marriage and it was a short walk from Dad's house. We sat in their tiny living room, and I explained what had happened between Mike and me.

'Do you love him?' Maria sipped on a mug of hot chocolate. There was to be no honeymoon until after the baby was born; neither of them could spare the time from their studies.

'I don't know. I think so.' I'd never loved anyone before, and I wasn't sure if what I felt for Mike was love or just lust or comfort. 'I love how he treats me. I love the way he makes love to me. I just didn't know if I loved him enough to commit for ever and now I'll never know.' He had been my first proper lover and had unleashed a passion I didn't know existed in me. 'You two are different. You've always been right for each other; I can't imagine either of you with someone else but what if we had got married and I changed? Or he did?'

'There's another reason isn't there?' Maria unconsciously patted her stomach. 'You said he made it clear he wanted to start a family as soon as possible.'

'Aye. The wanting children bit. Can you imagine me with a child?'

'That was the biggest obstacle, wasn't it?' Tom added. 'I don't think I've ever seen you with a doll never mind a baby.'

He was right. I'd never held a child, never changed a nappy; I'd never shown the slightest hint of being maternal in any way. 'Poor wean. Even if I'd wanted to carry a child for nine months, Mike would have had to give up work to look after it. And I really don't want to do that to my body, shoving a bowling ball out of a hole the size of a golf ball? I don't think so.'

Maria looked aghast. She threw a cushion at me. 'I've got that to look forward to. I'd managed to push it out of my mind before now.'

'Unfortunately, it's not your mind it will be pushed out of.' I plumped the cushion up and stuck it under my jumper. 'Look,' I stood up sideways on. 'Does that look natural to you?' They both laughed, and we changed the subject. I didn't want to go into details, I hadn't mentioned that Mike had found someone else. I didn't want their sympathy, especially not Maria's.

We stayed up late, catching up with the gossip I'd missed while in Nairn, drinking copious cups of coffee. At midnight I walked the half mile home. I'd dropped my bag off at Dad's earlier that day but the stench of cigarette smoke in the house and his complaints about his health had stopped my wanting to linger and chat and I had showered, changed for the wedding and left after barely ten minutes.

He was in bed when I got in, so I made tea and took his cup to his bedroom. I could hear his sonorous breathing even before I knocked on the door to his room. He didn't reply so I turned the handle and peeked into the room. The heat was oppressive and the air smelled stale. Dirty clothes lay scattered in piles where he'd dropped them, and a full ashtray sat beside the bed. Mum had never allowed him to smoke in the bedroom, but that rule had long since been discarded.

'I've brought you a cuppa.' I sat the mug on the bedside table, but he didn't stir. His lips had a blueish tinge and his breathing sounded forced. He opened one eye slightly but seemed to have trouble focussing. He clasped his chest and groaned.

'Having problems breathing? Shame that. Looks like a heart attack to me Auld Yin. What's that? You want an ambulance?' I feigned leaning in to hear his mumbled words.

He couldn't articulate what was wrong but the look in his eyes implored me to get help. His face was wracked with pain, each in-breath obviously agonising.

'Nah. You'll be fine. Maybe if you'd shown a bit more compassion to me as a child then I'd have some for you now but hard luck. You were only interested in appeasing your wife. You never wanted me. Pity that I'm the only one who can help you now.' The fear in his eyes pleased me. 'You cared more about those damn dogs than you ever did about me. Don't worry, I'll make sure they get rehomed. It's not their fault that you're a bastard.'

I drank half of his tea, ate one biscuit and nibbled the other, leaving the remains by his bed and walked back downstairs, shutting his door behind me.

I had read enough medical books to recognise when someone was having heart failure. What good would an ambulance do? If they could revive him, it would just draw out the agony. Even if he could have been saved it would have meant me staying and nursing him and I had no intention of doing that. Is it murder if you just don't get medical help for someone who's dying? I didn't consider it. I thought about the time he'd hit me, the times he'd neglected me as a child, the lies he had told me. I poured a whisky from his favourite bottle and settled on the couch with a book. I'd check him in the morning.

Chapter 58
TOM'S DIARY

September 24th, 1974

What a wedding day. Maria looked beautiful although she moaned that she was fat. Our celebrations were cut short this morning though.

Ginnie's dad died last night. Poor Ginnie. She seems to be surrounded by death. She's all alone now. I asked if she'd try to build a relationship with her real mum now, but she said no. She always seems so resilient, so happy with her own company. Maria wonders if she'll ever form any lasting ties with anyone but me.

She's having him cremated next week.

She's clearing the house. A big skip appeared this afternoon outside on the drive and she's dumping everything into it. Says she doesn't want anything from it. Nothing to remind her of her childhood or her parents. Mum says she'll regret that but, as usual, there's no telling Ginnie.

Tom 2015

Was the story about her letting him die a complete fabrication? Although morally reprehensible, not calling an ambulance was not deemed to be criminal behaviour. Even if what she said was true, she couldn't be charged with anything. He looked at the passage he had highlighted in the notes recorded by the investigating officers.

"Thou shalt not kill but needst not strive, officiously, to keep another alive." (Arthur Hugh Clough 1819–1861) in support of the proposition that the failure to act does not attract criminal liability.

Taken with all her other apparent fabrications it had been agreed that the death of her father could not be attributed to Ginnie. Even if she had done what she said, she hadn't physically killed him and probably wasn't even in the room at the time when it was accepted that he had died. The cup and partially eaten biscuit on his bedside table had corroborated the original findings that he had died during the night, after Ginnie had taken him tea. Her story now that she had been the one who had drunk the tea and eaten the biscuit was something that had never been revealed before but was it an afterthought? Had she made that bit up to try to put the blame on herself now?

Tom scratched his head and stretched his knee out. He had been sitting for far too long and his muscles and joints were beginning to seize up. He knew that Ginnie's relationship with her father had deteriorated after she had found out she had been adopted to the extent where it was obvious she couldn't stand to be in the same house as him. Could she be cold enough or uncaring enough to ignore a dying man? Did she think this was retribution for him failing to get help and putting trust in the family GP when her mother had died? Or had she simply transferred his death to a place in her mind where she could have some control over it. Had she wanted him dead so had imagined that she had been aware of his impending heart attack? The more he considered her behaviour the less he understood his friend.

The other thing that stood out in this case was the lack of a memento. Nothing in her collection had belonged to her father. She had been true to her word and had dumped everything from the house into the skip. He remembered various neighbours had helped themselves to furniture and items which had survived the clearance. When Ginnie had finished clearing the house she had asked him to take her to the station to get the train back to Inverness, leaving the house keys with a neighbour to hand back to the Council. She hadn't stayed for the funeral, a thing which had shocked his mother and Maria.

Chapter 59
FIONA
2015

She just throws this fact in as an aside in her story. She's saying she killed her father, and it comes across as if it's a normal occurrence in everyone's life.

'Don't you agree that what I did counts as murder Fiona?'

I'm not going to be drawn into this. 'Not according to the strict letter of the law.' I want to know more, 'What do you think you would have done if he hadn't died?'

'I've never thought about that. There was no need. I suppose I would have thought of something else. A house fire maybe?' She looks satisfied with her answer, a slight nod of her head agreeing that burning her father to death would have been acceptable.

'Why hadn't you done something earlier? Why wait so long if the reason you killed him was because he failed to show you any care as a child? You're usually quick in your retribution. This seems out of character.' I want her to tell me the truth. I'm beginning to doubt Ginnie's story, but it will still make a brilliant read when I'm finished with it.

'I guess the opportunity had never appeared. I was away, remember. Everyone knew he was ill. He'd been in hospital and had been told to stop smoking but hadn't. Maybe I had hoped he'd die without my intervention. He was just taking too long. Why are you asking this? Don't you believe me?'

'It's not my job to believe you Ginnie. I just want to tell your story, I'm just the transcriber.'

She looks perplexed. 'But you need to believe me. You need to explain why I did what I did. You need to believe these people deserved to die, champion my cause. I need you on my side. You know I'd never lie. I want our readers to understand that lying and stealing are not acceptable. Betraying someone's trust is worse than a physical assault. A person can recover from physical hurt but they never recover from the damage done by someone's perfidy.'

None of this rings true. This is the woman who has never shown any respect or care for those who she encounters and suddenly she's looking for sympathy. I nod to the recorder and pick up my pen. 'Carry on.'

Chapter 60
GINNIE'S TRANSCRIPT

1974

At Hogmanay I stood under the town clock in Nairn, surrounded by hordes of drunken youngsters waiting to cheer in the new year.

I craned my neck searching for the tall form of Mike. He had said he always came to the clock. I really wanted to see him again. I missed him, and slow realisation had dawned that I loved him. I had written to him again and again, but he never replied. I hadn't seen Taff for a few weeks so hadn't been able to catch up on any gossip about what Mike was up to. How was his romance with the nurse going? I had to see him. If I could talk to him, I could tell him I'd changed my mind; that maybe he really was the one for me. Then, in the crowd I spotted him and took a step towards him. As I got closer, I could see he had his arm round a small, mousy woman. Her tight curls bounced as she walked, gripping tightly to his arm. This must be her. He saw me so I waved before he had a chance to disappear into the crowd.

'Hi Mike.' I ignored the woman beside him. 'How are you?' I leaned in to kiss his cheek. He stepped back, pulling his companion into his side.

'Ginnie, this is Jean...' He paused before continuing, 'My fiancée.'

I glanced at the girl who was holding her hand out to shake mine. Ignoring the hand, I looked into Mike's eyes. 'Couldn't wait then?' My heart ached. Despite how I felt I managed a cynical smile, arching one eyebrow and shaking my head slightly. He was marrying my twin, my more dowdy, plain twin, but there was no denying the similarity. It wasn't just the names that were close. 'Jean? I suppose it saves you learning a new song.' I remembered him singing *Ginnie Come Lately* to me and imagined him changing the name to Jeannie. My heart pounded, I turned and strode away. I needed to go before I started to cry. I could feel the hot tears prickling at my eyes and my throat constricted. Ignoring the sound of the bells which rang in the new year and the lurching young men who tried to kiss me as I passed, I searched the crowd for Taff and spotted him chatting to a young man in the doorway of the fruit and veg shop on the High Street.

'Happy New Year Ginnie.' He swung me round and kissed me lightly. I hugged him back. 'This is Gary.' He turned towards the man at his side. 'Gary works at the Royal Marine. He's new to the area so I'm going to show him the sights.'

'Careful Gary. Taff might show you some sights you've never seen the likes of before.' I winked at Taff. 'Happy New Year.' We hugged then I dragged Taff off, telling him I wanted to dance the Strip The Willow with him.

'Back in a minute,' he called to Gary, as we were engulfed in the drunken crowds of revellers. Instead of joining the end of the line set up to dance the energetic reel I pulled him towards a side street. 'Whoa Ginnie, I thought you wanted to dance.'

I gripped his arms, 'You didn't tell me this Jean was such an obvious replacement.' I chided. 'Is he stupid? Does he really think he can replace me that easily?'

'Aye, I know. I take it you've met them. You're right, she is very like you sweetie. Not as gorgeous obviously. Have you heard they're engaged?'

'Yes – he had the cheek to introduce me to her. Have I made a big mistake Taff? Should I tell him how I feel?' The idea filled my head – if I declared undying love for him and ask him to take me back would I be able to win Mike back?

'Too late Gin. They're getting married and going to emigrate to New Zealand. Leave him be. You'll find someone else.'

I felt as if I'd been punched. Not only had the copycat Ginnie taken Mike from me she was dragging him across the world, so I'd never see him again. Could she not see that she was just a poor replacement? Did she really believe that he loved her?

'Come on sweetie, let's dance. Or do you want to get a drink. Gary has some ciders in his rucksack. I'm going to take him on the first footing rounds. Why don't you join us?'

'I'll pass thanks Taff. I'm going to grab the bus back home. I'll see you tomorrow. Don't feel like partying.

Enjoy the rest of the night. Cheerie.' I just needed to get away.

I ran towards the bus station. Late night buses had been laid on to get drunken revellers home. I sat at the back and leaned against the window. Tears pricked my eyes, but I fought them back. I watched as an old man in a torn kilt staggered along the bus towards the empty seat beside me.

'Hello darlin'. Gies a new year kiss.' He slurred leaning over me.

'Fuck off.' I hissed.

'Fell oot with your boyfriend did ye?'

'I said fuck off, what bit of that didn't you understand?' I slipped my knife from my jacket pocket and waved it at him. He took the hint and backed away.

'Only tryin' tae be friendly.' I heard him mutter as he retreated to the front of the bus.

I closed my eyes and dreamed of what I could do.

Chapter 61
TOM'S DIARY

24th Jan 1975
I'm a dad. Joe was born at 11am weighing 7lb 3oz. Mother and baby doing fine. That's what I'm meant to be telling people, but I can't face anyone. What the fuck am I supposed to do? I can't be a dad. I'm 18.
FUCK!!!!!

Tom 2015

Tom leaned back in his seat, pushing his glasses onto his head. He hadn't forgotten this period in his life, how could he? But he had buried them in the depths of his memory, a place to avoid. His hand shook as he placed the diary back on the table, straightening the edge so it sat squarely in the corner. Maria must never see this entry.

He had fallen apart after the birth of his son. He'd held it together for the photos with Maria and the baby and the congratulations from his family. Something his brother said had started his feelings of doubt.

'Well done wee man,' he'd boomed slapping Tom on the back, 'never thought you had it in you.' Jim, at seven years older than Tom, had a two-year-old daughter. 'Now the hard work starts. Wait 'til you're up during the night and have to get up to go to uni at seven. You'll never get a minute to yourself. That wee scrap will demand all your time.'

Tom had laughed, hiding his thoughts. Jim had no idea he was just confirming his brother's fears. What the hell was he going to do? How stupid were they to think they'd cope? His brother continued...'And it's the end of your sex life. You'll be too knackered to even think about it.'

He wasn't helping.

'Shut up Jim, you'll terrify the boy.' Jim's wife joined in, pulling her husband by the arm.

That was the problem. He was a boy, not an adult, not a man who could take bringing up a baby while studying for a degree in his stride.

That evening after calling all the aunts and uncles to tell them about the birth he had sat in his living room, a half empty bottle of scotch on the table in front of him and he cried. Maria and the baby were to remain in the hospital for two more days, the family had all gone home, and he was left alone, falling deeper and deeper into a black hole of depression. He couldn't do it. Maria would be better back with her parents, better to meet someone else, someone who was an adult and could provide for her and her baby. He had no place in this child's life, would just fuck up the whole thing. He opened the bottle of pills he'd found in the cupboard. Sleeping pills he'd been prescribed the year before when Maria had announced she was pregnant.

He stared at the small red pills in his hand. This was the answer. Philip had been right. End it. No more worries, no responsibilities. He had considered following his friend's method, going to the roof of Morven court and jumping, flying, easy. But it wouldn't be for him. He'd chicken out. He'd never even stood on the edge the way Francis and Ginnie had. No this was easier. Just sleep. This was easier. He picked up the phone, he had one more person to speak to.

Chapter 62
GINNIE'S TRANSCRIPT
1975

The feelings I had about Mike were alien to me. I hadn't wanted to marry him but didn't want anyone else to be with him. I thought he'd be sitting moping and mourning his loss but instead he'd just gone ahead and got engaged to another woman. A substitute me. Probably the woman who had split us up, the nurse who'd told him I'd got rid of his child. I tried to lose myself in work, studying long hours and when not immersed in a book I'd wander the hills around Inverness, retracing some of the walks I had done with Mike, missing the touch of his hand, remembering things he had said. I didn't want company, hardly ever went out with Taff, and barely spoke to anyone for months. Work was great but a little monotonous, an endless round of checking samples for cell changes and doing blood tests. Gregor was concerned that there were times when I didn't seem to be concentrating on the job. He thought I seemed distracted, that I rushed through the tests, and he was worried that I'd miss something, however when he checked my samples he realised that each result I had logged was precise.

'Don't worry Gregor, I may be quick but I'm accurate. I don't have to be totally engaged to do a good job.' He had agreed with me but from occasional worried glances I knew I had lost his trust.

In April I met Taff while I was waiting at a bus stop. I hadn't seen him often since I left the flat and was keen to know how Mike was doing. 'He and Jean got married last month. They're planning to emigrate to New Zealand, just waiting for paperwork to come through. I'm sorry that it didn't work out for you two.'

'Me too, Taff. Maybe if we'd met at a different time the outcome would be different. Then again, any longer and he would be a married man. He was telling me the truth when he said he wanted to settle down and marry and have kids as soon as possible. Anyway, he'd never forgive me for getting rid of his child.' I didn't want Taff to know I was still heartbroken. 'This Jean will give him what he wants. She moved quick though, didn't she? Engaged and married in less than a year?'

He mumbled a reply which I didn't quite catch. 'Need to go Ginnie.' Typical Taff. He never had a bad word to say about anyone and would always be loyal to his friend. If Jean was Mike's choice, then Taff wouldn't say a word against her.

I sat on the bus staring through the grime-stained windows as we climbed the hill to Raigmore. I imagined Jean's face beaming up at Mike at new year. The love had shone in her eyes. She didn't seem to acknowledge the likeness between us, didn't realise she was a substitute, that it was really me Mike wanted. Had she been the one who had told him about me being pregnant? If so, then surely she'd feel guilty at taking him away from me. She must know she was second best; that I was the love of his life and she a rebound lover.

That afternoon, scanning through the cervical smear test inbox, I noticed a vial with a familiar name on it, Mrs Jean Murphy. I made up the mounts, smearing the sample on several slides, staining and fixing them to highlight any unusual cells, ones that would indicate cancerous changes. I examined them under the microscope, scanning the stained cells, it was obvious that Jean had advanced cell changes. I paused and rechecked the slides. No doubt. I slipped the slides into my trouser pocket. I took another sample from a different vial, relabelled another set of slides and smeared the second sample on to the new slides with Jean's name attached. These were healthy cells; I recorded the results and stored the slides as was our normal procedure.

Placing the original slides in my box in my bedroom I wondered how long the happy married couple had left without medical intervention. I lay down in my bed and imagined the scenario. I would comfort the bereaved husband and he'd fall in love with me again. I drifted off to sleep, a look of contentment playing at the corners of my mouth.

Chapter 63
GINNIE'S TRANSCRIPT
1975

'Hold him a minute, will you?' Maria passed Joe to me. I held him at arms-length. I had never dealt with a baby before. He must have sensed my insecurity and started to scream and wriggle. Maria grabbed the traumatised child and cuddled him close. 'You were never cut out to be a mother.' She laughed. 'You're better off with puppies and kittens.' She dandled Joe on her knee, and he giggled and grinned toothlessly at his mother, the trauma of being held by Bad Auntie Ginnie forgotten. We were in a restaurant on the road up to Inverness castle. The new parents had brought their baby to the northern capital. It was great to see Tom again. The last time I'd seen him was the night Maria had given birth.

The fractious child now sat dribbling and smiling at his mother.

'He's teething.' She rubbed a finger along his gums, dabbing his chin with a bib. 'He's usually fine with strangers.'

'He'll be even more fine without this one.' I shuffled round the table, putting as much space as possible between the child and me. From my new viewpoint I spotted Taff with some of his mates at a nearby table and waved. He raised his hand in acknowledgement and came across to our table. I introduced him to Tom and Maria, but he pulled a chair close and leant into me, speaking in a hushed tone.

'Have you heard about Mike and Jean?' Taff could never resist some gossip.

I lifted my wine glass and took a slow sip of the Merlot. 'No. What about them?' I fixed my gaze on the glass, not wanting to meet Maria or Tom's eyes although they pretended to be deep in conversation, aware that Taff wanted to speak to me in private.

'They've had to cancel the move to New Zealand. She's been ill for months. Cervical cancer they say. Poor thing. It's spread to her liver.'

'Poor thing.' I echoed.

'According to his mum, Mike's devastated.'

'He will be. He so wanted children.' I tried to sound sorry. Working closely with the oncology department I knew the prognosis was poor. I also knew my part in it.

'Her doctors say it's a very aggressive tumour.' Taff loved gossip and always liked to get the full details of any story.

I was aware of all this. Her stored slides had been recalled for a check and my boss, Gregor, had agreed with my original result. Her slides showed healthy cells, no signs of even a slight change which would have raised the alarm. He had said sorry to me, explaining that they had to be checked and I had agreed and told him no need to apologise; I knew what the protocol was. I didn't mention any of this to Taff. I didn't want any suspicion raised regarding the fact that it was I who had checked her smear test.

'That's horrific.' I looked at him with as much shock as I could muster. 'Give him my love and tell him I'm so sorry to hear their news. Poor Jean. Such a nice woman.'

Taff glanced at me, but I averted my eyes. 'Really? Sympathy from Ginnie. You're getting soft honey.'

'I wouldn't wish that on anyone Taff. Don't be so harsh. Thanks for letting me know. Keep in touch, will you?'

'OK. See you Gin.' He returned to his table and his friends. I turned back to Tom and Maria as the waiter arrived with our food. Maria had strapped Joe into a high-chair and was spooning baby food into his mouth.

'You lying toad.' Tom raised his eyebrows. 'Sorry, I couldn't help but overhear you, "Such a nice woman".' He mimicked me. 'You hated her Ginnie.'

'Aye but Taff doesn't need to know that, nor Mike.' I spoke between mouthfuls of pasta washed down with the Merlot. 'I can be a supportive friend when I want to be, and you can bet anything Taff'll go back and tell him.'

'You're not still pining over Mike, are you? I thought you'd be well over him by now.' Maria joined the conversation.

I didn't answer. I didn't want any of them to know what plans I had for Mike and me.

Chapter 64
TOM'S DIARY

1st September, 1975

Oh God that was a disaster. Our trip to the Highlands didn't have the result Maria wanted. We've hardly been out since Joe arrived. Maria had decided it would be a good idea to let Ginnie meet Joe. That went down like a lead balloon. I knew it would. I'd tried to dissuade Maria, but she is trying so hard to accept Ginnie as a friend.

We had an argument as soon as we got home. She says Ginnie is selfish and only cares for herself, but she isn't.

When Joe was born Ginnie saved me, but Maria will never know that.

Maria thinks Ginnie could have shown a bit of interest in our son. It was her brusqueness that upset her but that's just Ginnie's way. She forgets to engage her brain sometimes.

I'll make it up to Maria in the morning, bring her tea in bed and deal with Joe's morning routine.

It's hard work being stuck between two women.

Tom 2015

He was still in the same position. Maria hated Ginnie, and now didn't try to hide the fact. She said she had tolerated her for Tom's sake, and she had tried for years to warm to his friend but long before Ginnie's incarceration she had given up giving Ginnie 'just one more chance'. Maria could never understand why Tom always took Ginnie's side. He had never told her the one thing that kept him tied to his childhood friend. Thinking about it now still caused his heart to pound. The memory of what might have been could still destroy him if Maria ever found out.

When he had called Ginnie to let her know about the birth, he had broken down. Had hardly been able to speak to her.

She had jumped in her car and arrived at his door at midnight. She had arrived just in time. Tom had drunk most of a bottle of whisky and had swallowed the contents of a bottle of sleeping pills. When she saw the state he was in she had made him drink copious amounts of salted water, sticking her fingers down his throat then rubbing the back of his head as he had vomited the drugs mixture into the toilet. She had known he wouldn't go to hospital, wouldn't want this on his medical record in case it affected his future in the police.

She had spent the night with him. Reassuring him that he'd be a good father, that he'd fly through university and police training, that he'd cope. She'd soothed away all his worries. She had promised to never mention it and she never had. He didn't want Maria to know, didn't want to worry her. Didn't want to appear incapable of being a father and bread winner. Ginnie had understood. She had saved his life in more ways than one.

He snapped back from the memory. No matter how much he loved Maria and Joe, Ginnie would always have a large piece of his heart. He would never let her down. No matter what had happened later, he wouldn't be where he was if Ginnie hadn't been there for him when Joe was born.

Chapter 65
GINNIE'S TRANSCRIPT
1975

Three months later Jean was dead. Her body ravaged by the cancer which had spread first to her liver then her brain. Taff and I travelled to the funeral together. He hadn't been sure that it was appropriate for me to go but I persuaded him I just wanted to pay my respects to the family. I watched Mike as he took his seat in the front row, he looked smaller and older than when I had last seen him. I watched him during the ceremony. His eyes were haunted, the deep shadows under them and his slightly gaunt look told a tale of a man who had been through a difficult time. My heart bled for him. I loved this man and to see him in such pain felt like a knife churning in my gut. I have no memory of anyone else being in the crematorium, my eyes were fixed on him. I sat in the second row in the aisle opposite him so I could see his face. His mother and sister sat on one side of him with Taff on his right. How I longed to be the one giving him comfort, supporting him when he needed it most.

I joined the file of mourners leaving the crematorium. When I reached him, I hugged him tightly, kissing him gently on the cheek and staring into his eyes as I mouthed the usual platitudes. He nodded, I wondered if he had even registered that it was me. The other mourners hustled me on, their gentle pushes moving the queue along and I was left standing on the steps of the crematorium looking back at Mike as he greeted each of the mourners with the same look as he had given me.

At the local hotel where the wake was held, I singled him out. 'How are you?' I held his hand as we sat in a quiet corner of the room. He looked at me but didn't answer. 'I'm sorry that your plans for New Zealand didn't work out. It was always your dream, wasn't it?'

'No. No. I'm still going. Jean and I discussed this, and she knew how much I wanted to go so we agreed that I'd still emigrate next year. Start a new life. There's nothing here for me now.'

'I'm here.' I squeezed his hand, but he drew it away. 'I love you, Mike. I always have and always will. Do you know how hard this is for me to say?' I gazed into his eyes, longing for the flicker of agreement, that he felt the same. Instead, his eyes flashed with disbelief. He stood up, the sound of the chair scraping against the wooden floor drew the attention of those nearby.

'For fuck's sake Ginnie. I've just buried my wife.' People turned at his raised voice. He strode across the room. I could see tears run down his face.

Taff saw the scene and came across to me. 'Are you ok?'

I patted my eyes with a tissue although there were no tears to dry. 'I think I'll go now.' I stood and pulled on my coat. 'You stay, I'll get a taxi.'

He tried to argue but I was adamant. I needed to get out of that room. All that planning had been a waste of time. I had lost Mike when I was eighteen and I was never getting him back.

Chapter 66
FIONA
2015

'We'll take a break there Ginnie.' I switch off the recorder and place my notepad and pen to the side. The sweat on my upper lip tastes salty, I feel physically ill. I have to get out of that room, the visceral reaction my body had on hearing Ginnie's words were surprising. I had heard many more gruesome tales in my time researching my books but never anything so cold and calculating. This couldn't be true. It was impossible to contemplate. I can't let Ginnie see the effect this part of her story had on me, so I excuse myself and as soon as I am out of her sight I run. I make it to the visitor's toilet just in time to vomit into the sink.

I press my wrists against the stark cold tiles and gaze at my ashen face in the mirror, dabbing the tears from my eyes. I've never been so moved by a client's story. Throughout my questioning I had endeavoured to keep my feelings neutral. I needed to get the truth from Ginnie, didn't want her embellishing her stories to elicit a reaction from me but this is too much. How could any woman do this to another for simply falling in love with someone? From what she says Jean and Mike had started dating after the breakup, this wasn't a case of someone wronging Ginnie. My breathing returns to normal, I need to get back into that room. If I leave now, I may never return and I have work to do.

I grab a couple of cups of coffee from the vending machine on my way back to the interview room. Some spills on the table between us, the tremor running through my body causing my hands to shake. A smile plays across Ginnie's face. Does she know? Can she sense her effect on me? I pick up my notepad and start the recorder again. Ginnie is playing with my pen, and her grip tightens as she hands it to me.

'It's amazing you're still using this.' She waved the pen at me. 'I had one like this at school. It disappeared. What a coincidence that you have the same one.'

I ignored her. All pupils who had achieved top marks had been given the inscribed pens. I'm surprised that she can even remember it.

'I would like you to think about what you've just described Ginnie and tell me exactly how you feel now about Jean and what you say you did to her.' At the beginning of the session, I had explained that I wasn't there to judge her or question what she said; that the investigation team had deemed her not guilty of any crimes, so it was not my job to contradict them.

She purses her lips and looks deep in thought before she answers.

'I think she deserved what happened to her. She knew she was a replacement but didn't think how that would hurt me, just went ahead and married the man I loved. She would have died anyway, just maybe not as quickly as she did.'

I wince when she says this. I try a different tack. 'Do you not think it's a bit of a coincidence that you were the one to find those slides? That you were given the chance to decide on Jean's fate?'

'Are you calling me a liar?' Ginnie snaps.

'It's just that I don't remember having smear tests in the early 70s. I'm sure it was later.'

'You're wrong. I routinely checked smear test slides. Maybe they weren't available to everyone but people with symptoms of cervical problems were given them. Maybe she'd had it for a while. I don't know. But I definitely covered up her test results. Why would I lie about that?'

Those were my thoughts exactly. Why would she lie about having a role in the death of a young woman?

She continues. 'My only regret is not playing it differently with Mike afterwards. Maybe I should have waited until he had time to grieve.'

I lean forward on the table, eyes directed towards the far corner of the room finding it hard to meet Ginnie's gaze. Those ice blue eyes cut through me, seeing deep into my mind. I mustn't let her in. It would be easy to believe her, but I have to search for the truth. I need to understand how her brain works.

'Can you imagine how Jean felt? She was a young woman in the prime of her life, about to start a new life together with her husband. She was a nurse and had followed all the medical advice about getting herself checked on a regular basis. Do you think she would have felt betrayed by the medical profession when the cancer wasn't picked up at screening? Betrayed that if she had been diagnosed earlier, she could have survived?'

'I don't care how she felt. I didn't cause her cancer. Perhaps if she hadn't slept around so much, she wouldn't have caught it. Isn't it a sexually transmitted virus that causes cervical cancer? Maybe if she'd not been such a slut then she'd still be alive.'

The legs of my chair screech as I automatically try to distance myself from this tirade. I gather up my notepad and recorder. 'I think that is enough for today. We'll continue this next week.'

Ginnie remains in her seat, head tilted slightly to one side, her eyes fixed on me.

She's enjoying this.

Chapter 67
TOM'S DIARY

January 12th, 1976

I phoned Ginnie last night. She'd been at Mike's wife's funeral. She was very quiet. I wish I could be nearer her. She has no close friends when she's upset and it's no use talking on the phone. She needs someone there to get her out of this depression she seems to be in. She tries to hide it but I know she's upset about Mike. Maria doesn't think Ginnie has a heart to break but she doesn't know her the way I do. I'll call Taff and see if he'll see her.

Tom 2015

There were hardly any notes about this part of Ginnie's confession. Yes, Ginnie had some slides in her drawer which showed cancerous cells, but she would have ready access to many similar slides as part of her training and there was nothing on them to suggest that they had ever been anything to do with Jean. No DNA could be extracted after the fixing process. The PF couldn't believe that anyone could plan and carry out such a heinous crime and after consulting with Jean's doctors he had ruled that there was no case to answer.

Tom couldn't believe it either. Surely no-one could harbour so much hate for a fellow human being. He knew Ginnie had seemed heartbroken that Mike had found someone new but this story she had made up was beyond understanding.

Tom had contacted Mike. Partly to get his stance on Ginnie's tale and partly to test the waters for his plan. Fiona had said it would be something that would help Ginnie move on. He had sent Mike the excerpt from Ginnie's story. The man's response was enlightening.

'When I started dating Jean, she explained that she had been diagnosed with cancer. We knew that we wouldn't have long together. This was long before Ginnie had met her. Whatever she saw in those slides, if she had even seen them at all, it had no impact on Jean's death. We made the plans to go to New Zealand as it was one of my dreams, but we knew we'd never get there. Jean made me promise that I'd go after she died. That's how I ended up in New Zealand. I married a couple of years later, but it didn't last long. Too soon after Jean's death and if truth be told, too soon after Ginnie. I never really got over her. She gets under your skin, doesn't she? I know I played things wrong with her. I was self-centred. I thought she'd want what I wanted but she was too young. I understand her better now. Time heals they say, don't they?'

Tom had agreed. There was something about Ginnie that when you got it, you got it. Mike's recounting of his version of the story had persuaded Tom that Ginnie had had no part in Jean's death. Mike had asked him to pass on his best wishes to Ginnie which is when Tom took the chance to ask him the favour he needed.

He closed the notes and straightened the piles of folders for the umpteenth time. He needed to walk a bit, to stretch out his legs and loosen up his joints. He found Maria in the kitchen. 'Fancy a walk?'

Maria put aside the drying cloth she had been using and put her arms round him.

'Course I do. Haven't seen you for hours. Just give me a second.' She kissed him briefly and left him to put on walking shoes.

He needed to talk to someone about this case but was Maria the right person? What would her response be to hearing about the latest crime that he was examining? He couldn't think of anyone else he wanted to speak to, Maria was his wife, his soul mate. As they walked through the fields surrounding their house, he told her the details.

Maria stopped and leaned against a field gate. He noticed her shoulders shaking and reached for her. Tears poured down her face, he searched in his pockets for a tissue.

'She's a monster Tom. What sick mind would do something like that?'

He held her at arms-length, he had expected this response. 'It wasn't proven that she had done this. The doctors said it wasn't possible.'

'It doesn't matter if she did it or not.' She shrugged away from him. 'Even if she made it up, what kind of monster would even imagine doing this to another woman? For God's sake Tom, she's sick. Wake up and see it. Your pal is a psychopath.'

He felt as if she had slapped him. He knew that Maria didn't share his thoughts on Ginnie, but he found it hard to not sympathise with his friend. Maria saw things from the viewpoint of the people affected by Ginnie's actions. Was he blind to them? Was he allowing his friendship to mask the truth?

'What does she need to do for you to realise what she is Tom? You need to think this through. I can't believe you still think she's the victim. Never mind what she did to you and Joe, just think about what she's saying she can do to an innocent woman.' The words caught as she spoke, her frustration clear in her voice. 'I'm going home. I'll see you later.' She strode off back down the path they had taken.

Tom watched her go. If he ran after her and said he agreed with her he would be lying.

Chapter 68
GINNIE'S TRANSCRIPT
1976

I moved back to Airdrie and into a small flat in the middle of the town. I would miss Taff, but I had to get away from the Highlands. Every corner I turned in Inverness I saw Mike; I heard his voice in shops and pubs; I was going mad. Tom suggested I go back home, closer to him and Maria. It would be good to have him nearby and I had agreed to come back south.

I got a job in a local bar. I needed to get away from everything about the Highlands and gave up my career in hospital labs. The Double A had been one of our favourites before I had moved to Inverness; frequented by a mix of youngsters, many not of legal drinking age, and middle-aged married men looking for something a bit more exciting than their boring wives.

I fit in easily. I was always a hard worker, and the clientele weren't the kind to want a lot of small talk like in some of the more traditional pubs. I could change a barrel as quickly as Graham, the boss, and carried heavy boxes of mixers with ease. Graham called me Little Miss Dynamite. I put up with this and his grandad sense of humour because the pay was ok and the tips better. The older customers always bought one for the staff when they paid for their rounds and the younger ones usually got too smashed to notice if their change was short.

'Can you do a couple of extra shifts this week Ginnie?' Graham came through from the office while I was re-stocking the shelves. 'Les has phoned in sick. Tonight, and tomorrow at least. Unless you've got a big date?'

Graham was always making comments about my love life. I sighed, 'No big date Graham. I'll come in.' Even if I did have a date, I'd not tell him, or anyone else for that matter. The dates I did have were with the married regulars in the pub. I had no intention of getting hurt again. Dating men who were already attached, who wanted exactly what I was prepared to give them was fine by me. A few gifts, jewellery or perfume, a decent meal out in Glasgow, away from local prying eyes. A quick screw in a cheap hotel was enough to satisfy me. No promises, no dreams of a future together, no lies.

This worked well for a few months, then I got a letter from Taff. I scanned through his words until I reached the main news. I knew he had something to tell me, hence the letter. Mike was getting married. He'd met someone in New Zealand. My head shook as I read his words. Seriously? Broken hearted Mike had recovered quickly enough to fall for someone who'd have kids with him? I scrunched the letter up and tossed it into the bin, digging my nails into my thighs, I sat on the bed, closing my eyes.

When I opened them again the light from the

lamppost outside my window illuminated the room. I must have been sitting there for a couple of hours, time passing unnoticed.

    I picked up the phone.

Chapter 69
GINNIE'S TRANSCRIPT
1977

'You're dating who?' Tom laughed when I told him.

Maria's cousin George had called me several times over the previous few months. I hadn't been interested in seeing him again, telling him I didn't want to get involved with anyone but after reading Taff's letter I called him and agreed to meet him. I had been sitting at the bar in the Double A when I smelled the presence of my date as he approached me from behind. The stench of Brut wafted over my shoulder and I swung round to be greeted by a grinning, moustachioed man, barely taller than me. I must have been drunker than I remembered at the wedding. Cousin George was no beauty.

He perched one cheek on the stool next to me, 'Drink, darling?' A real charmer.

'Rye and dry thanks.' I had to move on, I had already spent too long mourning Mike, but part of me hoped that if he found out I was with someone else he'd drop his plans to marry the New Zealand woman and come back to me. I'd tell Taff about my new love, and he'd be sure to pass this on to Mike. I looked at George as he ordered my drink, he was nothing like Mike and that attracted me. We went home together that night.

George and I were good in bed. We had little else

in common. We met up as often as we could, usually at my flat. We seldom went out, our relationship was based on sex and even when we did go out on a date we'd go home early, ripping each other's clothes off as soon as we got in the door.

I had dropped in to see Tom and Maria. They couldn't believe I was still seeing George.

'He's a moron. An arrogant moron to be exact,' said Tom, concern etched on his face.

'Aye but he's hung like a donkey.' I winked as I said it, but Tom didn't return my smile. He and Maria shared a look and not the one of shock that I had hoped would register, what did they know that I didn't?

'Seriously Ginnie. What on earth do you see in him?' Tom covered my hand with his and fixed me with a look that meant he was deadly serious. 'He's bad news.'

'Tom's right, Ginnie. I've known George all my life, you really don't want to get involved.'

'He's your cousin. I met him at your wedding.' I moved my hand but held Tom's gaze.

'And we told you then not to get involved. You can't always pick your family Ginnie. George's mum asked if he could come to the wedding. She wanted to know what he was up to. Typical Gozitan mother – wanted to make sure her boy wasn't being led astray.'

'We've been dating for weeks. We're fine together.'

'How come you haven't mentioned him before now? Why are you hiding him away?' It was Tom's turn to question me. What was this? The Spanish inquisition?

The thrawn part of my psyche took over. 'It's none of your business. I like him, you can tell his mother he's been led astray. Change the subject.' I didn't want to discuss George anymore. Whatever it was they had against him was of no concern to me.

Three months later we were married. A quiet ceremony in a registrar's office, Tom and Maria as witnesses, albeit grudgingly. Rumours were circulating that I was pregnant but that wasn't the reason for the quick wedding. George was going back to Malta, or to be exact going back to the small island of Gozo, to work in the family firm, and I wanted to get away. Mike was probably married again by now and I realised that I would never see him again. The idea of going to live in a foreign country had appealed to me but George's mother wanted her son to be married and would never consider us living together under her roof. Having lost Mike I had sworn that I wouldn't let anyone get under my skin the way he had. When George had suggested that we get married so we could be together on Gozo, I had said yes. It wasn't a romantic gesture; I didn't love him. This was a marriage of convenience, a way to get away from Scotland and try something new, see new places. Once the rings were exchanged, we went for a few drinks and a meal to celebrate but left after an hour in the pub. Our honeymoon was spent in my flat.

As he lay beside me on our first night as a married

couple, he took my face in his hands.

'God you're ugly,' he spat and turned his back on me.

Chapter 70
TOM'S DIARY

7th January 1978

Ginnie married George, Maria's cousin, today. We were the witnesses to the "happy" event. I don't get it. I don't get what she sees in him but typical Ginnie – tell her not to do something and off she goes. Even Maria's concerned. She's heard rumours that George left Gozo because he'd attacked a young tourist and his dad had him shipped off to Glasgow to study.

They're talking about going to Gozo to live.

I hope she'll be ok.

It's taken Maria's mind off babies for a few weeks though. She's desperate to have a brother or sister for Joe but every month she's disappointed. I hate seeing her face when she realises that another month has gone by, and she hasn't conceived. I feel so guilty.

Tom 2015

He still felt guilty. He knew why Maria had never got pregnant again. He'd had a vasectomy a few months after Joe had been born. Despite loving his son unconditionally, he had been terrified that another baby would bring on the return of his depression and didn't ever want to feel that way again. He had coped with studying and being as hands on a dad as he could but when Maria spoke about having another baby he would clam up and could feel his heart racing, the palpitations clattering through his chest. For a while he had made the excuse that it was too soon after the birth for them to have sex, but he wouldn't have been able to keep that up for long. So he had arranged a vasectomy, telling Maria that he had a benign cyst that had to be removed. His guilt was twofold – he had lied to his wife, a thing he had sworn never to do, and he had destroyed her dreams.

The only person he had ever told was Ginnie, knowing she was the only person who would never tell Maria.

Chapter 71
GINNIE'S TRANSCRIPT
1978

We moved to Gozo a month after the wedding. I'd never been abroad before and had no idea of what to expect. We stayed overnight in a hotel in Valetta. I was surprised that the menu in the hotel included lots of British dishes, reflecting the country's history under British rule. Road signs and advertisements were in English and all the staff I met spoke my language. The bus trip to the ferry to Gozo the next morning showed a different side to the country. The bus had a shrine by the driver's side, and I noticed that the locals entering the bus crossed themselves when they settled in their seats. The conversations I could hear were in a tongue I'd never heard before, Maltese seeming to be a mix of Arabic and Italian.

One of George's family picked us up from the ferry when it landed in Mgarr and drove us the few miles to his family's home. George called it a farmhouse, but it was nothing like the farms I knew. The animals were kept in small enclosures between the buildings, some appeared to live under the house. The place smelled of animal dung and dust.

His mother barely looked at me, I was obviously not her first choice as a wife for her son. She hugged him tightly but barely touched my outstretched hand, deliberately standing between us as she ushered us to the rooms at the back of the main house. This was to be our home. The walls were bare sandstone, the toilet Victorian. The furnishings were old and threadbare, the bed hard, the mattress lumpy and smelling of years of use.

Once unpacked we went through to the main house. This would be our routine for the next few months. I was never allowed to cook. George's mother chose what and when to eat. I had never been fussy about food, the stews and pasta dishes she produced were edible. I think she was disappointed that I didn't complain. Truth to tell I didn't care. This felt like my punishment for what I'd done to Mike. I wasn't sorry that Jean had died but I felt guilty that I'd hurt the man that I loved. Maybe I was due a bit of misery.

At the far end of the track we lived on was a stable yard. I had seen the men exercising the horses when I explored the area. Sometimes they rode them, trotting along the roads from the stable to the racetrack. Other times they sat in the open boot of a car or truck, leading the horses behind them. The first time I had seen this, George had explained they were racehorses, trotters. My memory went back to my day at Charlie's as a child. I had a plan for a way to get away from George's mother. I walked into the yard one day and asked for a job. Stephanie the owner, laughed.

'Why would I take on an English woman?' She looked me up and down.

'I've had experience.' I didn't mention how little, 'And I'm cheap. I just need a bit of spending money. And by the way I'm Scottish, not English. Different place.'

She cackled again. 'I like you. You might be in luck, I need a groom. You do know how to groom a horse?' She threw a curry comb at me. 'Here. Show me what you can do.'

I must have impressed her because she agreed to take me on as a yard hand. I was to ensure the horses were prepared and ready for the track. I was also allowed to exercise them; my slight but strong build was ideal for sitting in the sulky. Danny had been right; I was a natural.

George yelled at me when I told him. 'What the fuck do you want a job for? You could do more in the house.' He was always complaining that I didn't do enough to help his mother, despite the fact that she wouldn't let me when I offered and all but banished me to our rooms. I explained to him that I needed the exercise and that the little money I made would help us out. I could use it to buy the few necessities I wanted, British goods were few and far between in the shops and more expensive than the local products. I told him that I had seen his cousin Vincent at the stable. George was happy that more money was coming in and seemed content that Cousin Vinnie would ensure that I didn't step out of line. Reluctantly he agreed.

I got on well with Stephanie, the tiny, wizened faced, seventy-year-old owner of the stable. She could lift enormous hay bales that the rest of us struggled with and was the only person who could handle Odin, the breeding stallion which was stabled in the yard.

When mares were brought to the yard to be serviced Stephanie would lead him to them, controlling his movements to ensure neither he nor the mare were injured, and with a gentle word would be able to calm him down afterwards and let him loose in the field where he would gallop and buck releasing his pent-up energy. Every day she would enter his box to groom him. No-one else could get close. He'd bite and kick out at any of the other grooms who came near, his ears flat against his head and eyes rolling revealing whites which blazed with evil intent.

I spent hours with the horse, at first standing outside his stall, whispering gently to him, offering pieces of apple and the odd polo mint. Eventually he allowed me to touch him, leaning against my shoulder as he relaxed. Stephanie was delighted. It made her life easier if someone else could handle the stallion.

Soon I was working longer hours at the stable and helping out at the track when the horses were running.

George wasn't happy if he came home and I wasn't waiting at the door for him. He complained that I wasn't a 'good wife', he'd shout at me and push me around, his fingers stabbing into my stomach. He was like a petulant child, throwing tantrums if he didn't get his own way. I had never loved him, and now I began to hate him.

Chapter 72
GINNIE'S TRANSCRIPT
1978

George worked on Malta, in his father's business in Valetta, doing the books and dealing with orders. I loved when he was away and dreaded his coming home. Maria and Tom had been right. George was arrogant, a bully and a control freak. He'd talk over me, telling anyone who would listen that I talked rubbish and knew nothing about anything. He refused to teach me Maltese – even though it was the first language used in the house. He'd lie about things I had said. Using any opportunity to make me feel unworthy.

What started as verbal abuse, name calling, putting me down in front of everyone else, escalated into physical abuse. He'd punch me in the kidneys or squeeze my breasts until I screamed. I knew a psychopath when I saw one.

But I told no-one.

We were at the races one night and I was discussing the form of Truth, one of our horses, with Stephanie and Anthony the head lad. The horse had run second in his last three races, seemingly reluctant to pass the winning horse in each race.

'Needs a good whipping.' George spoke over the rest of the group. They turned to face him.

'That's the last thing he needs.' Stephanie's gentle

words were met with a nod from Anthony. 'Some horses just don't want to lead. Think of a race like a pack of horses in the wild. The lead horse is the boss. Some just want to be part of the herd. What we need to do is build his confidence. Get him to lead out of the yard. Make him feel worthy.'

George laughed. 'What a load of shit. A bit of encouragement of the painful kind would work.'

Stephanie shook her head. 'You have no idea,' she said, obviously annoyed at George's comments.

George turned on Stephanie, 'Listen. It's the same with that stallion of yours. All this whispering and gentle touch rubbish is just for show. A good punch would soon temper it. You lot haven't got a clue. You're as thick as she is.' He stabbed a finger towards my face. 'I'm going for a drink. You coming?' He staggered off to the bar leaving us staring in disbelief at his rudeness. I made to follow him, but Anthony held me back.

'Don't go.'

'I need to. Sorry...' I ran to catch up with George. I needed to be with him to try to stop him getting into a fight. I recognised the mood he was in.

'Managed to drag yourself away from your boyfriend?'

'What?' I had no idea what he was talking about.

'Anthony or whatever his name is. I saw the way you looked at him. Do you really think he'd be interested in an ugly cow like you?'

'I doubt it, I don't think his wife and children would

approve.'

George's face changed. 'Don't be so fucking smart. Home. Now.' He stormed off to the car park and I followed. I knew what would await me when we got home. His mood didn't lift on the drive back. He strode into the house grabbing the pile of mail that lay on the hall table.

'What's this?' George threw the phone bill at me. 'Calls to the UK when I'm at work? Who is he?' He punched my shoulder knocking me onto the couch.

'It's Maria's number.' I wasn't going to give George ammunition. He didn't need an excuse to batter me.

'How stupid do you think I am? You're forgetting that you're the idiot. Who is he?' Each sentence was punctuated with a punch.

I cowered on the floor. If I didn't move, didn't react, he would stop. He aimed one final kick at me. 'Whore,' he screamed, spit flying from his mouth in his rage. He slammed the door as he stormed out of the house. He'd be going to the local Band Club. I knew he'd continue his attack when he got home.

I rose slowly, each part of my body aching from the assault. I ran a bath and lowered myself gingerly into the hot soothing water. Bruises were starting to appear on my arms and body. None on my face. He never touched my face.

Despite George's behaviour towards me, I loved Gozo. Wandering through the narrow lanes of Victoria the capital, sheltering from the baking heat of mid-summer. The locals greeted me as I passed, always happy to stop and talk for a few minutes. The rocks overhanging Xlendi Bay provided perfect diving platforms, the clear Mediterranean water soothed my constantly bruised body.

There was a small Expat community who drank in St Patrick's hotel on the seafront, but I kept away from them despite their invitations to join them. If I made friends with the expats they'd question me; wonder why I wore long sleeves and scarves even on the hottest days. I didn't want sympathy or advice.

George's mother ignored my bruises, ignored the shouting and banging that came from our end of the farmhouse. She closed her eyes to what her son was doing to me on a daily basis. I didn't want anyone's sympathy.

When we had first arrived in Gozo, George had followed me into the tiny bathroom, emptying my toilet bag into the sink. He picked up the three packs of contraceptive pills I had brought from Scotland, placing them in his pocket until he could dispose of them, 'No more pills. I need a son to carry on the family business. My father expects it.'

I started to argue but he grabbed my hair and twisted my face towards his, 'Shut up. You have no choice in this. That's what a woman, what a wife, is for.'

He strode off down the sandstone corridor and slammed the door behind him.

George had lost all semblance of love, of decency;

I doubted if he had ever loved me. I think he just liked the idea of having someone he could control. Taking me to Gozo meant I didn't have friends around me, but he could show me off to his family, my fair skin and blond hair a real contrast to the looks of the wives of his brothers and cousins. He constantly put me down, making fun of me in front of his family, speaking in Maltese, unaware that I had started to pick up words from the staff at the stable, especially the derogatory words his male friends would snigger at when he ordered me to do things. He hadn't been pleased when I'd started work but was glad of the extra income coming in. He controlled every penny, dishing out a pittance for me to buy food and beer with; hell mend me if I didn't bring his bottles of Cisk from the shops in Victoria. More than once he'd hit me for being late, despite my argument that the infrequent bus service couldn't be relied on.

As the months passed and there was no sign of a pregnancy his rages became worse. When he saw the pack of tampons on the bathroom shelf, he'd scream at me that I wasn't a woman, that I was barren. What he didn't know was that there was no way I was going to be made pregnant. After the abortion I had had a coil fitted, a belt and braces along with the pill to ensure I would never conceive again.

Chapter 73
FIONA
2015

'Did you think you deserved to be punished for what you'd done to Jean?' Her throwaway line about George's abuse being what she deserved for what she'd done to Mike's wife is the part of her story I am interested in.

For the first time since I'd met her, Ginnie looks flustered. I take a note of her physical response.

'I never said that.' She slaps the table between us. 'Of course I didn't deserve George's abuse. There was no excuse for his behaviour –he was a bully and sadist. No one has a right to physically or mentally torture anyone. And no, I didn't think it was my fault.

She doesn't seem to see the irony. I replay the tape.

'That's not what I meant. Erase that. Jean deserved all she got. Why would I be punished for her manipulation of Mike?'

She was right. She hadn't said it was punishment for what she'd done to Jean, she had said she shouldn't have hurt Mike. Nevertheless, she had suggested that what she had done was wrong.

'You skim across the abuse Ginnie. Don't you want to talk about it?' Fiona softens her features, hoping to persuade Ginnie to open up to her.

'I'd rather not.' Ginnie drops her gaze. 'He knew

how to harm me without leaving evidence. Put it this way.' She leans back in her chair. 'Even if I had wanted children, I wouldn't have been able to.'

I put my pen down, blinking back the tears that threaten to spill over. What on earth had he done to her?

'Why didn't you just walk out? Or go to the police? You don't seem like someone who would put up with an abusive partner.'

'I'm not. I had to do it my way. He didn't deserve to be let off lightly. If I just walked out, he'd get away with it. The police wouldn't be interested in what I said. His family would have made sure of that. Remember this was in the seventies, on a tiny, Catholic island. A man was the head of the house then, I was his possession. He could do what he wanted to me, and no-one would have batted an eyelid.

Chapter 74
GINNIE'S TRANSCRIPT
1978

Rape became a constant in my life. If George wanted sex, then he took it. I soon learned it was easier to just give in, to lie as still as possible until he had finished. He no longer tried to please me, to make me come or make it any semblance of love making. It was rape.

'No.' I pulled away from him one night, 'I've got my period.' That didn't stop him. That night he raped me anally for the first and only time.

I'd had enough. I couldn't go on with that sham of a marriage. But how would I make it look like an accident? It never occurred to me to just ask for a divorce. He'd never agree to that. George should suffer the way he had made me suffer, should know fear and pain. Anyway, he wouldn't entertain thoughts of a divorce. The shame that would bring on his mother was something that he would have no intention of causing. I'd be stuck married to him forever.

As I trudged back from the bakery, I knew exactly what to do.

*

'Ok Anthony, I'll be there at six.' I hung up the phone knowing George had overheard me. What he didn't know was that Anthony wasn't on the phone, the team were at the racecourse. I had excused myself saying I had a headache and they had left at 3pm with three horses in the horsebox. The final race was at 9pm so I knew the stable block would be empty until they returned.

'I'll be back soon,' I said to George as I donned my jacket and boots. 'Just going to help at the stables.'

He glared at me. I knew he thought I was going to meet Anthony. He didn't believe me when I said Anthony wasn't interested so I used his lack of self-esteem to wind him up and I had dropped a couple of hints that something was going on between us. I wanted him to think that I was having an affair.

Half an hour later I drove to the stable. All was quiet; the horses had been fed and settled for the night, an occasional whinny or stomp of a foot were the only sounds which disturbed the peace of the barns. I went into the tack room and lifted the item I needed from its hook on the wall. A sign of good luck they said. I went into Odin's stall and began to groom him, running the curry comb over his flanks. His skin shuddered and he snickered, leaning into me so he was resting his weight against my body. Apart from Stephanie I was the only person who could handle the stallion, I was the only one the boss would trust near the horse. I heard a car draw up outside. As expected George had followed me, hoping to catch me with Anthony.

'Where is he then?' I pretended to jump at the sound of his voice.

'Who?' I asked, eyes wide in innocence.

'Your boyfriend. Where is he? You don't think I believed that crap about him being a happily married man do you? A whore will always attract even the happiest of men.'

'I take it you mean Anthony. He's at the course. He's working tonight, I told you that. I'm checking the stables for them.'

He grabbed me and pulled me from the stall. As he pulled me towards the stable door, he got too close to Odin and the horse stretched out and bit him on the shoulder. He yelled in pain and let go of me.

'Bastard.' He aimed a punch at the stallion's head, but Odin had stepped back into the furthest corner of the stall and his fist met with the edge of the door frame. 'Bastard,' he pressed his fist to his mouth. 'I'll show you who's boss.' He drew the latch and opened the half gate, stepping into the stall.

This was panning out better than I had expected. As he moved forward, I took the old horseshoe I had removed from the wall earlier and slammed it into the back of his head as hard as I could. He fell forward and Odin reared, bringing his hooves crashing down on George's head. I heard him cry out, he was still conscious. One more stomp of the stallion's hooves silenced him. As the horse continued his assault, biting and kicking my husband's prone body there was no doubt that George was dead. I washed and dried the horseshoe and replaced it on the wall.

I drove to the course and showed my owner's and trainer's pass. Anthony was leading Regina the mare into the saddling enclosure.

'Hi Ginnie. Feeling better?'

'Much," I said. I held the mare as he deftly manoeuvred her into the shaft of the sulky, straightening the girth, he lifted each of the horse's legs, one at a time to ensure she could stretch at full trot. He led her out onto the parade ring, and I joined Stephanie at the trackside to watch the race.

Regina won and along with the other two places earlier in the night the mood when we got back to the stables was one of celebration. I pulled up in the yard, exclaiming to Raymond the jockey I had given a lift to, that the car already parked there was my husband's. Anthony had also seen the car and jumped down from the horse box, running into the stables ahead of me.

'Alla tieghi,' he yelled and turned towards me. 'Stay there Ginnie. Don't come in.' He was pushing me back out into the yard. 'Stephanie. Ejja hawn issa.' The yard boss ran across to the stable, responding to the terror in Anthony's voice.

'What is it? Let me in.' I pushed past him. Stephanie was leading a trembling Odin from his stall, the horse snorted but calmed down as Stephanie whispered to him, rubbing his nose with her free hand. I peered past and saw George's body, his head a bloody pulp.

'George!' I screamed and fell to the floor of the stable, covering my face and wailing. I knew how a grieving widow should sound when confronted with such a horrific sight. Anthony lifted me from the floor and led me to the office where he called the emergency services.

'Sit here,' he said, fetching me a glass of water. I sat and stared straight ahead, not moving until the ambulance and police arrived. He sat with me while the police went over the events of the night. They took statements from everyone from the stables. The ambulance crew treated me for shock and Anthony drove me home. George's parents came to the door and led us inside. A young police officer, who had been sent from the local office, explained what had happened and comforted the couple. I called the only person I wanted near me.

Two days later Tom arrived, his face full of concern when he saw me. He held me tight while I told him what had happened. 'I came as soon as I could. I'm so sorry...' I let him comfort me. I had to pretend that I was heartbroken, too upset to talk much. It was difficult to keep up the pretence and I'm sure he caught me out on several occasions, but he never said anything.

I had been interviewed by the police again. Their questions framed with care when they saw how traumatised I was. They soon came to the decision that George's death had been a terrible accident, that he'd gone into Odin's stable for reasons unknown and the horse had attacked him. The statements from the stable staff all agreed that he had threatened to harm the horse and they thought he'd carried out the threat but had come off worse.

I stayed on Gozo until after the funeral, hiding behind enormous dark glasses I played the part of the grieving widow. George's parents made it clear they didn't want anything more to do with me now that their son was dead. They arranged the funeral, bells chiming at the local church and the wailing of his mother and the other village women irritating me beyond belief. I stayed in my bedroom, happy to play no part in the over-the-top grieving process that was expected. The day I left they ignored me completely. The only sadness I felt was when I said goodbye to the staff at the stable. I went to Odin's stable. The horse whinnied when he saw me, and I stretched my arm up to rub his nose. I took the scissors I had brought with me and clipped a few strands of his mane, placing them in an envelope. 'Good boy,' I patted his neck as Anthony approached, concern on his face. 'I don't blame him, Anthony.'

He nodded, taking my arm. He drove me to the ferry terminal, ensuring I had enough money to get home. No one on Gozo had known about George's abuse, I had made sure of that. Now everyone thought I was just a grieving widow, going home to Scotland for the support of friends and family.

Tom had arranged my flight back to Scotland, He

and Maria met me at the airport and took me to a local hotel. They had offered to put me up, but I refused their help. Maintaining the persona of distraught wife would be difficult and I was sure I would let the mask slip occasionally. I needed time alone until I could sort out the insurance claim. George's family had no idea I had arranged a life insurance policy before we left Scotland. Their sadistic, bullying son was worth more to me dead than alive.

'Are you sure you'll be ok?' Maria looked concerned as I said my thanks at the hotel entrance, ushering them out into the afternoon rain. Tom had walked ahead of her to their car and was watching our exchange. I'm sure I saw a slight shake of his head as he ducked into the driver's seat. I had told him about the abuse when we were in Gozo, I needed a reason for my lack of tears after a couple of days, keeping up the façade of being in shock proved too difficult. Did he realise I wasn't grieving? I had no idea what he was thinking when they left me alone at the hotel.

I closed the door behind them and smiled.

Chapter 75
TOM'S DIARY

August 13th, 1978

I love my wife. I know Maria doesn't really like Ginnie, but she agreed that I had to go to Gozo for George's funeral. She said she'd stay at home with Joe but knew I had to be there for Ginnie.

I haven't told her what Ginnie told me. She doesn't need to know our concerns were real. George was a wife beater. It took a while to get Ginnie to admit it and she had asked me to not tell Maria. I think she feels a failure, that it was her fault.

Maria asked why Ginnie didn't look as if she was upset when we picked her up last night and I struggled to keep my promise to Ginnie. I'll pray to Maria's God for forgiveness, but I can't break my promise.

I'm so sorry Maria. I love you.

Tom 2015

He recalled that when he reached Gozo, Ginnie had been her usual self, no tears, no signs of grief and he had tried to get her to talk to him about how she felt. Eventually she had broken down and told him about

George's abuse. He had listened to her as she poured out her tale, aware that this was unusual for Ginnie. He realised he had seldom had serious discussions with her, she always put a light-hearted skew on even the most horrible things that had happened to her. Had that been her way of dealing with the horrors of losing her parents, best friend and husband? Or had she been playing him all along? The night she had told him about George she had talked for hours, his gentle prodding extracting every detail of their life together.

She had made him promise not to tell Maria saying that she didn't want the family upset. He hadn't thought at the time that this was totally alien to Ginnie. She had never shown any concern about anyone in the past. Even when she had told Fiona about her friend Christine being raped and beaten by her family, she hadn't shown any real sign of caring about the situation that her friend was in, had just told her to deal with it herself.

Now he found himself questioning why she had made him promise. Was she ashamed of what had happened? Had it been a way of distracting him from what had happened to George? If he had questioned the result of the Maltese police investigation, would they have found evidence that she had a part in his death? He hadn't been a detective at that time, but he knew how they worked, and he had thought that the Maltese force had been quick to come to their conclusion that it was an accident, that George had been at fault for his own death. Nowadays DNA evidence would have been sought but would anyone have checked a single horseshoe in a room full of horseshoes? He doubted it. The stable hands all said Ginnie was with them at the track on the night that George died, there was nothing linking her to her husband's death apart from her confession. Had they been covering for her? A sense of loyalty among friends? It was known that George wasn't widely liked but was he hated enough for people to lie to the police and cover up the cause of his death? Time of death had been inconclusive. There's no way now that he would be able to find the truth. Many of the people who'd been involved were dead. The couple he'd been able to contact said they could barely recall the circumstances of the night George had died. It was thirty-five years ago and although his police senses believed that anyone viewing such a horrendous scene would be unlikely to forget it, he had been unable to elicit any further evidence from them.

None of the statements taken from George's family or her workmates at the stable had mentioned that they had thought she was being abused. Working in a stable, handling several tons of horseflesh, falls from the sulky, all resulted in bruises and Ginnie appeared no worse off than anyone else. Had there been abuse, or was this another fabrication by Ginnie? Had she weaved the whole abuse tale to explain her lack of emotion at having lost her husband?

He worried that Maria would soon discover he

had lied to her, as soon as she read the book she would know. How could he explain why he had never told her about the abuse?

He wasn't his wife's favourite person at the moment. They had agreed to disagree on their thoughts about Ginnie, but she was finding it harder each day to believe anyone could have sympathy for his friend. How was he going to tell her? What was he going to tell her? Where did he start? He had always said he would never lie to his wife but as the years went on, he realised he had often withheld the truth. Could that be construed as not really lying?

Chapter 76
FIONA
2015

The similarity between George and Ranald's deaths screamed out of the page. Once again, she had relied on an animal to kill her victim. 'How could you be sure the horse would finish off what you started?'

'He didn't have to. George was almost dead when he hit the floor. It wasn't a racing plate; it was a normal horseshoe. You forget how strong I am... was. All I needed was for Odin to mess up his head so my blow wasn't obvious. I saw a horse stomping on a dog years ago, I knew Odin would do exactly the same. I feel sorry for the horse though, he must have been terrified.'

Typical of Ginnie's behaviour. More worried about the horse than her husband. I note that she denied saying she should be punished. Ginnie is showing textbook traits of a psychopath but sometimes she slips. I need to check with my books. Would a true psychopath care about animals? The books I've read say that most start their killing ways by torturing animals but there has never been a sign that this is the case with Ginnie. Would she feel she should be punished, or would her narcissism mean that she was above the law? Had she slipped when she spoke about George's abuse? Or is she playing with me?

'Why did you put up with so much abuse from

George? Surely you could have left him?' This didn't make sense. She dealt with people who had slighted her but had let a man abuse her for months.

'It was my fault. I shouldn't have married him and felt that I deserved what I got. I could deal with the physical pain, or I thought I could. I had been warned that George was bad news. Maybe I should have found out more – listened to Maria. I didn't want to admit that she'd been right, so I dealt with it in my own way. By not letting George get to me I felt in control. I never cried when he hit me. I didn't go running to his mother to complain.'

'So why the change? Why did you decide that he needed to die?' For the first time I feel like I'm getting into her psyche. Beginning to understand how her mind works.

'What he did that night wasn't done just to hurt me. He wanted to humiliate me and take my final ounce of self-worth. Taking that from me was worse than any pain I had endured.'

She is speaking quietly, almost to herself.

'I think that's enough for now, Ginnie. I can see you're upset. Let's take a break there.' I am starting to feel for this woman. I don't know if that's a good thing.

Chapter 77
GINNIE'S TRANSCRIPT
1979

Once my insurance claim was paid out, I bought a small cottage on a shooting estate southeast of Glasgow. I didn't want to move back to Airdrie, the place was depressing, and I had few good memories to draw me back to the area. The cottage was within driving distance of the village Tom and Maria had settled in, close but not too close. I began filling it with furniture and art works to my taste. I even rehomed a large ginger cat from the local Cats' Protection group. Riley was as close as I'd get to a family, he didn't need a lot of attention, as long as he had food and water, he was happy to share the cottage with me.

I had called Tom and Maria and invited them out for a meal, ostensibly to celebrate some good news. They had laughed when I said I'd rather pay for a meal than cook. I looked around the restaurant. The dark red décor and leather upholstery felt warm and intimate. I considered how this would look in the cottage. Tom poured me a glass of wine.

'The good news is I've got a job.'

The couple lifted their glasses, 'Congratulations. Where?'

'Kelvingrove Gallery. I'm going to be working on the herbaria collection, cataloguing it to be put into a country wide data base.'

The interview had been fairly short and painless. They were looking for someone with a biology background, someone who understood the Linnaeus method of naming plants and had a good eye for detail. I had researched the job thoroughly and had obviously used the right words during the question-and-answer section. They had offered me the job immediately.

'Sounds interesting. It'll be good for you to get back out into the land of the living. Not often you get an offer during the interview. Were you the only candidate?' He winked at Maria. I knew when I was being wound up.

'Of course not, but it was obvious they wouldn't get a better candidate. Why waste time?' They laughed, but I wasn't joking. Since returning from Gozo I'd lived quietly, doing up the cottage. Really only seeing Tom and Maria, and even them only very occasionally. We rarely spoke of George. If his name came up it was quickly glossed over. They seemed to have planned that I should forget about my time on Gozo and move on. It suited me to wash over my failed marriage. The quicker I got on with life the better.

'You need to meet some new people.' Maria waved her fork in the air as she ate. 'I don't mean in a romantic way – you just need to get out there more.'

I nodded, concentrating on eating the prawn cocktail I had ordered. Eating out in the 70s and early 80s in Lanarkshire was limited to steak houses or greasy cafés.

The former is what we had chosen for my celebrations.

I looked at Maria. 'Thanks for your concern but I'm ok. I like my own company.'

'Either way – here's to your new job, and a new start.' She sipped at her red wine, obviously savouring the taste.

'How's the wee man?' I pretended that I couldn't remember their child's name, hoping to wind up Maria. It was easy to rile her. I mentally slapped my wrist – I had to stop that. I needed to keep her on my side. I doubted if she'd drive a wedge between Tom and me. After all I'd been in his life longer than she had but it made sense to not alienate her completely.

'Joe is fine. He's just started primary school and he's loving it. You'll have to come and see him; you'll notice the change.' She reached across and took Tom's hand. 'We were wondering if you'd do something for us?' She glanced from Tom to me and back again. Whatever it was, was obviously her idea. 'Would you consider being one of Joe's Godparents? Well not Godparent as such as he already has them but we both think you should be a part of his family.'

I burst out laughing, spluttering some wine over the table as I did so.

'Godparent? Me? You do know I'm an atheist?'

'Told you.' Tom shook his head.

'No no, not in a religious way. I shouldn't have said Godparent, but I can't think what else to call it,' Maria said. She wasn't giving in.

'I never wanted my own children. Why on earth would I want to be part of your child's upbringing?' I could see that this cut her deeply.

Maria jumped up from the table, excusing herself as she strode towards the toilets, her face burnt red.

'That was a bit harsh.' Tom had stood to follow her but turned to me as he realised his wife didn't want him to see how upset she was. 'She's trying really hard to be your friend.'

I glared at him. 'I don't need her as a friend. She'll be ok. We're total opposites. Doesn't understand that some of us don't want or need children in our lives. But ok, I'll try to be nicer.'

Maria returned to the table. Her nose and eyes were red rimmed. Hormones have a lot to answer for. I continued to eat my starter, ignoring the drop in mood my outburst had caused.

'Of course I'll be there for Joe, Maria. I'm only messing with you. I'm really sorry, I didn't mean to upset you.' I raised an eyebrow and glanced at Tom. The look said "I'm trying. OK?"

Maria nodded. The things I did for Tom; he owed me.

'How's life as a cop?' I looked directly at Tom, giving Maria time to compose herself.

He looked at Maria whose imperceptible shake of her head told him to forget what had happened and just get on with the evening.

'It's difficult. The other guys hardly speak to us.

They think we have an easy time just because we have a degree. They know we'll be promoted quicker than they will.'

'What do they do? Are they bullying you?'

'No, nothing obvious. They just ignore us, it's as if they want to avoid us as much as possible. Like in the canteen, they're always sitting at a full table and there's never space for the grad trainees. It's not a problem. I'm finished at Tulliallan in a few weeks then it's the real thing. Doubt if I'll see any of them again. Must admit I won't miss them.' His expression said that it did bother him. Tom had always sought the friendship and recognition of others. There was nothing I could do to help; he'd need to get on with it. Whatever his chosen career had been he'd have to put up with difficult times, I couldn't be there to protect him. That was Maria's job now.

Chapter 78
GINNIE'S TRANSCRIPT
1979

On Monday morning I turned up at the imposing sandstone building in the west end of Glasgow. As I gazed at the massive pipe organ which rose majestically at one end of the entrance a smiling guard approached me. 'Can I help?'

I explained that I was due to start work and he showed me to a suite of offices at the far end of the hall, handing me over to my new boss. Rosemarie was in her fifties and wore Laura Ashley dresses, large multi coloured beads and walking boots. Her grey hair was tousled like mine, but she had clipped it up with two intricately carved bone clasps, the resulting look bohemian and quirky. I felt under-dressed in jeans and tee-shirt beside her, but I had been told to dress casually. The vaults where the archived materials I would be working on were dark and dusty.

'Follow me. We'll go down to your room and I'll tell you what you need to do. Coffee?' I took the pass and keys she handed me and followed her downstairs away from the public view, grabbing two cups of coffee from what was her office as we passed. We wound our way through various corridors. She pointed to a small courtyard with rooms beyond. 'That's taxidermy, I'll introduce you to Fred and Malcolm later. They smell a bit, so we keep them out here. Along that end are the art restorers. They're working on Dali's St John of The Cross at the moment. Come and meet them.'

She led me further along the corridor and into a small, cosy office. 'Bill, Stuart, this is Ginnie. She's working on the herbaria collections.' The two men stopped their various tasks to greet me.

'Poor thing.' Stuart held out his hand in greeting. I took it in mine and felt a tingle run through me. I looked into his eyes. I guessed he was in his fifties, his curly, red and silver hair made it difficult to determine for sure, he could have been older.

'Nice to meet you.' I held his gaze for a fraction longer than necessary before moving on to the other man. I turned to Bill. 'Can I see the Dali? Rosemarie says you're restoring it.'

'Of course, through here.' Bill ushered me through to a large airy, workroom where the painting of Christ of St John of the Cross hung. 'Just touching it up a bit. Some headcase decided it was blasphemous and threw paint on it. This is the third time I've restored it.' I remembered seeing this painting on a school visit; it had been hung at the top of a staircase and drew gasps of wonder from visitors as they looked up at the depiction of Christ hanging on the cross. Dali had painted the scene from above, as if the viewer was looking down from heaven on to the body of Christ. It was a stunning piece of work. Even here, on an easel in a cold, austere workroom it had a mesmeric effect on the viewer. Why anyone would call it blasphemous was beyond me.

Bill picked up his palette and began work again on the painting. He glanced over his shoulder to where I stood. 'Nice to meet you, Ginnie, pop in for coffee any time. You'll need a break away from the joys of botanical collections.'

'Will do. Thanks guys. See you later.' I aimed my comment at Stuart. He looked up as we left, and I caught his eye and winked.

Rosemarie led me back along the corridor to the opposite end of the building. 'This is yours. The designers are next door and gilders on the other side. Keep your radio down, the designers like peace and quiet to create.' She raised her eyes, obviously not in agreement with the need for silence in the workroom. 'They complained so much about your predecessor that he left.'

The room faced the back, or what is actually the front, of the building – it was well known that the museum had been built back to front – looking on to the car park and the river Kelvin beyond. It was filled with over-sized dark wood furniture, tables and desks which could have been there since the building opened. Stark light bulbs hung from the ceiling but provided little in the way of light; two angle poise lamps sat on the table. I would need decent light for my work.

'Back out this way and I'll show you where the collections are stored. Basically, you just go through them, corroborate the identity of the plants, and enter the details into the index cards. Some lucky soul in Edinburgh gets to input the information into the data base. If the artists think this work is mind numbing, imagine what the life of those poor souls is like.'

She led me to a long corridor filled with chart drawers. In each drawer were hundreds of pressed plants, each with a Victorian label attached detailing what it was, where it was found and when. Having these details on computer would mean botanists could check the spread of wild plants and see where they were either thriving or being destroyed. It was obvious from the start that reading the faded, scrawled notes on the labels would be the hardest part of the job.

Bill had been right, it turned out to be a soul-destroying job. Trawling through hundreds of plant specimens, checking with the latest botanical tomes, examining specimens through the microscope and deciding whether the original identification was correct became boring. Thankfully the other staff in the museum recognised this and tried to keep me sane.

The taxidermists would take me on trips into the countryside outside Glasgow to find dead animals for mounting, and fresh plant specimens for displays. They taught me the basics of taxidermy, allowing me to stuff flat mounts to get me away from my microscope for an hour each day. One of them, Danny, was helping students at Glasgow University who were conducting a project on variations in polecat colouration. Members of the public and gamekeepers handed in dead polecats which had to be treated and stored as part of the study.

The skins were stored flat, no need to build mounts like the animals which were on display upstairs. I loved going through the process of removing the skin, drying and sterilising the pelt and stretching it to store for examination at a later date. The only down-side to this was that the overwhelming musky smell of polecat remained on your skin and clothes for hours.

Rosemarie took me on fungal hunts with the Museum foraging group, her speciality was mycology and she taught me how to identify different mushrooms, some edible, some which could prove fatal. This intrigued me. The mechanics of Amanita poisoning was fascinating, the small greenish Death Cap and beautiful, pure white Destroying Angel belying their deadly capabilities. Stuart and Bill often joined us on these forays, sharing recipes for the plants and fungi we found. We photographed the specimens and freeze dried some for displays in the main gallery, taking the edible ones home for dinner. The team was working on a Highland flora and fauna display, the taxidermists mounting white hares, red deer, and grouse to add to the rocks, dried heathers and gorse which made up the moorland panorama. I was given the task of providing the heathers and mosses used as the base of the display. The restorers painted frescos as backdrops to the displays.

I was sitting at my bench painting bright green lichens on polystyrene rocks. As I tried to match the exact colour of the crusted lichen I was working on I realised how limited the palette was that I was working from. It gave me the excuse to go along to the restorers to borrow some paints from them. I had seen Stuart in the corridors on several occasions but hadn't had time to stop and chat. Something about him drew me to him although he was probably old enough to be my father and wore a gold band on his wedding ring finger. He was alone having lunch at his workbench when I arrived.

'Come on in Ginnie. The rest are away to the pub. What can I do you for?'

I explained what I needed, showing him the photographs of the lichen I was painting. He pulled out several tubes of oil paints and began mixing the colours. I leaned in close to examine the palette.

'Here, you do it. Bit more of the cobalt green I think.'

I brushed his hand with my fingers as I reached for the tube of paint. I squeezed a small portion on to the palette and stirred some into the mix, noting which ones we had used. 'Perfect. Can I take these along to my room? I've got quite a bit to cover.'

'No problem. Any time.' He smiled showing white, even teeth, the front two crossed slightly giving a quirkiness to his look. I reached across and pecked his cheek. Stepping back quickly, the paint tubes in my hand.

'Thanks Stuart.' I turned and left the room before he could react to the kiss. I could feel his gaze on me as I walked away. I knew how to lure someone in.

Chapter 79
GINNIE'S TRANSCRIPT
1979

'See you tonight.' Rosemarie called over her shoulder as she climbed into her bright yellow Volkswagen Beetle.

'I'll pick you up at seven. Cheerie.' I still used the Nairn term for goodbye even though I'd been away from the town for a few years by then. I had agreed to swing past Rosemarie's flat on the way to the retirement do at the People's Palace on the south side of Glasgow. The head of our department was retiring after forty odd years in the museum. I didn't drink much so was happy to be the driver on the night.

Getting ready for the party I paid a bit more attention than usual to my makeup and clothing. The dress I had chosen was white, the sheer fabric glistening in the bedroom light as I swirled in front of the mirror. I dabbed Chanel No5 on my wrists and neckline. As soon as I had been able to afford decent perfume this had been my scent of choice. I may not have had Marilyn Munroe's figure, but I had her hair and smell. There was method behind my get up. I wanted Stuart. Since the peck on the cheek, I'd flirted with him whenever I had the chance. Running into him on the stairs when he arrived at work; I was well aware of the times of his train. Brushing close to him as he held the door open for me, ever the gentleman. When we spoke, I held his gaze a fraction long before dropping my eyes to look away, apparently embarrassed. I listened carefully to what he said, laughing at the right time, quietly seducing him.

At half past six I drove back into the city to Rosemarie's flat in the West End. She climbed into the passenger seat, throwing a brightly coloured gift bag on the back seat. 'You look lovely Ginnie. Nice to see you out of your work uniform.' She was, as usual in a Laura Ashley, her hair piled high and a blue streak of colour across each eye. 'You smell better than usual.' She laughed. I had discovered it was a common trick in the museum to give the rookie taxidermist the polecat job. I laughed but didn't return the initial compliment. Apart from the eyeshadow she didn't seem to have made any effort.

'Were we meant to bring gifts?' I nodded towards the back seat.

'No, no. It's just a book I know Gordon will enjoy. I've worked with him for twenty-five years. You didn't need to get him anything, although a glass of malt will go down well if you're near the bar.' She reassured me.

The People's Palace was a magnificent venue for a party. The glass walls, luxuriant greenery and sheer magnificence screamed opulence. I scanned the room but there was no sign of Stuart. Bill waved to us, pointing to several empty chairs at a large round table he was seated at. 'Grab a seat ladies. What can I get you?'

I caught Rosemarie's eye, this was a first, Bill getting a round in. He pulled out a chair for Rosemarie.

'First drink is on Gordon,' he continued.

Rosemarie laughed. We both knew Bill was as tight as a fish's arse. There would be a kitty on the table for future drinks. He took our order and disappeared towards the bar.

I spotted Stuart coming through the main entrance and caught his eye. Then I noticed the woman he was with. She wore a long skirt and high-necked top, her grey hair hung limply over her face. She was nothing special to look at. Bill yelled at him that there were seats at our table. This would be fun.

Stuart sat opposite me, introducing me to Maggie, his wife. She knew Rosemarie and the others and acknowledged me with a brief nod of her head before turning to Stuart and whispering in his ear. I caught his eye and winked, not caring if she noticed.

The chair beside me was scraped backwards and Malcolm the youngest of the taxidermists sat down with a thump. His long black hair was tied back in a ponytail. Not a good look. 'Good to see you Ginnie. I didn't think you'd come tonight. Bit of an old fart's convention, isn't it?'

I turned towards him and flashed my brightest smile. 'Better now you're here,' I said, my voice raised enough for Stuart to hear. I placed my hand on Malcolm's arm and turned to face him. I could feel Stuart's eyes on me.

As the night went on. I danced with Malcolm, leaning into his body in time to the music, my eyes searching for Stuart to see what effect my flirting with this younger man had on him. I caught him staring and blew a discrete kiss towards him. He looked flustered. I wasn't surprised when I saw him helping his wife on with her coat. It was only 10pm. 'Looks like Stuart and Maggie are leaving.' I shouted in Malcolm's ear. 'Let's go say goodnight.' I took his hand and led him towards the door where the couple were saying their goodbyes to Gordon. I reached out and took Stuart's hand.

'One dance before you go auld yin.' I dragged him onto the dance floor and placed my hands on his shoulders. I held myself away from his body but stared into his eyes. 'Malcolm will keep Maggie amused. Shame you had to bring her tonight.' I left the meaning of my comment unsaid. I could tell the effect my closeness was having on him. Slipping my arm through his I led him back to Maggie and Malcolm. I dropped the hold I had on Stuart's arm. 'Bye you two. Nice to meet you, Maggie.' Although I'd hardly spoken a word to her all night, I wanted her to know who I was. I cuddled into Malcolm and returned to our table.

By 10.30 I'd had enough. I leaned across to Rosemarie. 'Do you mind if we leave now? Got a headache coming on.' I rubbed my forehead and donned a look of regret.

'No problems. Just let me say goodnight to Gordon and I'll be right with you.'

'You're leaving?' Malcolm took my hand. 'I thought

maybe we'd go on somewhere? Or back to yours.'

'You thought wrong then.' I pulled away from him. 'Night night, sweetie.'

Chapter 80
TOM'S DIARY

October 23rd, 1979

Have I made a mistake? The first few weeks in the force were difficult and it's not getting any easier. We were given easy jobs, supposedly to give us time to study but the others thought we were on a cushy number. It's obvious the other student police look on the grads as potential bosses so keep away from us. Our sarge said it's because they want us to be nice to them when we're the bosses but I'm not so sure.

I chose the detective route. Now I'm in plain clothes and no-ones boss - yet.

At least I've got Maria to come home to, she believes in me and always has a word of encouragement.

I think Ginnie's seeing someone but she's keeping it quiet for some reason. She's unusually cheery and she even took Joe for the day to let Maria and I celebrate her birthday.

Tom 2015

He remembered Maria's face when Ginnie had offered to babysit. Joe was five years old, Ginnie had said she'd be fine as he was no longer in nappies and could talk if he needed something. Ever Miss Practical. Maria had been reticent at first but as she watched the two of them playing football in the garden, she had relaxed. Ginnie seemed to be getting on well with Joe and when he had asked later if he could visit her, Maria had conceded that maybe Ginnie was changing, growing up. Joe had loved playing with Riley, Ginnie's big ginger tomcat. His son had pestered Maria consistently since he had come home, asking for a puppy or kitten but she had never liked cats or dogs and didn't want the responsibility of one at home as they were both working long hours. He stretched down and patted Bert. The labrador had been his retirement present to himself. Maria had finally agreed when he had explained that the dog would be the perfect excuse to get him up and out of his chair. Not that he was doing that as often as he should at the moment.

After that first successful child-minding episode Ginnie often took Joe with her on walks, or on visits to the museum. Joe loved seeing the stuffed animals, dinosaurs and Chinese warriors and had always looked forward to his trips out with Ginnie. At the time they had known that Ginnie had allowed their son more freedoms than they had. He had often wondered if he and Maria were too strict with Joe. As an only child they had maybe been overprotective. Tom had been glad that finally Ginnie was showing some normal behaviour around their son. He hoped that maybe this would soften the relationship between his wife and friend, he felt they tolerated each other rather than there being any closeness or friendship.

His time as a trainee detective had meant long hours and he had been glad that Maria had been afforded some free time by Ginnie since Maria's mother had moved to the west coast town of Largs when she retired. They had missed having a regular babysitter.

Joe had come home from the museum visits talking about someone called Stuart, said he was always with Auntie Ginnie and asking if he was her boyfriend. When Tom had asked Ginnie about Stuart she had denied any relationship with him. Just that they were colleagues.

Now in her transcript Ginnie was saying that they had been conducting an affair. He wracked his brain, trying to remember back thirty odd years.

'Maria,' he called to his wife who was busy in the kitchen. 'Can you remember Ginnie going out with anyone when she worked at Kelvingrove?'

'I don't think so. I can't remember her ever mentioning anyone at that time,' Maria came into his office carrying a plate of sandwiches and a mug of tea. 'She certainly didn't introduce us to anyone. Why?'

'It's one of the cases that Fiona has asked me to look at. Ginnie says she had an affair with someone. If she was that serious about anyone, I'd have thought she'd have told us.'

'She may have told you, but Ginnie never shared anything of her life with me. Unless I just happened to be in the room when she was telling you.'

Tom knew Maria was right. Ginnie had tolerated Maria; never trying to get close to his wife. He tried to recall anything about an older boyfriend but nothing came to mind. If Ginnie had been seeing anyone when she worked at Kelvingrove they had never met him. They had seen a lot of Ginnie at that time, Joe had loved going out with his Aunt Ginnie as he called her, and he felt pangs of guilt that neither of them had paid any attention to her love life at that point. Had they merely used her as a child minder? He put his head in his hands. What kind of friend was he? Had he ever really been there for Ginnie? Had he ever really listened to her? How could he have missed so many traumatic times in her life, times that she said had led her to kill. Even if, as he believed, she had never committed any of the crimes the fact that she could imagine killing people to avenge harm done to her was evidence that she had been an extremely troubled person. A good friend would have recognised that, wouldn't they?

Chapter 81
GINNIE'S TRANSCRIPT
1979

Stuart and I grew closer. We'd stop in the corridor and chat, resting fingertips on each other's arm as we spoke, bumping into each other in the canteen and spending too long over a coffee. I didn't ask about Maggie. I had removed my own wedding ring as soon as George was dead, I had no wish to be reminded of that time. If Stuart was married it was no concern of mine. I didn't care if he had a wife at home, I wanted him, and I was hell bent on getting him.

One wet, freezing December night I offered him a lift to the station. As I pulled up into the drop-off point, I turned and leaned over to the passenger seat and kissed him. Gently at first then I moved in and pulled him closer to me, kissing him passionately. There was no going back. He knew exactly how I felt. 'Call me.' I pressed my phone number into his hand, then turned back to the steering wheel. He sat, mouth agape for a few seconds. A honk of a horn from the car behind roused him from his dwam. He grabbed his briefcase and jumped out of the car. I drove off, catching a glimpse of him in my rear-view mirror as he watched me. *'Got him.'*

At work we kept our burgeoning relationship under wraps. This was on his insistence but if it meant we could have time alone elsewhere I was happy to comply. I flirted with other members of the team so that any time Stuart and I were caught sitting too closely or exchanging glances everyone dismissed it as just my way.

Malcolm obviously fancied me. He had taken my dropping him at the retirement party as a challenge. He'd pop into my office on any pretext and asked me out on a date several times. I always refused but that didn't deter him.

He was a martial arts expert and one lunch time I heard noises coming from the taxidermy work room. I peeked in. He was stripped to the waist, his body shining in sweat. He held two thick sticks joined together by a chain and was swinging them about his body, posing at the end of each movement. He saw me and motioned for me to enter the room.

'What're they?' I asked pointing to the swirling weapon.

'Nunchakus. Also called rice flails.' He continued to twirl them, slapping them against his hand as he grunted in time with the movements.

I bit my lip. Was this a strange mating ritual? Was I meant to be impressed? 'Carry on,' I said and turned to go. He stopped what he was doing and caught my arm, his fingers digging into the flesh.

'Come on Ginnie. Admit it, I'm hot.'

I laughed out loud, pulling away from him and walking to the door. 'Aye, hot and sweaty.' I laughed.

He leapt towards me, grabbing my arm again. 'Come on. Don't be a cock teaser. You know you want me.'

I pointed at the rice flails. 'Let's see them then.' He released me and handed me the sticks. 'Show me how to use them.'

He stood behind me, his arms wrapped round my shoulders and proceeded to move the nunchakus. 'You swing them round like this.' He demonstrated the move slowly and gently until I had built up a rhythm. 'Now you keep it going,' He stepped back, and I swung the sticks round, clattering him across the face.

'Oops.' I placed the rice sticks on the table. 'Sorry.'

Fred walked in to see Malcolm, blood pouring from his nose.

'What's going on?'

'Malcolm was showing me how to use his toys.' I grinned at the sight of the bleeding wreck in front of me. 'He had an accident.'

Chapter 82
GINNIE'S TRANSCRIPT
1980

In early January Stuart called at 11pm, speaking quietly into the phone, declaring that he'd never met anyone like me. Too right he hadn't. I knew that the whispers were because his wife would be in the house, perhaps had just gone to bed and was waiting for him to lock up and join her. He'd be far better coming to my bed, and I told him this.

'Can you come over tomorrow night?' I asked. I didn't invite him for a meal, we both knew what was on the menu.

Next day I wore my shortest skirt to work. 'Ooh Ginnie's got legs,' Malcolm commented when I walked into the canteen. I glowered at him.

'Very nice.' Stuart whispered when I sat next to him, pressing my thigh against his.

'I'm allowed to show them off occasionally Malcolm. I'm meeting Chris straight after work. I'm sure he'll appreciate a bit of effort.'

I had invented a boyfriend, Chris, as part of Stuart's and my attempts to deflect any suspicion from our colleagues. I even took Joe into the museum on my days off, telling everyone that he was my partner's son. Joe had been great for most of the visits except on one memorable occasion. He loved the dinosaur display, prattling on for ages about the differences between a Velociraptor and an Iguanodon. The taxidermists had laughed, Fred their boss and Malcolm were showing Joe the exhibits, 'I think we've found our next head of department Ginnie. I'm sure Chris is proud of him.'

'Who's Chris?' Joe piped up. I skelped him on the back of the head.

'Very funny Joe. They don't use first names at home but I'm sure he knows his dad's name.' I glared at Joe as I dragged him away. I had weaved stories of my imaginary lover, Chris. He worked in town, and we often met at lunchtime or after five; these were the times that Stuart and I sneaked off to spend time together, kissing and cuddling, holding hands in quiet café's and on benches in the park. I didn't need Joe putting doubts in the minds of the guys I worked with.

'You'll need to bring this Chris to the pub some night Ginnie,' Malcolm continued. 'It'll be nice to see what your type is. I'm sure he, or is it she, will get on well with us.'

'Ah I get it. You think because I don't want you then I must be a lesbian. You are a twat.' I clasped Joe's hand and headed to the stairs and the museum shop, dragging Joe behind me. I could hear Stuart and Bill laughing behind me.

'Did I do something wrong Auntie Ginnie?' He rubbed his head.

I ruffled his hair. 'Not at all Joe. I was just joking. I didn't hurt you, did I?' The boy was fiddling with a toy dinosaur and didn't meet my gaze.

'No,' he said hesitantly. 'I'm ok. I didn't mean to say anything wrong.'

'It's ok Joe, no harm done.' I wanted to keep Joe on my side, if Maria thought I was softening to her child she'd give Tom an easier time. I had noticed her sharp tone when we met up. I pointed to the toy he was playing with. 'Would you like that one?'

'Yes please.' He brightened noticeably. I slipped the dinosaur model into my pocket. Joe's eyes widened.

'Close your mouth, you look like a fish.' I laughed as we walked back to my car.

'But you stole that toy, Auntie Ginnie. Is stealing not wrong?'

'Did no-one ever tell you it's ok to steal if you really want something?'

'Mum says stealing is a sin.' Despite his words he grabbed the dinosaur tightly when I handed it to him.

'Better not tell her then.' I started the car and drove off.

That evening Stuart arrived at my house at 7pm. I jumped into his arms, wrapping my legs around his waist, and kissing him deeply. I was making sure he was under no illusion of what was on offer that night. We had never slept together, and I couldn't wait any longer.

'What did you tell Maggie?'

'She thinks I'm at a darts match with the guys.'

'Ah so no staying over?' I nibbled his ear.

'Oh God. Don't do that. You know what it does to me.' He had closed his eyes and I could feel exactly what it was doing to him. 'I'll need to leave at elevenish.'

'Shame. Better get started then.' I laughed and led him towards my bedroom. I undressed in front of him, ensuring he could see every inch of me then I kissed him again, undoing his belt. He pushed me gently on to the bed and stripped off.

'I can't believe you're really here.' He lay down beside me and I reached for him.

That was as far as our passionate embrace got. No matter what I tried he couldn't maintain an erection.

'Oh God Ginnie. I'm so sorry.' He could hardly look at me. I sat back against the headboard, if I'd been a smoker, I'd have lit one then.

'It's ok.' Although it was far from OK. I'd never had that effect on someone before. 'I think Mr Guilt is affecting you.' I got up and threw on my dressing gown. 'Better get off then. Back to Maggie. You can tell her the darts match got cancelled.'

He reached for me, but I pulled away. 'I'm so sorry,' he said, 'I'll make it up to you another night. I just need to get my head round the fact that a gorgeous young woman would want me.'

'Forget it. We'll just have to be friends who flirt.' I picked up his clothes, dropping them on the bed. 'I think you should go now.'

He dressed quickly then, as I walked him to the door, he tried to kiss me.

'Don't start something you can't finish. Go on, I'll see you tomorrow.' I turned my head, and his lips brushed my cheek. I ushered him out of the door, locking it after him.

I threw myself on to the bed, unsure of what I was feeling. Why was I so angry? Stuart hadn't done anything wrong. He was a married man whose conscience had got the better of him. He had always said that he and Maggie had more of a platonic relationship now. He said they'd stopped sleeping together once their third child had been born and although they loved each other, the physical side of their marriage had stopped. So what was his problem?

Was he hiding something from me?

Had he lied?

Chapter 83
GINNIE'S TRANSCRIPT
1980

From then on things cooled somewhat at work. If Stuart saw me in the corridor he would turn and disappear into one of the rooms. He was seldom in the canteen at our usual meeting times and the secretive kisses and touches stopped. I guessed that Mr Guilty had really taken over. Had he realised what he would lose if Maggie found out about us? He didn't seem to know that it probably wouldn't have gone much further than a brief affair. Knowing that didn't stop me hurting though. If anyone was going to cause the break-up it should have been me. Break-up? We hadn't even started. If he'd given me the chance to be the good one, the sensible one then what eventually happened probably wouldn't have. I'd have left the relationship on my terms. I decided that I still would.

I bumped into him in the long gallery one morning. He was changing the cartridge in the humidifier as he always did on a Monday at ten.

'Stuart. Can we talk?' I stood directly in front of him. 'Can we still be friends?' I ran my fingers over his arm. 'Nothing more, just friends. I miss our chats.'

'I'm sorry Ginnie. Of course we can. I didn't mean to hurt you.' He wiped away the tear that began to trickle down my cheek. 'I'm really sorry.' He actually did look remorseful.

I sniffed, looking down at his feet. 'Can I see you tonight? Come to mine for dinner. No sex!' I giggled through my tears. 'Just pals. I promise I won't try to accost you.'

'Ok. Tonight would be good. It's Bill's birthday and we're all going to the Shish for a curry, but I can get out of it.'

'Thanks Stuart. I really do miss you. It will be great to catch up. I'll see you at mine at seven then?' I stared into his eyes, a smile brightening my face.

'OK. I'll be there.'

Got him.

The doorbell rang exactly on seven. I do like a man to be punctual. Stuart stood at the door, a bunch of flowers and a bottle of wine in hand.

'Ooh thanks,' I gushed. 'Come on through, dinner's nearly ready. Risotto ok?'

He followed me to the kitchen, and I passed him the corkscrew. 'You know where the glasses are, I'll be right with you. Just got to finish this off. Have to keep stirring.'

I returned to the cooker where I added the finishing touches to our meal. He poured the wine and we sat at the small dining table in the corner of the farmhouse kitchen. I had placed his flowers in a vase and sat it between us. 'No candles. This isn't a romantic meal.' I wanted him to feel at ease. 'Just two friends enjoying each other's company.'

He relaxed at my words, taking a large mouthful of the wine.

'So, tell me how you've been. How's Maggie?' That shocked him. 'Stuart. You can't ignore the fact that you're a married man and that you obviously love your wife. Why else would what happened have happened? If we want to be friends, you have to be open with me. Tell me about her.'

He knew I had a long-term friendship with Tom and that Maria just took it for granted that Tom and I would do things together and meet up. I had told him I wanted the same type of relationship with him. Why shouldn't a man and woman just be friends? My approach worked. For the rest of the evening we talked about his family, his work, his life. He didn't seem to notice that we didn't talk much about me. After the meal we sat on the couch and finished the wine.

'Nightcap?' I fetched a bottle of malt from the living room. I had developed a taste for good whisky after my dad died. I poured two large glasses. We talked about our workmates, both of us laughing drunkenly at his stories about Malcolm and Bill.

'This has been lovely Ginnie. I think we can do this.' His words slurred slightly.

'I'm not so sure. You know you shouldn't play with young women's affections.' I placed my glass on the table and topped his up.

'You're the only one...'

'Seriously Stuart,' I interrupted, 'you could really hurt someone. Making them think you love them when you're really not interested.'

'I never...' He looked dejected. 'I'm sorry Ginnie. I've never done anything like that before. But you were the one coming on to me. All blue eyes and big smile. I was flattered. It was exciting.'

'You're the married man. You could have said no. Stopped it before I got hurt.' My voice quivered. 'I'm sorry. I thought we could just be friends but standing here, right now, I know I really love you. I want what I can't have. I think we should really just call it a day, forget the friends idea. I think it would hurt too much.' I stood up and fetched his jacket from the hall.

He staggered slightly as he walked to the door.

'Goodnight, Stuart.' I reached up and kissed him. 'Goodbye.'

'No need...' but I had already shut the door.

I leaned against it for a few seconds, then I walked to the kitchen and washed up the dinner dishes and cooking pot. Scrubbing them thoroughly before stacking them back in the cupboard.

Chapter 84
GINNIE'S TRANSCRIPT
1980

I bounced into the Restorers' workroom. 'Is Stuart in yet? He said he'd help me with some painting I have to do.'

Bill looked up from the painting he was working on. 'Nah. He phoned in sick this morning. Said he'd been up all night. Stomach bug.'

'Must have been the Shish curry.' I laughed.

'I'll have you know the Shish is the best curry house this side of Bombay. Whatever bug he's got he must have had it yesterday. He didn't come out with us last night. Anything I can do to help?'

'It's ok, you're busy. I'll come back when the auld man's back. Actually, can I borrow a paintbrush please?' I needed something of Stuart's.

'Help yourself,' Bill pointed to the tub of brushes on Stuart's desk. Perfect. I picked one at random – anyone would do, I just needed it for my collection.

'Thanks Bill. See you later.' I went back to my room and spent the rest of the morning cataloguing plants.

Stuart came back to work a few days later. He looked hellish and I told him so.

'Horrible bug. Were you ok? I wondered if it was something we ate,' he asked.

'No, I've been fine. Don't you go blaming my cooking. I'm renowned for my mushroom risotto. Must have been a bad pie at lunch time.'

'Think it must have been just a flu thing. Seems to have gone now. I wouldn't wish that on anyone. Thankfully no one else in the family got it.' He looked at me, his brows wrinkled. 'Did you really mean what you said about us not being friends?'

'It's the best thing really. I'm looking for another job, best if we don't keep bumping into each other. I've applied for a post at the Southern. In the lab.' I stepped closer to him, running my hand down his chest, I could see the effect that had on him. 'I could have loved you, Stuart. I wish I'd met you years ago, wish I was older.' I looked up at him, hurt and longing etched in my face, I should have been an actor.

He gulped and shook his head. 'I'm sorry...' I raised my hand to stop him speaking then turned and ran along the corridor to the loos. He wouldn't follow me there.

*

A month later I was on holiday when I got a call from Rosemarie. Stuart had died. Liver failure.

'They think it was possibly Amanita poisoning. The autopsy showed there were toxins in his blood. Margaret said he had often had mushrooms for dinner before he became sick. How could he have made a mistake like that? He's been foraging for years.'

I sounded suitably distraught. 'Oh my God.' I sobbed. 'Poor Maggie. Are you sending a card and flowers? When's the funeral?'

'It's only family and close friends. I'm sorry Ginnie, but I'll send your regards.'

'Thanks Rosemarie. So sad. He was such a nice man. Thanks for letting me know.' I hung up.

Chapter 85
TOM'S DIARY

September 20th, 1979

What a difference in Ginnie. She's been taking Joe into the museum to give Maria and me a break. Joe loves his 'Auntie Ginnie'. You should see her face when he calls her that though, I don't think she's delighted by the term, but she never says anything. He always comes home with a wee gift. Maybe she's softening in her old age.

Maria wasn't sure about leaving Joe with Ginnie at first but even she realises we need some time on our own occasionally.

We thought Ginnie might start seeing someone, but she says there's no-one in her sights. She's happy on her own.

I think George has put her off starting a relationship again.

Maria's period came on Tuesday - I'm not sure how to lift her mood.

Tom 2015

He had known nothing about Ginnie's relationship with her co-worker. Reading the autopsy report on Stuart there was no suggestion that his death was anything but a horrible accident. He was a forager. In the investigation notes it said that his wife had said he often collected mushrooms and plants to cook with, but she and their kids had never liked mushrooms so when he did eat them, he was the only one in the household. He had made a couple of mistakes in the past, the resultant sickness and diarrhoea had made her even more determined not to share her husband's culinary experiments. His death had devasted her. The bout of sickness was no different to any he had had in the past. The realisation that by the time they knew what was wrong he was in complete liver failure and slipping in and out of consciousness was unbelievable. As Tom read the medical report and the explanation of how Amanita poisoning worked on the body and the thought that nothing could have been done to save Stuart, he was shocked.

When Ginnie had told her version of his death the staff had been questioned but none had ever suspected that the two were having an affair and the dead man's wife completely refused to consider that her husband of thirty years would cheat on her. The paint brush in Ginnie's drawer could have come from anywhere and was ignored as evidence.

Surely if Stuart had suspected that Ginnie may have poisoned him he would have confessed to his wife about the affair when he became so ill? What would he have to lose?

Fiona had asked Tom if he could remember Ginnie ever mentioning Stuart and he could honestly say that no, he'd never heard of the man. Reading his diary there was no mention of Ginnie ever speaking about seeing someone in the museum. He would have written something, especially if she was seeing someone so much older. Stuart had been nearly sixty when he died.

Chapter 86
FIONA
2015

'What do you think Stuart did to deserve to die Ginnie?'

'He cheated on me. He said he and his wife didn't have a happy marriage and that we would be together.'

'Surely you mean he cheated on his wife? You knew exactly what his circumstances were.' I want to challenge Ginnie. I'm concerned that my readers won't have any sympathy for her. I can see that she is the result of an abusive childhood and marriage and that she seems unable to accept affection from anyone, that she's damaged, but will my readers get it?

'He led me to believe that he would leave her, but he didn't. He broke my heart.'

I look over my notes. I can't be positive, but I don't remember anything in her transcript about Stuart promising her a future with him. Does it just suit her narrative to make me think she was the wronged party in this affair? I've spoken with Tom. There's no evidence that she had any part in the death of Stuart. Was there even a relationship? Am I going to have to change the title of this book to *The Liar Inside*?

'How did you know that the meal would kill him? Surely it would depend on the amount he ingested?'

'Have a look online. Every forager knows the potency of the Death Cap mushroom. It's well recorded. One small mushroom mixed in with the others wouldn't be noticed, especially if chopped up, and eating even a tiny quantity will kill. The good thing about it is that the victim thinks they're recovering. Once liver failure is diagnosed it's too late, there's no cure. Stuart would know what was happening. That's the best bit. None of my other victims were aware of their impending deaths but Stuart was. That was very satisfying.'

She's getting worse, seemingly relishing in this man's death. I can't see Ginnie as heartbroken. Surely having any feelings for Stuart would prevent this obvious joy she is showing when she describes his death? According to Tom, none of their colleagues was aware of any relationship between the two and Stuart's wife had suspected nothing. Is this whole tale a figment of her imagination? I need to work on how I'm going to present her story. I usually play the part of the psychiatrist in my books, getting to the heart of my protagonist and explaining their behaviours. I think I know where I'm going with this, how to make my readers like, never mind love, Ginnie, is going to be difficult.

Chapter 87
GINNIE'S TRANSCRIPT
1985

The next few years passed relatively quietly. I dated a few men, usually married, the relationships never lasting long. I had decided that I maybe wasn't cut out to be a wife or girlfriend. Safer for all involved.

I was sitting in the porch, the late autumn sun warming me through the glass as I read the latest Stephen King novel when my peace was shattered by the noise of two loud shots ringing out from across the field. I was used to the sounds of gunfire on the estate, the pheasant shooting season had started and parties of rich Americans were continually being ferried back and forward from the estate house to the shooting area to the north of my cottage, but this was much closer.

I walked out into the garden and looked around for Riley. I liked to keep him in when they were shooting but there was no sign of him. When he still hadn't appeared for his food that evening, I walked up to the head gamekeepers lodge house. He was an elderly man, had been on the estate for years and drove around the area as if he owned it. I explained that I was looking for my cat. His round, florid face split into a grin.

'Shouldn't have cats on a shooting estate, we've lost dozens of young birds since you moved in. Haven't seen it but if it comes round here it'll learn.'

I glared at him. 'Seriously? Is that a threat?' I think he wanted to scare me. 'I think you've killed more pheasants with that Land Rover of yours that you career around in than my cat will have. Just let me know if you see him.'

'I've no' got time to look oot for a cat.' He opened the back of his car and half a dozen spaniels spilled out. He growled a command to them, and they rushed towards his house, squeezing past my legs. He followed them, hitching his shotgun over his shoulder. 'Fuck off townie. I've no' got time to staun here gabbin' to you.'

Charming I thought as I walked back down the hill. I couldn't believe someone could hold such old-fashioned, bigoted views.

Three days later Riley limped into the kitchen. His foreleg was bleeding, a deep gash round the leg cutting through the fur and exposing the bone. His mouth was torn and bleeding. I took him to the vet who suggested that he'd been caught in a snare although he thought it strange that he'd been able to get out of it. 'He must have chewed through the wire. Poor boy must have been trapped for days. They're supposed to check the traps daily, I doubt if they ever do. I'll try to save the leg but that's a nasty wound and it's infected.'

Riley lost his leg. The vet did what he could, but the damage was too bad. Had the gamekeeper trapped him and left him to suffer? Was that a warning to me?

Time to send out my own warning.

I had spotted a dead buzzard on the roadside a few

days before, probably hit by a car when feeding on roadkill. If it was still there, I could use it to teach the gamekeeper a lesson. That night I drove to where the bird was and scooped it into a box and into my boot. It wasn't too decomposed, the cooler nights keeping it fresh, perfect for my plan. There was a big shoot planned for the next morning, everyone on the estate would be working.

In the morning I drove to the gamekeeper's lodge. There was a rickety old shed to the side of the garden, inside hung several gin traps and boxes of rat poison spilled their contents on to the shelves. I took one of the traps and rubbed it over the dead bird's body, picking up some blood and feathers on the teeth of the gin. Other boxes and tubs were labelled as DDT and Carbofuran, the skull and crossbones on the packaging indicating they were poisons. I didn't need to set him up anymore, he was doing a great job on his own, even I knew that these were controlled substances and there were rules on how to keep them. The same applied to his guns. Two shotguns sat propped in the corner and there were boxes of shot on the shelf beside the poisons. I stuffed a few cartridges into my jacket pocket and grabbed one of the guns. I have no idea why I took them, but I couldn't let the chance of causing the gamekeeper grief go past.

I took the buzzard and dumped it on the compost heap at the back of the garden, partly burying it so it wouldn't be seen unless you were looking for it.

Back home I hid the shotgun and cartridges in the back of my wardrobe and called the RSPB and reported that I had seen a man bludgeoning a bird to death in the field in front of my house. The inspector took the report seriously, wildlife crime was a new and important issue, there had been reports of court cases where landowners and gamekeepers were prosecuted for killing raptors. The offence was fairly new, and a few test cases were being run to ensure that the warning went out to the estates that they were being watched. The inspector arranged to come and take my statement that afternoon.

When he arrived, I invited him in and made tea as we discussed what I had seen. Riley jumped up on to his knee, his missing leg another piece of evidence of poor practice on the estate, I explained the vet had said it was a snare injury.

I described the man I had seen. 'I think he's the gamekeeper on the estate, I've seen him driving around. The poor bird didn't stand a chance, it was horrible,' I sobbed.

He took notes and thanked me for my help. 'I'll go now and speak to the landowner and the gamekeeper, Miss Queen. Don't worry, I'll say it was an anonymous tip-off.'

I had asked not to be identified, saying I was worried about my and, more importantly, Riley's safety. I stood on the doorstep waving as the inspector drove off towards the lodge and estate house.

The next day I spotted a police car and the inspector's car on the track, he must have found the bird. I was hoping that would be enough for them to investigate the gamekeeper, there would be plenty of evidence to charge him, the man was a dinosaur, the poisons and traps, along with the dead buzzard would be enough to convict him.

A week later the inspector called me. I wouldn't need to go to court. The gamekeeper had pleaded guilty to keeping illegal traps and poisons and for keeping a loaded firearm in an unlocked area. He had denied killing the bird, but the RSPB had decided that they would drop that charge as it would be harder to prove him guilty. They were satisfied that he would receive a big enough fine for the breaches of other regulations to deter him. That would be his punishment; a fine. He probably wouldn't even pay it himself; I was sure the estate would cover it. I thanked the inspector for letting me know but I wasn't satisfied, that wasn't enough. He deserved more than a fine.

*

The result from the shot had been spectacular, I had doubted that anyone could have recognised the man from what was left of his face. I had been careful to not get any blood on me when I untied him and placed his hands in the required position, washing my hands before pulling my top on, showering and changing when

I got home. He had been happy to join in my game, happy for me to bind his hands with my bra, the arrogance of the man thinking I really fancied him and wanted sex was laughable. The look on his face when I had picked up the gun he had left on the kitchen table and placed it in his mouth urged me onwards. I would have liked to make him suffer more but the stench as his bowels emptied wasn't conducive to spending time in his company. Pulling the trigger had been easy, no aim required although the recoil had made me drop the shotgun. I had picked it up then pressed it into his untied hands before letting it fall to the ground.

His body had been found two days later when the landowner had wondered why his employee hadn't turned up for work. The local police had been round the estate asking if anyone had seen or heard anything, but a single shot on a shooting estate during the hunting season wasn't out of the ordinary and they had quickly come to the conclusion that it was a suicide case.

I scratched Riley's ears. 'You'll be safe now.'

The big ginger cat purred.

Chapter 88
Fiona
2015

'So you shot the man and staged it to look like suicide?'

Ginnie nods her head, 'That's it, Fiona. Exactly that.'

I can't imagine what it would take to pull the trigger of a shotgun, knowing that the blast would blow her target's head off. This wasn't the same as giving someone a poisonous mushroom or hitting someone over the head and hoping an animal would finish him off, this was close up and personal, taking someone's life, no dubiety in the outcome.

'How did you feel when you pulled the trigger?'

'Elation. That's the only way I can describe it. The look on his face was brilliant. He knew what he was dying for, knew who was doing it. I felt vindicated.' She pauses, leaning forwards slightly, 'Do you know what? I felt excited, it was as good as an orgasm. Do you know how that feels?'

I don't answer her question, instead I carry on with my questioning.

'Don't you think that the fine was punishment enough?'

She looks at me as if I've asked the most ludicrous question yet. 'He wouldn't learn his lesson. He had to be stopped. And I stopped him, permanently!'

This was the first time Ginnie had shown real excitement when relating her version of her life. If she did really kill this man, she was becoming more and more dangerous. She was enjoying the act of killing. This was more like the typical actions of a serial killer, a psychopath. The enjoyment of the kill is something that has been recorded in many of the books on real life serial killers I have read. Ted Bundy, Dennis Nielsen, Peter Sutcliffe – they had all relished the deaths of their victims. Prior to this Ginnie had seemed to just see the deaths as something that had to be done, a wrong righted. Now her whole demeanour suggests that she is getting a thrill from ending her victim's life. What would she have gone on to do if she hadn't been arrested for what she did to Tom and Joe? If she's telling the truth that is.

Or is she imagining she had anything to do with the death of the gamekeeper? Was his death purely the suicide it had been recorded as? Did she just grab the coattails of that story and weave a monstrous tale round the man's death? I look at my notes and unconsciously rub my forehead. Ginnie tilts her head to one side, a move that she does often, a quizzical look searching my face for signs of what I am thinking. I have to make a decision soon on the tack I'm going to take with my book. Is she a cold, calculating killer, taking pleasure in causing the deaths of those around her? Or is she delusional, making up stories to try to retain some control of her life?

'I listened back to some of your transcript. Going back to Philip's death. You said you'd had sex with him then changed what you meant when I challenged you about it when you were telling me about Mike. You need to be truthful with me Ginnie. A lot of people have died around you; friends, lovers, family, strangers, but were you really responsible for those deaths? Isn't it possible that you just wanted to be in control, so you've fabricated all of this?'

'You're right that a lot of people have died around me. But there's no fabrication,' she replies. 'They die because I want them to, because I am seeking retribution. If you are tending to think otherwise, you're playing a dangerous game, Don't dismiss me as a delusional idiot.'

'I didn't say you were an idiot. Nor delusional. I think you're deeply troubled. Please let me help you.'

'The only way you can help me is to tell my story. To let people out there who ride roughshod over other's feelings by lying, bullying and betraying them that maybe, one day, that person will get vengeance. Perhaps if they were to realise what the result of their actions maybe then they'll think again.'

The look in her eyes is one of pure menace. I need a drink.

Chapter 89
GINNIE'S TRANSCRIPT
1985

'Did you know him?' Maria nodded towards the lodge house.

'Not really. I saw him driving by occasionally, but I never spoke to him.' I handed Joe an apple. 'Go and play with Riley, he's in the bedroom. Just watch his leg, he's just had the stitches out.' The boy ran off, calling for the cat.

Tom and Maria had dropped in to ask me to look after Joe while they went Christmas shopping. The death of the gamekeeper was the talk of the village. His apparent suicide the week before had shocked the community.

'Seems he'd been through the courts recently and had been fined.' Tom sipped his coffee, 'You wouldn't think that would be enough to drive him to kill himself.'

'Maybe there was more to it.' I joined in the gossip, 'Someone said he had been sacked.'

'That might explain it. They said he'd been here most of his life. If he lost his job, he'd lose the house as well. Still, he must have been really depressed to shoot himself.' Maria shuddered as she said it. 'Horrible way to go.'

I bit into my jam doughnut, the scarlet jelly oozed

out and I wiped my lips with my finger. I sucked the sweet sauce off, relishing the look on Maria's face. 'Really messy I'd imagine.'

'What's messy Auntie Ginnie?' Joe had reappeared at the kitchen door. 'Riley's not in the bedroom, I looked everywhere.'

'Brains.'

Tom ushered his son into the garden, glaring at me over his shoulder. 'Ginnie!' He tried to distract his son. 'Jam doughnuts Joe, look how messy Ginnie is. Let's see if Riley's in the garden.'

'What?' I shrugged my shoulders at Maria, I could tell she wasn't pleased by the loud tut. 'I wasn't going to say anything. Just kidding. On you go. I'll look after Joe; I promise I won't tell him about what happens when you blow your brains out with a shotgun.' I shushed her out of the door. Tom was waiting by the gate, watching Joe who sat on the bench with Riley. 'Enjoy your shopping; Joe and I will be fine. I promise I'll look after him, no horror stories.'

Tom took his keys from his pocket. 'Thanks, Ginnie. We won't be long. Just want to pick up his bike and don't want him to see it.'

Maria glared at her husband. 'We could get it on Monday, I could go into town at lunch time.'

'Don't be daft Maria. On you go. He'll be fine, I'll take him for a walk round the pond. We can feed the ducks.' I loved winding Maria up, she was so easy to rile.

'Yayy,' Joe ran towards me. 'Can we take bread?' I

nodded and pushed him towards the kitchen.

Tom took Maria's hand. 'Come on.' He tugged her towards their car. 'Ginnie won't say anything to give Joe nightmares, will you?'

'Course not. See you later. Come on Joe, bring the bread,' I called into the kitchen. 'We've got birds to feed.'

Chapter 90
TOM'S DIARY

November 23rd, 1985

We picked up Joe's Christmas present today. Ginnie took Joe for us. I think Maria still doesn't trust her, even after all these years. She thinks she's a bad influence on Joe, but he loves his Aunt Ginnie. Probably because she lets him do things Maria doesn't.

I like Joe spending time with Ginnie, his mum cossets him too much, doesn't like him taking risks whereas Ginnie lets him have a bit of rough and tumble. I wish I could spend more time with Joe. No-one warns you about the hours you spend away from your family when you're a detective. A couple of big cases have eaten in to my 'free' time over the past few months.

Maria seems terrified that Joe will get hurt. I know it's because he's an only child and she's terrified that she might lose him. And yes, I feel as guilty as hell about that.

I need to take Joe back to Ginnie's tomorrow, he has something to return to her. I'm not looking forward to it.

Tom 2015

Tom would never forget that day and the events that followed. He had been tucking his son in after reading him his favourite bed-time story on a rare occasion when he was home in time for bed. The metal braceleted watch had been tucked under his pillow.

'Where did you get this?' Tom had asked, reading the inscription on the back – *Ranald 21*.

'I found it in Aunt Ginnie's bedroom when I was looking for Riley. I didn't think she'd mind if I borrowed it.'

'Did you steal this, Joe? You know it's wrong to steal.' He had raised his voice slightly; enough, he thought, to show Joe that he was serious.

Joe had looked shocked. 'I'm sorry Dad. I meant to put it back, but we went out and I forgot.' He looked as if he was about to cry.

Tom comforted his son. They had always tried to instil a sense of right and wrong in their son but his contriteness seemed overblown. 'It's ok, it's ok. Don't worry darling. We'll take it back tomorrow. You can apologise then. I'm sure she'll be ok. The main thing is that you are sorry for taking it. It was stealing, and you know that stealing is wrong.' He hadn't wanted to scare Joe and felt guilty that he'd made him almost cry. He hugged the boy tightly. 'Come on wee man, you're ok.' The child nodded, wiping his nose on his pillow.

'Yeuch. Don't let your mum catch you doing that.' He ruffled Joe's hair. 'Night night. It's ok, Aunt Ginnie won't mind. Sleep tight.' He kissed his son on the forehead and tucked the duvet round him.

He sat on the couch and picked up the beer Maria had poured for him while he had seen to their son's bedtime.

Maria picked up the watch. 'What's this?' She sat beside him on the couch tucking her knees up and leaning on his shoulder.

'Joe had it. Says he took it from Ginnie, he found it in her bedroom. He's really upset though. He knows he's done wrong but he was really upset before you came in. I'll take him round to apologise tomorrow. I think it's best if I go with him.' He examined the watch. 'Look though, the inscription on the back says Ranald 21. That was the name of the farmer who died, remember the one who was eaten by his pigs. Ginnie's dad's pal.'

'Vaguely.' Maria examined the watch. 'How did Ginnie get it? Did he leave it to her for some reason?'

'Doubt it, not the kind of thing you'd leave a twelve-year-old. Maybe her dad got it and passed it on. It's not an expensive one though. Hardly worth keeping.'

Chapter 91
GINNIE'S TRANSCRIPT
1985

I was surprised to see Tom and Joe at my door. Tom looked concerned and Joe was obviously upset. We walked through to the kitchen, and I put the kettle on, pouring a glass of milk for Joe.

'Two visits in two days? I'm honoured.'

'Joe has something to say to you.' He looked at his son who reached into his pocket and placed Ranald's watch on the table between us.

'I'm sorry Aunt Ginnie...'

Before he could say more, I grabbed the watch and shook it in his face. 'Where did you get this? You little thief...' I couldn't keep the anger from my voice, and he flinched away from my raised hand, starting to cry.

'Come on Ginnie, he's sorry he took it. He's apologised.' Tom indicated to Joe to come to him, and the boy buried his face in his chest.

I tucked the watch into my jean's pocket and turned to him, composed my face and lowered my tone, 'Just want to make sure he has learned that it's wrong to steal.' I reached out towards Joe, but he moved away.

Tom hugged Joe and told him to go and wait in the car. The boy didn't look at me as he left. I doubted if he was in the slightest sorry for what he'd done.

Tom turned to me. 'What's so special about it anyway. I didn't think Ranald was that close to you.'

'He wasn't. He was a bastard. He abused me.'

My words had the effect on Tom that I had hoped. His face softened, 'Oh god no Ginnie. I'm so sorry. I didn't know.'

'No-one knew, Tom. I didn't even realise what he had been doing. Got what he deserved.' I told him what Ranald had done to me. Tom sat in silence. I had never opened up to him like this before. Part of me still wanted to keep this one of my secrets but I knew I would have to distract Tom from what he would see as my over-reaction to Joe's action. And Joe's over-reaction to having to admit that he'd stolen from me. I had lost control when I saw the watch. What else had he found when he had been rooting around in my room? I would have to check that he hadn't taken anything else. My revelation seemed to both shock and sadden Tom.

'Why have you never told me about this?'

'Why have you never asked?' I retaliated. I wanted to shift the focus from me to him. 'I was ashamed. I let that old pervert abuse me. I was stupid but I wanted to forget it.'

'Why keep his watch then? Did your dad give it to you?' Tom's face showed his concern.

'Can't remember. I've had it for ages. I suppose it reminds me that I survived it.' I picked up the glass from the table and rinsed it in the sink, thoughts of coffee and a chat long forgotten, 'I need to get on Tom. Thanks for bringing it back. Tell Joe I'm sorry if I frightened him. Tell him it's ok, we're ok.'

But we weren't. Joe wasn't in the slightest remorseful for stealing from me, he was just upset that he'd been caught.

Chapter 92
TOM'S DIARY

24/11/85,

I have to tell Maria. The thought that Ginnie had been going to hit Joe has disturbed my sleep and she has been asking what's on my mind. Neither of us has ever raised a hand to our son and his instinctive movement when Ginnie had raised her hand and shook the watch in his face is worrying. I can't believe she would hurt Joe, but his reaction makes me worry that she has hit him before. Is this why he was so upset? I'll talk to him tonight.

Tom 2015

'She did what?' Maria had screamed at him when he told her. 'I'll kill her. That's it Tom. We're finished with her. I don't want her near Joe again and I don't want you seeing her. You can't excuse her this time.' He knew by his wife's stance and tone that she was deadly serious.

'Speak to Joe first. Maybe it was an automatic response. He's never been scared of going with Ginnie before, I'm sure she has never hurt him. I've never seen her so angry before, I think the memories the watch triggered had a bigger effect on her than we realised.'

'Seriously? You're looking for excuses?' Maria had turned away from him, but he could see her fists clench and shoulders shake.

'No, no I'm not. I just think she has problems. She's never shared so much before. Maybe I can talk to her and get her to see her doctor or whatever she needs.' He had told Maria how angry Ginnie had been and what she'd told him about the abuse. He knew his friend needed help but persuading her to speak to a professional wouldn't be easy.

'She's using you Tom, manipulating you to get your sympathy. I can't believe that you can't see that.' Tears shone in her eyes. 'It's your choice. You support me and your son or you take Ginnie's side. You can't have both.'

Maria glared at him and ran upstairs to Joe's room. Tom sat at the kitchen table. His mind had been in turmoil. He had to protect Joe, which was his main purpose in life, and he had to support Maria, but Ginnie had been a part of his life since childhood and he felt a strong tie to her, knowing she was hurting tore at his gut. He wanted to help her, but Maria and Joe came first.

The look on Maria's face when she came back downstairs told him everything he needed to know. 'Joe has something to tell you.' She sat the boy down beside Tom. 'Tell your dad why you were so upset when he found the watch.'

Joe looked at him, he enormous grey eyes prickled with tears. 'I was scared that Ginnie would hit me again. Mum says that she won't let her. The man in the museum said that you were Ginnie's boyfriend so I told him that wasn't true, and Ginnie hit me and told me not to be silly. It wasn't very sore, but I got a fright.'

'When was this?' Tom had to know.

'It was when I was little but I've never forgotten it. What she did was wrong wasn't it, dad?'

'Yes it was wrong,' he pulled his son towards him. 'Don't worry. It won't happen again.'

Maria took Joe's arm. 'She told him not to tell anyone and gave him a gift to shut him up. The bitch hit our son Tom. Wake up. Deal with it. I'm taking Joe to your mum's. Come and get us when you're done.'

*

Tom sat his diary down. The memories of that day were forever fused into his brain. He had known that this would be a big turning point in his life, but nothing had prepared him for what was to come.

Chapter 93
GINNIE'S TRANSCRIPT
1985

I ran my fingers over the watch's dial. Tom had asked why I had kept it. I couldn't tell him the reason, that I had always had a compulsion to keep something of my crimes. I'd need to tell him about my victims to do that and that would open up a whole bucket full of worms. Most people wouldn't understand what I had done and I'm positive that a detective would definitely not understand. The last thing I wanted was to lose Tom's respect, the realisation of that hit me hard. I'd never cared about what anyone thought of me before now, but the thought of Tom not being there for me hurt more than I cared to admit.

I'd had to make him believe that I had forgiven that wee bastard of his. The thief had sat there in front of me. Big watery eyes pretending that he was sorry for having stolen something belonging to me. He must have been rummaging in my memento drawer.

The first thing I had done when they left was check that he hadn't stolen anything else. I lay the knife, slides, bracelet etc on my bed. Nothing missing. I returned the watch to its place.

It could have been worse; Joe could have found the shotgun I had stolen from the gamekeeper's shed, and I have no idea how I would have explained that one to

Tom. It wasn't the gun that had killed the gamekeeper; I had had to leave that one beside the body, placed in such a way to indicate suicide. The one I had taken was enough to remind me of the look on the man's face when he had realised what was happening.

Chapter 94
GINNIE'S TRANSCRIPT
1985

Tom sat opposite me at the old pine table, his face grave. He hadn't greeted me in his usual fashion when I had answered the door to his forceful knocking, and he had brushed past me into the kitchen.

'Sit down Ginnie. We need to talk.' His eyes fixed on mine, boring into my soul. 'Joe told us you hit him when he was little.'

'He...'

'Shut up. I don't want excuses. There are no excuses for hitting a child. I want you to get help. Now sit down.'

I pulled the chair opposite him out, the noise of the legs scraping against the stone floor screeched into the silence between us.

I returned his gaze. 'I don't need help. Since when were you the psychology expert?'

'I'm trying to help you Ginnie. Please listen. If you don't get help, we're finished. I can't have you round my family if I think you're going to hurt them.'

'Should this not be Maria sitting in that chair.' I pointed to him. 'This is her doing, isn't it?'

Tom shuffled in his seat. 'Stop it. It doesn't matter if it's from Maria or me, don't try to deflect this. You're lucky it's not Maria here, she wants to kill you.'

I laughed. Maria kill someone? Not a hope, she

doesn't have it in her. She'd rather send her husband to do her dirty work.

'It was only a tap. And it was years ago. He...'

'Stop it. I don't want to know why you hit him, don't need to know that. Can't you just see that what you did was wrong? The way you screamed at him when you found out about the watch wasn't a normal reaction. You're losing it Ginnie. You know I've always supported you, excused your rudeness, stood up for you when others slagged you off. I'm on your side but you need to acknowledge that you have a problem.'

Realisation crept in. Tom was threatening me. I was going to lose him because of that snivelling little shit of a child of his. I stood up and walked away from him.

'Ginnie, sit down. You can't just walk away from this. Listen to me.'

I continued walking; I knew what I had to do. He stood and followed me into the living room.

'Fuck. Where did you get that?' He stared into the barrel of the shotgun I was levelling at him.

'It was in the loft when I moved in. Thought it would come in handy one day.' 'Ginnie, listen to me. Put the gun down.' He reached out his hand towards me.

The trained cop in him taking over his movements.

'No way Tom. You're not getting rid of me. You're the only one who has always been there for me. I'm not losing you. This isn't how I wanted this to go but I need to do something and I need to make sure you won't stop me.'

Tom dropped his hands. 'Put the gun down Ginnie. Put it down and we'll talk this over.' He took a small step towards her.

'Stay right there,' she yelled. 'Don't move. You always take Maria's side.'

'It's not about taking sides. Look at you. This isn't the Ginnie I know. I owe you everything, You know that, but this is crazy. You need to put the gun down and we'll get you the help you need.'

'I know what I need. I need to make sure Joe knows he has done wrong. He needs to learn how to fly.' Tom's face showed me he knew what I meant. I dropped the barrel and aimed at his leg and pulled the trigger. I didn't want to kill Tom. He had never wronged me, but I had to make sure he didn't stop me. He fell, striking his head against the edge of the table. He was silent, knocked unconscious.

I ran.

Chapter 95
GINNIE'S TRANSCRIPT
1985

I parked outside Tom's house, my mind racing. How could I get Joe from his mother? I was under no illusion that if Maria saw me, she'd either attack me or phone the police. I wasn't sure how long I had. Tom would be able to call for help once he came round. The wound in his knee would stop him running for help, I had deliberately aimed off to the side, I didn't want to kill him, just stop him following me. When he fell and was knocked out it made my escape easier. Maria's car wasn't in the driveway, I had to see if it was in the garage. I kept close to the hedge using the thick Leylandia to shield me from the house in case they were inside. Standing on tiptoes I could just see through the dirty, side window of the garage. It was empty. Where would she go with Joe?

I got back in my car and headed to the local park. Joe loved to feed the ducks and play on the swings, but the park was empty, the threatening rainstorm keeping folk away. Maria had no family nearby, but Tom's mum still lived in Airdrie, in the house opposite my childhood home. Fifteen minutes later I pulled into the bus stop a couple of hundred yards from the house. Maria's red fiesta was parked in the street. There was a back lane which ran behind the houses, there was no reason for Maria to be looking out for me, but I didn't want to take any chances. My luck was in, Joe was playing in the back garden on his own, his stupid mother thinking her beloved son would be safe there. She had no idea of my plans, unless Tom had got help quickly and the fact that the boy was in my sight suggested that he hadn't been able to raise the alarm.

I snicked the gate open. 'Joe.' I kept my voice low.

'Aunt Ginnie.' The idiot seemed pleased to see me. Then his face fell. 'Are you still angry with me?'

'Of course not. We're still best pals. Want to go to the park? Your dad has sent me to get you, he's waiting at the pond for us.'

Joe ran towards me then turned to face the house. 'Mu...' I placed my hand over his mouth.

'Shh. Your dad wants to surprise your mum, he's got a present for her, and I've got one for you.' I had knelt down and was looking at him directly, keeping his face turned towards me so he would concentrate on what I was saying. I handed him the watch. 'You can have this. It's a gift from me.'

'Thanks.' He held the watch up. 'Are you sure?'

I nodded and he slipped the watch into his pocket. He relaxed and walked with me back down the lane to my car. I needed Joe to come with me, but I'd have to gain his trust. I didn't want to scare him; a screaming child would look suspicious, or at least be memorable. I took him to the park as promised.

When he saw his dad wasn't there, I could see a look

of concern on his face. 'Maybe he's gone to the shop to buy your mum's present.' This cheered the boy up and despite his dad not being there he happily tucked into the choc-ice I'd bought him from the ice-cream van.

'I think your daddy's playing hide and seek with us. I know where he'll be. Let's go.' I took his hand, ignoring the stickiness from the melted ice cream. I knew what I wanted to do with the thief.

Chapter 96
TOM'S DIARY

24/11/85,

This has been the worst day in my life. I need to sleep now.

Tom 2015

The memories of that fateful day came flooding back. He hadn't believed that Ginnie would shoot him. When he had seen the gun pointing at him his training kicked in and he had tried to reason with his friend. Ginnie wouldn't shoot him. But she had. The shot had blasted a hole in the wall to the side and behind him but enough shrapnel had lodged in his leg to cause damage he still suffered from. Had the gun gone off by accident?

He couldn't remember exactly what happened next. He had been knocked unconscious when he fell and had no idea how long he'd been unconscious. He remembered crawling to the front door, he thought he must have blacked out a few times while he lay in the hall. He remembered calling the station then had blacked out again. His next memory was of being in a hospital bed, his leg heavily bandaged and a drip in his arm replenishing the lost blood. The doctors told him he was lucky, most of the shot was in his calf and had missed the popliteal artery and chipped the kneecap. When he came to, he had pulled the drip out and screamed at the nurses for a phone.

When he got through to the station, he discovered that Maria had already called them, Joe was missing. His legs buckled when he realised that Ginnie had his son. 'I need to get out of here.' He was still arguing with the doctors when Maria arrived on the ward.

She had persuaded them to let him leave, he couldn't do anything stuck in the hospital. They'd lent him a wheelchair and set of crutches and he had sat in the chair reluctantly, knowing he had to follow their instructions if he wanted to be part of the search for his son. Maria drove him to the station where his boss had appraised him of what was happening.

Joe had been missing for almost three hours. An appeal had been put out on TV and local and national news with a warning not to approach the tiny, blond woman. Her cottage had been searched but there was no sign of Ginnie nor Joe. The team was interviewing her neighbours and checking her workplace and haunts. All airports and ferry terminals were on alert although Ginnie's passport had been found at her cottage.

Tom had argued with his DCI to let him help with the search. McIntyre had been reticent at first. Tom wasn't fit for work; he would be signed off as soon as the paperwork was complete. The blast from the shotgun had peppered his kneecap and destroyed the soft tissue of his calf; he was strapped in bandages from ankle to hip, the hospital was waiting for the swelling to go down before operating. He could hobble short distances with the crutches but was mostly confined to the wheelchair. He was also too close to the case. His friendship with Ginnie was seen as a conflict of interest. He had argued that his friendship was what made him the best person to find the missing woman and his son. He knew how her mind worked, at least he thought he did. He was beginning to doubt that he knew her at all. How could she shoot him in cold blood? Why hadn't she killed him? Her eyes had dropped as she lowered the weapon and fired. From six feet away she shouldn't have missed, no matter how inexperienced she was. Why had she taken Joe?

He shook his head. These were the actions of a cold, calculating sadist, not his childhood friend.

Chapter 97
GINNIE'S TRANSCRIPT
1985

'Not far now.' I tried to keep my voice light. Joe had started to gripe about the distance we were walking. It was only half a mile across the fields to the quarry but, unlike his dad and me as children, Joe wasn't used to running wild. It wasn't the done thing now to let your kids wander the countryside looking for adventures. At ten we had been walking miles each day, visiting the quarry, climbing trees, sliding down the pit bing.

'This is where me and your dad used to play. We used to come here and catch fish and frogs. Has he ever told you that?'

The child shook his head. 'I don't like frogs.' He scrunched his face up in distaste.

I led him over to the edge of the quarry. 'Look how deep it is Joe. Would you like to go for a swim?' I placed my hand on his shoulder.

He shook his head. 'I can't swim yet. Dad's going to teach me. Says everyone has to learn to swim but it's too cold here.'

'Did he ever tell you that this is where our best friend Francis died?'

Joe gasped. 'What happened?'

'He was a bad boy. He lied to me. He was the age you

are now, and he could swim but he still drowned.'

'That's horrible Aunt Ginnie,' he said, his voice trembling. 'I don't like it here. Can we go now? It's starting to rain.'

Typical. Whinge, whinge. So like his mother. I wonder what she's doing. She must have noticed he's missing by now. I'd need to be careful and avoid busy places, she's bound to have called the police. When I had imagined killing Joe, my first thought had been to bring him here and drown him in the same way I had drowned Francis. Then I had plotted different ways of making him pay for stealing from me and lying about me. The child needed a bit of excitement in his life. He'd been mollycoddled too much. He'd never screamed in joy nor had the thrill of danger making him shiver. He deserved to have one moment of elation before he died.

'Have you ever dreamed you could fly Joe. Imagine soaring through the air like an eagle. Wouldn't that be brilliant?'

He nodded. 'Yeah, like Superman.' He pulled away from me and swooped across the clearing, his jacket held out like wings.

'Come on then.' I held out my hand, 'Let's go fly.'

Chapter 98
TOM'S DIARY

25/11/85
It's 4am. I can't sleep.

Tom 2015

He remembered writing this short entry. He had slipped from their bed and gone to Joe's room, holding his sleeping son, trembling at the thought he had almost lost him. Even now he had nightmares about it. He would wake screaming and Maria would hold him, soothing him until he dropped off again.

He recalled that dreadful day. He had been unable to sit at home waiting for a phone call from his colleagues and had spent time with the officers who were looking for his son. Maria was at home, in case Ginnie phoned. She had a family liaison officer with her. Truth be told he hadn't wanted to see the look of fear mixed with hatred he had seen in his wife's eyes.

'Tell me again what she said to you Tom.' DCI McIntyre had sat with him. Tom knew his boss was just humouring him. Making him think he was doing something to help. He had wracked his brain. Most of what had happened at Ginnie's was a blur. He placed his head in his hands. The thought had been like a lightning bolt, it was accompanied by a rumble of thunder from outside. He knew where Ginnie had gone.

'I need to go home boss. Can you get me a car to drop me off please? I need to be with Maria.'

His boss had been happy to let him go but when Tom got in the car, he had asked them to drop him at his mother's in Airdrie. If his hunch was right, he knew exactly where Ginnie would be.

The "flying" comment had been her clue.

He had waved the car off and turned the wheelchair away from his mother's house and headed up the hill towards the flats. He hadn't told his boss where he was going. If his guess was right, he didn't want the team rushing in and making things worse. He could talk Ginnie out of what she had planned.

The three blocks of eight story flats towered above him. Which one? He guided the wheelchair into the foyer of the left-hand block, Cairngorm, and into the lift, the smell of piss and decaying carry outs caught his breath. He hadn't thought through how he was going to get on to the roof. The lift only reached the eighth floor, the roof accessed by a set of concrete steps. The door padlock and chain were exactly the same as he remembered as a child. Too narrow for an adult to access unless that adult was tiny. He threaded his crutch through the chain and twisted, wrenching the padlock from its fixings on the door. He slid from the wheelchair and, using his left leg and crutch, pushed himself from step to step. Each movement caused him to gasp in agony, cold sweat ran down his back and he fought to stop himself crying out loud. If Ginnie was here with Joe, he didn't want to panic her.

He scrambled through the door on to the roof, using the door handle as support. He scanned the concrete area; the roof top was empty.

'Shit.' He hobbled to the air conditioning unit which took up the centre of the space.

'Yeehh!' The yell had come from his right. Had he heard that or was his pain filled brain playing tricks? His head swivelled trying to pinpoint where the call had come from. On the parapet of the middle block of flats stood Ginnie and Joe. They were holding hands, arms stretched out to the side, and they were screaming. Not screams of fear. Excitement rang across the void. He had to get to them. Adrenaline coursed through his veins, and he half fell, half hopped down the steps to the lift, abandoning his wheelchair. The light above the lift door indicated the lift was on the third floor. He hit the call button repeatedly and fell into the space when the door opened, jabbing furiously at the 'ground' button. The lift descended, the indicator showing the fall from floor 8 to 7, 6 then 5, interminably slow. 'Come on, come on.' Tom screamed. The lift bounced to a stop on the second floor.

A young woman with a pram stood glaring at him, mouth open.

'Keep out.' He yelled at her. 'Police.' He realised he didn't have his ID. He realised that he'd need help. 'Phone 999. Tell them DS Tom O'Brien has found Virginia. Tell them she's on the roof of Morven Court. Tell them to get here now!' As he shouted at the startled woman, he once again began battering the Ground button. He knew he would need back-up eventually but had to get to Ginnie first.

He lurched across the grass between the blocks of flats and into the darkened hallway. There was no light on the lift. Despair and agony coursed through him. He could feel warm liquid running down his leg, his efforts ripping the stitches which held his torn flesh together. 'Please, please, not a power cut. Please God.' He stabbed the call button, his knees buckled when he heard the whir of the lift mechanism.

The door to the steps to the roof lay open, he scrambled up the concrete stairs and, his injured knee screaming, stepped through the door to the roof. 'Ginnie.' He tried to speak clearly but gently, not wanting to startle either of the people on the parapet.

'Dad.' Joe looked over his shoulder. 'Look dad, we're flying.' He waved his free arm causing Tom to cry out in fear.

Chapter 99
GINNIE'S TRANSCRIPTION.
1985

We stood on the parapet of Morven House. 'Hold my hand, Joe. Now stretch out the other and feel the wind. It's like flying isn't it?'

Joe copied what I was doing. He flapped his free arm up and down and screeched like an eagle.

'That's it. Imagine we're soaring the thermals,' I called over the noise of the wind.

'Ginnie.'

I turned when I heard another voice behind us. Tom.

'Ginnie. Please Ginnie. Bring him down. Please,' his voice keened across the space.

'Why?' I shouted back at him. 'He's a thief, Tom. Do you want a thief in your family?'

'He's a child Ginnie. Let him go.' He moved a step closer. I could see blood dripping down his leg and on to the roof of the building.

Tom held his hand out. 'Please Ginnie, he's all I have.'

'Whatever happened to your police training Tom? Isn't it against the law to steal? Shouldn't he be punished?'

Tom rubbed his eyes as if his vision had begun to blur. How much blood had he lost? He swayed against the wall of the air conditioning unit. 'Maria and I will deal with him Ginnie. This isn't your problem. Give him to me.' He held his hand out, but kept his distance. Was he afraid to get closer to us in case he startled me? He took a deep breath, I could hear the gasp despite the noise of the wind. 'Ginnie, listen to me. I'll make sure you're ok. Let Joe go.'

I turned to Joe. 'What do you think Joe? Do you think a thief should be punished?'

'You said it was ok to steal Aunt Ginnie. You said if you wanted something you couldn't have then it was ok to steal.' Joe's bottom lip stuck out, trembling slightly.

I looked at him, remembering saying this to him when I'd given him the dinosaur. Was it my fault he had stolen from me?

'So I did Joe. So I did. But you shouldn't steal from people you know, especially not your auntie. That's not forgivable.'

The sound of a police siren filtered up from the road eight floors below, Tom called to me, his throat raw, eyes blinded by tears, 'Please listen to me Ginnie. If you throw Joe off the edge, I'll follow him. I can't live without my son.'

I stared down at my old friend. What was he saying? I can't let him do that. I turned to face the boy. 'Right Joe.' I gripped his hand tighter. 'Let's jump.'

Tom collapsed, his hands covering his face. He lay sobbing, obviously afraid to look up. Joe reached out to him, pulling his fingers from his eyes. 'Daddy. Look

Daddy'.

He looked across to where I leaned against the door. 'Thank you,' he gasped. 'Thank you.'

I realised why I had stopped. 'I couldn't let you kill yourself Tom. You know I'd never do anything to hurt you, you've never wronged me. I'm sorry. Please...talk to me.' The door to the stairwell burst open and two uniformed police officers grabbed me. 'Tom...' I tried to get his attention but he was wrapped up in his son. The third officer was on the radio calling an ambulance. One of the officers who had grabbed me was trying to staunch the flow of blood from Tom's leg.

I watched Tom with Joe while I was handcuffed and read my rights. The look of love on his face caused a pang of jealousy in my chest. He had never looked at me like that, although we had been as close as I'd been to anyone else. The young officer dealing with me was gentle, covering my wrists with my jacket sleeves before clicking the cuffs shut. I tried to catch Tom's eye, but he refused to look at me. 'Tom...'

The constable hushed me; he cautioned me again as he took me by the arm and led me down to the waiting car, reminding me of my right to remain silent.

Chapter 100
TOM'S DIARY

26/11/85

I couldn't write any more yesterday. All I wanted to do was cuddle Joe and Maria, but the docs gave me some serious painkillers and I kept dropping off. Maria's hardly speaking to me, she hasn't left Joe's side. The poor wee man knows something's wrong between us. Maria won't let him come through to see me. I can't concentrate on anything, think the drugs are still working. The pain in my leg is a dull throb but nothing compared to the ache in my chest. Will Maria ever forgive me? Do I deserve to be forgiven?

Tom 2015

Tom wiped the tears from his eyes. Despite it being thirty years since that day the memories still tore his heart apart.

Lying in his makeshift bed in the dining room, he could hear voices from the living room taunting him. He had struggled into the wheelchair which had been retrieved from the top floor of Cairngorm court.

Maria looked up from the couch where she had

been reading with Joe and his son had rushed to him, clambering on to his good knee. Maria followed her son across the room and lifted him from Tom. 'Go and finish your book Joe, Daddy needs to rest.' Tom had tried to argue with her, but Maria was adamant, he could see she was struggling with her feelings.

'Not yet Tom. I'm sorry, I need to get my head round this. Your friend tried to kill Joe. I'm not sure I can forgive you for putting him in harm's way.'

He tried to take her hand, but she pulled away, grief staining her face. He hadn't been able to form the words he needed to say and had returned to his bedroom, aware that he had to give Maria time. Everything was still too raw, the only saving grace was that Joe didn't seem concerned about what had happened. He had gone with Ginnie willingly, happy to be with her, having fun. The only thing that bothered him was seeing his dad in pain. Even the appearance of the police bursting on to the roof and grabbing Ginnie had been part of the excitement for the boy. Maria had insisted that Joe see a psychologist, concerned that he was hiding any trauma and worried that it would resurface in the future. She had been surprised when the results came back that Joe seemed to be unfazed by the events.

Even now Tom struggled with the memories. Time had done its part in reducing the flashbacks, but the diary entries drove his feelings at the time to the surface. He wondered if Maria still had the dreams which had haunted her for months after that day. Fortunately, she had agreed that they would face the issues together and he had managed to save their marriage. Ginnie being in prison and refusing to see him helped. He could honestly tell Maria that he wasn't in communication with Ginnie, and that she was no longer in their life. Eventually the two had agreed to put the event behind them but now he was dragging it all back. Had he done the right thing by agreeing to help Fiona?

Chapter 101
FIONA
2015

Tom had told me what had happened after Ginnie had shot him. His strength and bravery made me see him in a different light. When I first met him, I had thought he was a quiet, slightly obsessive man who had allowed Ginnie to treat him, and especially his wife, with contempt.

I'm completely confused by this part of Ginnie's story. Joe had wronged her, at least to her way of thinking, but she couldn't kill him because she couldn't hurt Tom. This is so far out of character for the person Ginnie was pertaining to be. I don't understand this.

'Did you change your mind about killing Joe because he was only a child and all he did was steal an old watch?'

'No, I've just told you. I couldn't hurt Tom. I could see what losing Joe would do to him, and he threatened to jump, so I let the boy go; I couldn't let Tom kill himself. And by the way, it was a big deal that he stole my watch. That watch meant a lot to me. That was Ranald's watch. Held a lot of memories it did. I'd never have been able to replace it would I?'

I have a list of the items found in Ginnie's house. The items she insists were taken from her victims. The shotgun she used against Tom was never traced to the gamekeeper. It wasn't on the inventory of the shooting estate although they had said that gamekeepers sometimes had their own guns, and they couldn't be totally positive that it had come from his house. Ginnie had told Tom she'd found it in her loft. It was thought it may have belonged to the previous tenant of her cottage and had been left behind when they moved. The only prints on it were Ginnie's. Which version was true? Has she been caught out in another lie?

Every other item could have been part of a normal collection; bits and pieces accumulated over a lifetime. Even I have my memory box which holds the ticket stub from the first rock concert I had attended, a favour from my wedding, the first Valentine card I'd received. No-one had considered Ginnie's collection to be anything other than the normal detritus people pick up throughout their life, things which trigger fond memories of people and places they had been. Things which had helped form them into the adults they became.

'How do you feel about Joe now? Have you forgiven him for stealing from you?'

'Of course I have. It was a long time ago. What is it they say? "Time heals all wounds", or is it "old wounds"? You know what I mean. I've changed. You're not the person you were as a teenager, are you? You don't seem like a bully now.' Again she's deflecting my questions, focussing on me instead of herself.

'I think my readers will sympathise with much of your story Ginnie, but do you really think someone should die for a minor slight? Lying? Stealing? Are they really capital crimes?' I look over the top of my glasses, challenging her to explain her actions.

'They are to me. I put my trust in people. If they betray that trust, am I not within my rights to take out whatever revenge I see fit. I don't kill everyone who wrongs me. After all, you're here, aren't you?'

Once again, my blood freezes. Am I lucky to still be alive? I don't remember bullying Ginnie at school but as I note her current comments I'm aware of her watching me intently.

Ginnie grins. 'I'm nearly done now. Let's get on.'

Chapter 102
GINNIE'S TRANSCRIPT
1985

There was nothing I could do to argue my case. I had shot a cop and kidnapped a child. I sat in the back of the police car contemplating what I would do next.

At the station I had been charged with attempted murder and abduction of a child, and had been given the number of a solicitor to call. The woman on the phone had told me to say nothing or say 'no comment' to any questioning until she could get there. I thought that would be a waste of time and declined her help. I was guilty, no point in making things more complicated. I spent the night in a cell, curled up on a hard, uncomfortable mattress. Someone brought me a fish supper, still hot and steaming from the chip shop next door, they must do a roaring trade. The next morning, I had stood in court and pleaded guilty to shooting Tom and kidnapping Joe. I had been remanded in custody and taken back to the station for processing and to await sentencing. This all took time but eventually I was sentenced to twenty years, ten with good behaviour. I had been transferred from Polmont to Cornton Vale women's prison in Stirling. There I shared a cell with a ruddy faced, red-haired woman.

She pointed to the top bunk, 'Yours. Ah'm Senga. Whit are ye in fur but?' Her broad Stirlingshire accent and use of the word 'but' as punctuation were the eventual cause of my sentence being extended to thirty years.

When I said I'd shot a cop she laughed, 'You'll be aw right in here hen. Naebody'll mess wi' a cop shooter but.'

A few days after I was admitted the warder handed me a letter. I didn't recognise the handwriting and waited until Senga had left our cell before opening it.

Ginnie.

I don't know what hold you have over Tom but I want you to let him go. He wants to keep in touch with you while you're in prison and nothing I can say will dissuade him so I'm writing you to ask you to not reply to his letters. He needs to move on and concentrate on his family. If you stay in touch, you'll always be foremost on his mind, and I can't have that. Joe and me should be the ones he has to concentrate on. I want my husband to get on with being the father he should be and to forget about you and whatever has gone on in the past.

I'm begging, please forget about Tom. Let him forget about you. I don't know if I can cope if you're still there in our lives.

Maria

I read her words, cringing at how needy she was, how much she undervalued what she had with Tom. And "Joe and me" – For fuck's sake, this was a supposedly educated woman. 'Joe and I, Maria,' I shouted.

I know more about Tom than she ever will. She may

have tried to destroy our relationship, but some ties are never-ending, Tom and I are bound forever by the secrets we share, and although Maria thought that she had won, I know he will be there for me. But I did it. I tore up the letters Tom sent and never once replied to him. Eventually he stopped writing.

Over the next few weeks, I told Senga about the other crimes I had committed. It felt good to share the secrets I'd held for so long. Senga loved my stories, laughing uproariously when I described the look on Ranald's face when I hit him with the bucket.

'You're a fuckin' bampot,' Senga announced when I told her about George. 'How the fuck did you no' get caught for that yin but?'

I described the police on Gozo and how they preferred to have an easy time, the less paperwork the better. She particularly loved my description of shooting Tom, although she didn't understand why I hadn't just killed him. She didn't get the fact that he had never wronged me so how could I kill him?

I never asked her what she was in for, although she held a high position in the prisoner ranks. Other women deferred to her, bringing her packs of cigarettes and sweets. Even the guards spoke to her differently. Whatever she was in for, she was there long term, she had told me that she didn't expect to see her grandchildren until they were grown-up.

When I told her about Jean, she looked at me with a hint of fear in her eyes.

'You really are a fuckin' head-case, aren't you?' She moved further away from me on the bunk where we'd been sitting chatting. 'You should tell them about this. You'll get sectioned. Carstairs is a much mair cushy number. You'd get an easier time there but.'

Her words started me thinking. Was she right? If I had to spend time locked up, would it not make sense to make my life as easy as possible? I had never heard of Carstairs but her description of it as a softer sentence appealed. I had seen a psychiatrist as part of the court case – she hadn't deemed me unfit to plead.

Three months into my term I approached one of the prison warders in the sewing room. 'I have something more I want to confess to. I've killed nine people...'

The warder looked at me, raising her eyebrows. She was younger than me but had the demeaner of a much older woman. Her role gave her the confidence she needed to deal with all kinds of behaviours. I think someone confessing was outside her realm of understanding, most prisoners complained that they were innocent and had been set up.

She held up her hand and stopped me. 'Stop there Ginnie. I can't take your confession; you'll need to speak to CID. We'll have to do a cell intervention.'

She then left me alone, giving me time to formulate my speech. It was time to confess, time to tell someone in authority that I was a killer, that the deaths surrounding me were my doing. If they found I was insane then I could be out of there soon, no more of Senga's 'buts'.

I was called to the governor's office where I repeated what I'd told the warder. Again I was offered the presence of a solicitor, this time I had accepted, and a duty solicitor was called to meet me at the station. The two cops who drove me to Stirling police station hardly spoke to me. I stared out of the window as we drove in the shadow of the castle, past the infamous Raploch. Boarded windows and skeletal cars bore testament to the depravity of the area. Senga had told me she was from the scheme which was a home to the majority of Stirling's drug dealers and thieves. I had thought I had been brought up in a fairly rough area, but it was nothing compared to the notorious housing estate in Stirling.

We drove on and into the car park of the station and I was guided through the heavy-duty, blue doors and into the custody suite where we waited for the solicitor. He arrived just after I had been settled into a cell which looked exactly the same as the one in Airdrie, small, grey, cold and furnished with a single bed and a bucket in the corner. He was a grey man whose suit wore him like a sack. He ran his hand through the greasy strands of hair which sat in a conspicuous comb-over. I briefly outlined what I intended to say to the police. He advised me to say nothing. I fixed him with a glare, what bit of, 'I want to confess' didn't he understand?

An hour later two suited officers came into my cell and led me into a sparse, pale blue painted room and sat opposite me at a long table. Conor Muir, my solicitor sat beside me, his leg rubbing uncomfortably against mine under the table. The taller and older looking of the two detectives introduced himself and his colleague then explained that the interview would be recorded and that at that time I wasn't under any charge and that I was there under my own free will. I agreed to all of this. My solicitor once again cautioned me, whispering in my ear. His breath was foul, a mixture of stale cigarette smoke and poor dental hygiene made me recoil when he leaned in close.

'Can I ask you to leave please?'

He looked at me dumbfounded.

'I am here to represent you Miss Queen, if you will not take my advice then I suggest you seek representation elsewhere.' He pointedly closed his notebook and sat back in his chair.

'Ms.' I said, narrowing my eyes. 'It's Ms Queen. Please just go now. I don't need your advice.' I didn't want him interrupting me constantly, I needed my statements to be clear and unambiguous, his constant shuffling and huffing, and his proximity distracted me.

The two detectives watched this exchange, slight smirks twitching at the sides of their mouths. The lawyer stood and bid farewell in his annoying stilted manner. I was glad to see him go.

'OK Ginnie, is it ok to call you Ginnie?' the older officer asked. I nodded. He went through the formalities of explaining what would happen again. Turning to the tape recorder he noted the time and who was present and asked me to start.

I listed the people I had killed, giving brief details of each crime. The two men sitting opposite me recorded my confession and one took copious notes. At one point, my dad's killing I think, they had exchanged glances and the notetaker had placed his pen down and closed his notebook. His sigh was loud enough for the tape to pick it up.

'Let's have a break there Ginnie. This may take some time. Tea or coffee?' They had left the room and I thought I heard laughter in the corridor.

When they returned there was a definite shift in the atmosphere in the room. They seemed to be taking me more seriously. They let me finish my list then took me back to the start to get more details of dates and places, garnering as much information as they could. They explained they would have to carry out more investigations and would come back to me if they needed anything else.

What I thought would be a straightforward 'I'm guilty' acceptance turned into six months of questioning and psychiatric tests. In that time, I was back and forward every few days between Cornton Vale and the police station.

Senga was enthralled by the whole business. 'Dae they believe you?' she had asked one morning as I got ready to leave for the station.

'Hard to tell. They do a lot of eyebrow raising and teeth sucking but they never give anything away.' I didn't mention to her that I was loving every minute of the process. Getting away from her for a few hours was the best part.

'Dae ye ken you're in the paper?'

I shook my head. 'How..?'

'Dinnae ken.' She was lying. 'Sumdy must have telt them but.' She looked away from me, staring at the door of our cell.

I could spot a tell a mile away.

Chapter 103
Fiona
2015

'Did you make this whole story up to get an easier sentence?' I decide that questioning her directly on this may elicit the truth.

'Of course not. Every word I said then and now is true. Don't you believe me Fiona?'

She looks concerned. 'What's the point in me telling you all this, all these hours of recordings if you don't believe me. You're supposed to be telling my life story.'

'And what do you think the outcome will be? Do you want them to re-open the cases? Look for more evidence?' I don't tell her that Tom is doing exactly that. I spoke to him, and he is of the same opinion as I am.

'I want people to understand me. Want them to say I had every right to do what I did. Take my side against the bullies, the thieves, the liars.'

Once again I shiver when she mentions bullies. If I'm wrong and she is capable of committing these crimes, am I under threat? Does she still see me as the bully who taunted her as a child? My plan is to elicit the sympathy of my readers, to portray Ginnie as the victim, as a sad creature who is living a fantasy life. How will she take that?

Chapter 104
TOM'S DIARY

18/2/86

I can't believe what I heard today.

Nine victims? No way.

Ginnie had been sitting there for hours listing the people she claims to have killed. Even the guys questioning her don't seem to believe her. They kept going out to stretch their legs and I could hear them in the corridor laughing.

Tom

2015

Tom couldn't remember much about the few days after the arrest. Ginnie had been charged with wounding with intent and kidnap and had been up before the sheriff the day after her arrest. She had pleaded guilty; everyone had thought it was going to be a straightforward case and she had been remanded in custody. Referred to the high court for sentencing it had come as no surprise that she had been sentenced to twenty years, it would have been life if the judge had considered that she had intended to kill Tom. As it was it was a hefty sentence.

A few months later, while serving her time at Cornton Vale, she had said she had something to tell them. McIntyre had called Tom at home, knowing that he would want to hear what Ginnie was saying and agreeing it would be a good way to ease him back into his job after a prolonged period of sick leave. Although he could take no part in the interviews McIntyre knew Tom was the person best placed to understand Ginnie.

Tom had sat in the room next door to the interview room, listening in as the two detectives took her statement. He could tell by their body language when he met them in the corridor or tea-room that they thought she was a lunatic. They took frequent breaks, laughing as they made copious cups of coffee and sharing what they were hearing with whoever was in the station.

Her appointed solicitor wasn't much better. Tom knew Ginnie could afford a much more experienced representative but had seemed happy with the man who had been called in to advise her until she dismissed him. She was hell-bent on confessing and the solicitor's constant interruptions before she had even started had seemed to rile her.

He had listened with ever increasing horror at what she was telling the detectives. They had seemed to think the whole thing a joke until he had spoken to them in the corridor.

'Trust me guys. She's not joking. I know about all of the deaths she's mentioned so far, they are real. Whether she had anything to do with them is another thing but there are bodies out there. Everyone she has mentioned so far has died.' He explained to them that each case had been investigated at the time but that none had been deemed to be suspicious, Until now. 'You've got a lot of work to do. And I suggest you order a psych evaluation.' He had relaxed when he realised his words were getting through, the two jokers changed their behaviour, straightening their ties, swearing under their breaths.

He had been kept updated on the course of the investigation and hadn't been surprised when the Procurator Fiscal had concluded that there were no cases to answer. There was not a jot of corroborating evidence that any crimes had ever been committed or that the deaths of the many people surrounding Ginnie were anything but accidental or suicides. It was widely held that she was telling these tales to get committed into a psychiatric unit from where she could be released following treatment. Many believed that she thought being committed to Carstairs would be an easier sentence. Someone had leaked her confession to the papers and some Sunday rags had produced articles about the 'Tiny Terror' as they had named her. There had been a flurry of excitement about the story but it had soon blown over when the PF had dismissed her stories as pure fabrication.

He had heard that she had been upset when she had been told that no further action would be taken and that she would continue her stay in Cornton Vale. But why was she continuing to tell the same story now? Was the chance of monetary gain behind it? Fiona had said she had secured a lucrative deal with her publishing house and there was a bidding war for the film rights. Ginnie would be a very rich woman when she was released.

Chapter 105
GINNIE'S TRANSCRIPT
1986

'Seriously? That's it?' They hadn't believed me. The hours and hours of recounting my story were dismissed. They said I was a liar and was trying to manipulate the court. I threw myself on to the bed and turned my back to the detective and court representative who had been sent with the news.

Senga came back from the lunch break and sat on the bunk below me. 'Ah heard that yer stayin' wi' us Ginnie. Can't say Ah'm sorry, Ah could have a much worser cell mate.' Her joviality stung like a hornet.

'Fuck off Senga and give me peace. How did you find out anyway?'

'I've got my sources. I'm only sayin' but. Jist wanted ye tae know ye'll be fine here but.' I could hear her petted lip from my position above her.

'Enough with the "buts", can you not form a sentence without swearing or finishing it with a "but" for god's sake.' I wasn't in the mood for Senga's platitudes.

'Reel your neck in hen. I'm just tryin' to be nice but.'

I chucked a book at her.

'I'll leave ye the noo. Maybe you'll be in a better mood when you see what's in the paper.' She threw the newspaper at me and stomped out of our cell.

My case had been leaked to the press and the Sunday papers had picked up on it. I had sworn to my investigators that I hadn't released any information but a few words to Senga were more than enough to get the gossip mongers started. The headlines screamed that the 'Tiny Terror' as they had dubbed me, wasn't to be charged. For a few days I was headline news yet again, then everyone seemed to forget about me.

I settled into prison life. With good behaviour I'd be out in ten years but in year nine I had heard one too many 'buts' and had stabbed Senga with a fork as we stood in the dinner queue. When she took the last fruit scone on the pile and had retorted, "It's just a scone but." when I had complained about it, a wee nerve went twang and I stabbed her, first through her hand then I swung the fork into her neck before I was bundled off by a burly warder. The cow sat on me while her partner prized the fork from my fingers before rushing to help the squealing Senga. She was ok, I'd missed the carotid in her neck, deliberately obviously. I had no intention of killing her, she hadn't wronged me, she'd just got on the final nerve I had left, the stress of getting close to applying for parole had affected me more than I thought.

A week later there was another incident that earned me an extra five years and ended my chance of early release. I had attacked a new, very butch guard who had come on to me in the library. She obviously hadn't heard about my reputation and thought she could touch up this delicate wee prisoner and not bear the consequences. Who knew so much damage could

be done with a date stamp?
> It got me on the front pages yet again.
> "Tiny Terror attacks again".

Chapter 106
FIONA
2015

Her attack on Senga was the first corroborated instance of Ginnie being violent since her attack on Tom. Was this the behaviour of a possible killer or just someone at the end of their tether with an annoying fellow prisoner? How had being locked up for so long affected Ginnie? I know I'd be climbing the walls with boredom. I could understand why she had stabbed the woman. I decided to ignore this part of her story for now and concentrate on Ginnie's feelings.

'Are you saying you never had a visitor until I contacted you?' I can't believe that in almost thirty years no-one from Ginnie's past had been near her. She was truly alone. Even Tom appeared to have abandoned her.

'Not a soul. I didn't want to see anyone. Maria wrote to me at the start and asked me to forget Tom.' She levels her gaze at me. The steel blue eyes cutting through me like ice. 'I got a letter from Taff once. Thought I'd like an update on Mike. Told me he was coming back to Scotland; his marriage hadn't worked out. He said Mike knew I hadn't had anything to do with Jean's death – that he wanted to see me. What the fuck did he think I'd be able to do about that? Invite Mike to come on over? Play Little Miss Innocent?'

I can see a glint in her eyes. 'How would that make

you feel Ginnie? Do you still have feelings for Mike?'

'How the fuck do you think it made me feel? If I'd married Mike none of this would have happened. I wouldn't have spent half my life in prison. Trust me Fiona, it's no fun being stuck in here. If I'd just trusted him and let myself be loved I'd be a different person.'

For the first time since I'd met her, Ginnie began to cry.

Chapter 107
FIONA
2015

I've finished the first draft of the book and I think I know the tack I'm taking is correct. I'm in Tom's living room, we've spent hours discussing the book. 'I just know there's more to this than meets the eye. I've done a load of research on childhood trauma and it's obvious to me that this is where Ginnie's behaviours come from. When a child has no control over circumstances, for example the death of a family member or friend, they build their own boundaries.'

Tom nods. 'Just because she was annoyed at Francis, do you think she blamed herself for his death?'

'Perhaps she was there when he fell in. We know she couldn't swim, had never been allowed to because of the chance of epilepsy. Maybe she carried the guilt of not helping her friend. Maybe this is all a call for help. A way to ask us to understand that she was never able to help those around her. What happens to a child who has no parental love? Does she apportion the blame to herself?'

'I had never thought of that. Whatever her reasons it's obvious that she's not guilty of any of the crimes she's admitted to.' Tom looks puzzled. 'How do you get to the root of her psyche? The psychiatrists she has seen over the years never forwarded an argument that she suffered from any type of psychosis.'

'They were right. Ginnie shows many of the traits of a sociopath, she's manipulative and callous while at the same time she's engaging. Her fearlessness and lack of empathy are symptoms but there are things about her that don't fit the mould. Her relationship with you for instance. She genuinely seems to love you, not romantically obviously, but you are an enormous part of her life. She's a narcissist, that's obvious, but the thing that I keep coming back to is her delusional behaviour. She still insists she killed people but I'm positive that that's her coping mechanism. She had little control in her life, and she has transferred her daydreams to what she believes to be reality. However, people who suffer from Delusional Disorder usually show signs of a God Complex, believing they have been born to sort out the wrongs of the world. I have seen no signs of that in Ginnie. She's a paradox. She may simply be a liar with an over-active imagination. I noticed a couple of lies when I went over the transcripts while writing the book. She said she was a virgin when she met Mike but earlier on, she says she slept with Philip. She was also caught out on the story about her birth mother. If she lied on those occasions maybe the rest is made up too.'

Tom is nodding his head. 'Her version of where she got the shotgun also varies. If she had been responsible for all those deaths I would surely have noticed, I'm supposed to be a detective after all, that's meant to be my skill set. If she's a killer, then she's a mastermind.

Her ability to destroy forensic evidence, years before it had even been recognised as an important science in crime detection was something neither the police nor I had ever come across before. The investigating team doubted that it was even possible.'

The parole board had agreed on Ginnie's release. After almost thirty years in prison, it would be difficult for her to adapt to freedom, but Tom had agreed to support her. He had brought his wife, Maria, to meet me, and we had tried to persuade her that Ginnie was no longer a threat to her family and that inclusion into their circle would further aid her recovery. I don't think we succeeded; Maria had been very quiet when we met although by the look on her face, she was biting back what she really wanted to say.

Tom still hadn't told Maria about his attempted suicide, unsure of how she would take the news that he had almost abandoned her and her new-born child. I'm happy to keep his secret. I like Tom, he's a gentle soul, he deserves to be happy. This passage in Ginnie's life isn't in the book, at Tom's request. His secret is safe.

'My publisher's timed the launch of my book to coincide with Ginnie's release. I've got a plan that I think will help Ginnie move on. What do you think of having Joe at the launch? It would give her the chance to forgive him for stealing the watch but also to let Joe forgive Ginnie for kidnapping him and shooting his dad.' I'm hoping Tom will agree to my plans. It will make great viewing. 'I'll leave it to you to tell Maria. I'll need both of you and Joe to agree.'

'I'll try.' Tom looks sceptical, 'If you're sure it will help. I can't promise. Joe's an adult now, he can make up his own mind, but Maria might be harder to persuade.'

'It will help. I'm sure of that. But I've been thinking. Maria wants you to have nothing to do with Ginnie when she's released. I think she may be right. Maybe we need someone else to take care of her.'

Tom looks deep in thought. 'I've been in touch with someone more suited to the task. Leave it with me. There may be more than one surprise for Ginnie at the launch. I know the very person that Ginnie would accept help from.'

Ginnie has read my book and has agreed on the stance I have taken. I was surprised that she hadn't argued more but I explained that it would be up to the reader to reach their own conclusions. If she wanted their sympathy, wanted them on her side then putting doubts in their minds was the way to do it.

I have put my worries aside. I have to believe that Ginnie is innocent of the crimes she insists she has committed. Ginnie has woven her stories in such a detailed way that she believes them. She has had to find a reason behind the deaths of so many of her friends and lovers and is blaming herself.

I no longer feel under threat that she may want to exact revenge on me. She hasn't mentioned anything about bullying recently. I think she was just trying to frighten me, game playing.

Chapter 108
TOM'S DIARY

October 26th 2015
Appointment 2pm. Stirling

Tom hadn't told Maria where he was going, better to give her the news after the fact. He wasn't even sure what he was going to say. The fact that Ginnie had agreed to the visit had surprised him. Since Maria had written to her so many years before he had heard nothing from her. He had eventually stopped writing when Maria had told him what she had done. He had accepted that Ginnie had severed all ties with him although the acceptance had left him bereft. At times over the intervening years, he had yearned to call his oldest friend, needed her reassurance that everything would be ok, needed the advice she'd give him, advice with no baggage, no subterfuge, just what he needed to hear and do.

He handed his phone to the warder at the desk and followed her to a small, comfortable room, taking a seat to wait for Ginnie to appear. He wondered what so long in an institution would have done to her. Would she still be the woman he knew? He needn't have worried. Ginnie strode into the room, plonking herself on the chair opposite him, an enormous grin on her face. Her hair was grey, cut short but wayward curls still dropped over her strikingly blue eyes. Her face was relatively unlined but the main thing he noticed was that the essence of Ginnie was there, the unremitting energy emanated from her tiny form, this was the same woman he had last seen thirty years previously. She reached across and took his hand.

'God you're old,' she spoke with a laugh in her voice.

He relaxed. 'Can't say the same for you. Where's the painting?'

Ginnie laughed. 'Ah the old ones are the best. Must be the easy life inside,' she said.

'Really?' Tom knew prison life was anything but easy.

'No. It's been shite but it's almost over now. Thanks for coming, Tom. Fiona told me you were going to be at the launch but it's good to have a bit of time with you. I'd imagine the lovely Maria will be delighted by that.'

'Maria's fine with it,' Tom lied. 'Joe persuaded her that we all need to move on.' Tom chose to ignore the dig at Maria; a habit he had never grown out of.

'So I heard. How is Joe?'

Tom gave her a brief resume of his son's life, his face softening as he spoke about his grandchildren.

'He sounds like a good father, just like his dad. I told you things would be fine. Remember that night? You scared the life out of me, I thought I was going to lose you.'

How could Tom ever forget that night? If Ginnie hadn't rushed to be with him he would have killed himself, the cocktail of drugs and booze he had lined up would have felled an ox. He had been half-way through the pile when Ginnie had arrived. He had chucked the lot down the toilet the next day, terrified by what his intentions had been. Even more terrified than he was at impending parenthood.

'I'll never forget what you did then Ginnie. I owe you my life.'

'Why the visit now though, Tom?' As ever Ginnie was abruptly to-the-point.

Tom looked into her eyes, seeking the truth in their azure depth. He took a deep breath. 'One thing I need to know. Did you really mean to kill Joe?' The scene on the roof of Morven Court had haunted him. Things had blurred. He could remember Ginnie and Joe on the edge of the parapet, could see them standing with arms outstretched as she had done with Francis when they were children. He couldn't remember what they had said, the loss of blood had made him fade in and out of consciousness and he struggled to recall the details. His doctors had said it was his brain's way of blotting out the trauma, but no amount of counselling had unlocked it. The only person who knew exactly what had happened on that roof sat in front of him. Her version which appeared in the book terrified him. Could she really have wanted to kill Joe?

Ginnie stared back into his uneven eyes. 'I don't know what I was thinking back then. I didn't mean to shoot you, just scare you, but when I saw the blood I just ran. I wanted to see Joe, to apologise for hitting him. I thought he'd like the excitement of doing the things we did as children. He seemed to enjoy himself, he loved standing on the edge, pretending we were soaring like eagles. I didn't think it would be construed as kidnapping but in court I realised how wrong I had been. That's why I pleaded guilty. I didn't want to put you through any more trauma. I'm so sorry. The story I told Fiona was nonsense. I thought it would sound more exciting in the book if she thought I would want to kill Joe. Please believe me, Tom. I would never hurt you.'

'Thanks Gin. That's what I needed to hear. The whole thing's a blur but I knew that you'd never harm Joe. He doesn't remember it being anything but fun.' He relaxed in his seat. What Ginnie had just told him persuaded him that he and Fiona had been right. Ginnie's story was a fabrication. The reason behind it was what would have the readers empathising with her.

Ginnie looked at the clock. 'Nearly time up. Will you all be at the launch?'

'Of course we'll be there. And a few more familiar faces.'

'Who? Who else would want to see me?' she asked, a look of concern on her face.

Tom grinned. 'That's the big surprise. You'll see. Trust me.' He stood up, reaching to hug her briefly, 'Thanks for letting me visit, Ginnie. And thanks for your honesty.'

He drove home, reassured that he was right to support Ginnie despite Maria's misgivings. The woman he had just spoken to wasn't a killer. She needed love and understanding. He hoped she would find that soon.

Chapter 109
Ginnie
2015

Tom's visit was a surprise. When I'd been told he had requested a meeting I knew I had to clear things up with him. It had gone exactly as I had expected, and he had left, reassured that I had never intended to hurt Joe. He wasn't listening.

The book is finished. They've made up their minds that I'm innocent; that I've concocted this tale to take control of the aspects of my life that I had no control of at the time. Parents who didn't love me, sexual predators and abusers, incompetent professionals, people who have hurt me or lied to me – I couldn't do anything about them; I was a child, a vulnerable young woman. Only I know if they are right. Fiona sees me as a pitiful creature. A poor abused, neglected child who has formed a shell around herself to protect her. Maybe she should have consulted the psychology experts instead of relying on her own 'expertise'.

I've told Fiona that I'm happy with the spin she has put on it; that it's lies, fantasy, whichever way you want to look at it; a cry for attention from a damaged woman.

When I originally confessed my crimes, it was to get an easier sentence, a spell in a secure unit due to diminished responsibility. That didn't work and now I need to get out of prison. Not because I hate it in here.

It's fine actually. I have my job in the library, no-one bothers me, I'm warm, dry and fed. What more does a body need? But I've got something to do, unfinished business. I won't be out for long if things go to plan.

As I said at the start of the book. I've never forgiven the thief.

Chapter 110
FIONA
2016

And here we are. The final edits are done, and the book is due for release. *The Killer Inside* is a sure-fire hit. Readers love to act the psychiatrist, love to second guess the outcome. The films of my previous books have won numerous awards and *The Killer Inside* has already been snapped up by the same film company with Emmy award winner Christine Huntley lined up to play Ginnie. Fans are clamouring for this next instalment in my series. They can't wait to see the real woman behind the book. The launch has been sold out for months and the tour my publicist has organised has been hyped as the "go-to" event in 2016.

Ginnie had been reluctant at first, she was wary of being under the public's gaze, but I had persuaded her that she was what would really sell this book. I think a bit of flattery was what she'd needed. We've gone over the questions which she'll be asked so that she's prepared. A bit of nervousness and fragility will serve her well though. I need the audience to empathise with her, to feel her pain.

Everything is organised. Everyone knows their role. I can't wait to introduce Ginnie to her public.

Chapter 111
TOM'S DIARY

November 21st, 2016
  Book table for Saturday
  Collect prescriptions
  Pick up Joe from airport – 10am
  Ginnie's book launch 7pm

Tom 2016

TOM'S DIARY was now more of a to-do list. He no longer poured his heart on to the pages but instead used it as an aide memoir to remind him of the basics of life, birthdays, appointments. Maria laughed when she said he was getting forgetful but there were times when he worried that his memory really was failing. He noted down a reminder to mention it to the doctor next time he was in for a check-up.

He lay his shirt and jacket on the bed, straining to fasten the button on his suit trousers, it had been a while since he'd worn them, but he wanted to look smart for the launch. Fiona had warned him that the press and TV crews would be there, such was the interest in Ginnie's story. Fiona had done an excellent PR job. Everyone wanted to know more about her client; wanted to meet the real woman behind the book and film's portrayal.

It had taken a lot to persuade Maria that their plan for the launch was a good idea. A reconciliation between Joe and Ginnie had horrified her at first.

'For God's sake Tom. She shot you and tried to kill our child, I can't forgive her that and I don't know how you can.' Maria battered the sofa cushions into shape. 'I know it's been years but it's not something a parent can forget. I'm tired of this. Do what you need to do.'

Tom sighed. He found it difficult to put into words what he felt about Ginnie. He would never change Maria's mind about what happened. He had tried to explain that they thought Ginnie was lying but she wouldn't listen.

'She was always there for me. She protected me when we were children, always fought on my side. I can't forget that. Her face when she was being led away and she said she could never hurt me was heart-breaking. I can't give up on her. I never could.' His eyes pleaded with his wife to understand.

Eventually Joe had spoken to her and explained that it would bring closure and would allow them all to move forward. He had seen Maria cringe at the term, but she had relented and agreed. As the time neared for them to leave, Maria had broken. She sat on the couch beside him.

'This is it, Tom. After today you break all ties. She can get on with her own life. You haven't seen her in years, although I know you tried. Let her go.' She took his hand. 'I mean it. No more.' She took a deep breath, smoothing her dress as she stood up. 'Let's get this over with then. The taxi will be here in ten minutes.'

They were meeting Ginnie and Fiona at the venue. A well-known TV personality was interviewing them, and he scanned the list of questions she had sent. Most aimed at Ginnie but a few to him. He had rehearsed his answers, had noted a few bullet-points he thought would be interesting. Maybe he wouldn't get a chance to say much. Fiona tended to take charge, although he was sure it was Ginnie they all wanted to hear.

He shrugged on his jacket and ran his hand through his hair; he'd do, no-one would be interested in him.

*

The venue was packed, it seemed everyone wanted a piece of Ginnie. He picked up two glasses of orange juice from a side table, declining the champagne on offer. On the other side of the room was a table laden with hard back copies of the book waiting for the signature and dedication which would ensure the readers would go home satisfied. He took his seat and turned as the room fell silent and Ginnie was led into the room. She stopped at the signing table and arranged a couple of the books then made her way to the stage.

As he sat watching the reaction of the audience to Ginnie's story of her time in prison, her childhood and what impact it had had on her life, he relaxed. This would bring resolution to his life with Ginnie. Joe had happily agreed to their plan, knowing that his appearance and apology would help Ginnie move on. He saw Ginnie smile when she saw Taff sitting in the audience behind Maria. This was part of Fiona's plan to reintroduce Ginnie to someone from her past who could help her.

As Ginnie told the story about her father and his death he saw many women nodding, understanding the teenage Ginnie's feelings about a father who had never shown her any love and had allowed her to be abused by a family friend. They understood when she said she had taken him tea and biscuits on the night he died, abused children often showed love to their abusers, this was a daughter ensuring her father was comfortable and trying to gain his respect and love, that small act of kindness resonated with the audience. Even if they believed that she had killed him, they would have supported her. Fiona had never allowed the ending to the book to be revealed. She wanted her readers to make up their own minds on whether Ginnie was telling the truth or not.

He saw those same women wiping tears from their eyes as Joe stepped on to the stage.

Chapter 112
GINNIE
2016

Fiona leads me into the signing room and shows me the pile of books waiting for my signature. I've practiced my signature; GQ with a flourish.

'Ready?' she asks.

'Ready.' I rearrange the books slightly, take a deep breath and turn to her.

We walk to the stage, Fiona's hand resting on my arm. I'm sure the writer has planned this to make me look tiny, vulnerable. She needs to get the audience's sympathy for this poor, wronged woman. It took a lot to agree to accepting her take on my story. At first I had wanted to argue. Like everyone else she didn't believe that I'd done what I'd done. She stole my life and twisted it to suit her needs. I'm not sure who this delusional woman the book portrays me as, is. I don't recognise her but keeping quiet and accepting her conclusions have meant I'm here now. I'm wearing Maria's bracelet; the one she had lost so many, many years ago. On the day she had taken Tom.

Our interviewer, Sharon Lewis, arts correspondent on late night TV, leads the applause and welcomes us. I take my hand from the pocket of my dress, why had no-one ever designed pockets in dresses before, and shake her hand. She winces slightly as I grip her hand. Fiona had chosen her specifically because of her reputation for championing the underdog, knowing she'll make me look good. This is purely a PR stunt. When they had told me how they had intended to finish the launch I had been surprised and hadn't answered immediately. Seeing Joe would be interesting.

'It'll be all over social media; you couldn't get a better hook,' Fiona had explained. She didn't need to persuade me. I couldn't have planned it better myself.

I sit between my guardians, taking a sip of champagne, nothing is too good for Fiona's clients, and scan the audience. Cameras flash until Sharon asks for them to be switched off until the end of the interview. Maria sits in the middle of the front row, I raise my hand slightly in acknowledgement, the bracelet shines in the spotlight. I'm glad she is here.

I don't want her to miss this.

Behind her I recognise the figure of Taff. This must be Tom's surprise. It's good to see him, however fleetingly.

Fiona starts the launch by introducing the book and answering a few questions setting the tone. Sharon steers the questions expertly, eliciting laughs and looks of horror from the audience in equal measure as I tell my story. I read an excerpt from the book, explaining how my childhood and my adoptive parents' covert negligence had affected me. I wiped the tears from my eyes and notice the rise in Tom's eyebrow when I do so. Oh yes, I can cry. Fiona has mentored me well.

'We'll have a short Q and A session before we go.' Sharon stands up at the end of the interview, 'But we have a surprise for Ginnie first.' I feign a questioning look, although I know what is about to happen. 'Please welcome Tom's son, Joe to the stage. He has something to say to Ginnie.'

The tall man who had been sitting next to Maria rises and walks on to the stage. He looks like his mother. Everyone stands to greet the newcomer. I join them, a broad grin on my face. 'Hello Joe.'

'I have something for you Ginnie.' He fumbles in his pocket and removes Ranald's watch. 'I'm sorry I stole this from you. I'm sure if I hadn't then none of what followed would have happened.'

I take the watch from him and stare briefly at the dial. Someone has had it renovated and the second-hand slides smoothly over the face. I smile up at the thief's handsome face. 'Thanks Joe. You don't know what this means to me.' I hold out my arms towards him.

'We have another surprise for you Ginnie.' Sharon beams across the stage, 'All the way from the Highlands...'

A familiar song begins to play, Brian Hyland's "Ginnie Come Lately" ringing out around the room as I step towards Joe to embrace him, slipping the fountain pen from that oh-so-handy pocket in my dress. Fiona had used that pen, my pen, throughout our meetings, taunting me yet again. She had left it on the signing table at my request. I see Tom and Maria moving towards me but before they reach me, I turn and plunge the pen into Fiona's chest. I knew exactly where to strike – I had played *Operation* as a child.

'Thief,' I hiss.

As her knees buckle, I look beyond her to the side of the stage. There, older, greyer but unmistakable, stands Mike. This had been their surprise. Not Taff, not Joe. Mike. My Mike. The only man I've ever loved. He is here for me.

I bury my face in my bloodstained hands and weep.

Epilogue

'Welcome back, Ginnie. Didn't expect to see you again.' The warder welcomes me like a long-lost friend. She escorts me to my cell. The secure wing this time. No "buts" from Senga to rile me.

I sit on the bed and look around the bare room. I was still declared sane. No cushy psych ward for me. "Doing a Ginnie" had become a thing on social media, meaning someone over-reacting to something.

The headlines in the papers screamed – MAD, BAD OR SAD? They asked me why I had picked on Fiona that day and not Maria or Joe. They haven't been listening. I would never hurt Tom. His family was always safe. But Fiona – now there's a different story. She had been the ringleader in the group of bullies at school; other women came forward when the book was published and joined the 'MeToo' group. She had stolen my pen. People said she had been jealous of me, she would never be dux, never win an achievement award.

I had asked the court for it back, but as a murder weapon it has to remain in the evidence files. I would like to use it to write to Mike. I still love him.

I pick up my copy of *The Killer Inside*.

It's about time I read it.

Acknowledgements

In 2012 I wrote a short story about three children. In 2017 this morphed into Ginnie's memoirs and *Liar Thief* was born. Massive thanks to Luca Veste who 'got' Ginnie, chose me as the winner of Black Spring Press's debut crime novel competition, and helped me through the whole editing process. Also thanks to everyone else at Black Spring Press for giving me this chance – thanks Todd.

I have a list as long as my arm of the people who have moulded me as a writer and helped me get Ginnie on to the page. If I miss anyone, please forgive me, you know you have my unending gratitude.

Where do I start? At the beginning obviously.

To my mum, the real May, who encouraged my love of reading and introduced me to the crime world of Ed McBain when I was 12.

Maggie Elliott and Cheryl Grassam who told me that 'of course you can write a novel' when I had struggled to even finish a short story.

To my writing buddies at Moffat Crime Writers and my lovely Twisted Sisters for guidance, beta reading, support, love and for introducing me to Crime and Publishment writing weekends in Gretna run by author Graham Smith.

Special mention to Linda Wright, Ann Bloxwich, Jackie Baldwin, Fiona Quinn, Christine Huntley, Hayley Rebecca Kershaw, Kriss Nicol, Jo Abbott, Alice Mae Jamieson – I'd never have done it without you.

To Graham Smith, Michael J Malone, Caro Ramsey, Mike Craven, Les Morris, John Langley and everyone who has appeared at C&P, sharing their knowledge, tips and support.

Most of all to my husband Kris Koren who puts up with me getting up at 5am and scribbling in a notebook when characters poke me awake to tell me something; who feeds the cats, hens and me when I'm writing, and who has supported my dreams to be a published writer since day one.

The Black Spring Crime Series

Curated and edited by the best-selling author Luca Veste, and endorsed by the likes of Lee Child, Mark Billingham, and Val McDermid, the Black Spring Crime Series is filled with fantastic reads, waiting to be discovered. From psychological thrillers, to historical crime novels, to classic noir, we have something for everyone, with many, many more to come ... some of our selection are listed below!

A Crime in the Land of 7,000 Islands, Zephaniah Sole

This psychological literary fiction tells the tale of Ikigai Johnson, a Special Agent working out of the FBI's Portland, Oregon field office, who pledges to bring justice to children abused by a monstrous American in the Philippines. Amidst an expertly accurate police procedural, Ikigai recounts her tale to her eleven-year-old daughter through fantastical allegory.

This is a powerhouse crime thriller written by a serving FBI agent fused with folk tales and the influence of anime. Described by bestselling author Stuart Neville as 'an extraordinary feat of storytelling'.

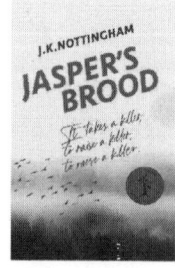

Jasper's Brood, J.K. Nottingham

It Takes a Killer, To Raise a Killer, To Raise a Killer...
Jasper is a killer. Raised by a man who is not his father, but a serial killer to become just like him. Only, he is different. He wants to help people. The only way he knows how. To be just like him.

Cormac McCarthy meets North-East England in this unforgettable novel, with a fresh and exciting voice from a debut author.

The Salt Cutter, C.J. Howell
Bolivia. 1991. A soldier arrives in the small town of Uyuni. A place people endure rather than enjoy. The soldier knows they're coming for him. Hunting him down so they can deal their own brand of justice. He needs to get out. To make it to the border and escape what is waiting for him. He's prepared to do anything to survive. Even kill.

This is noir fiction at its finest. With characters that you will root for, heartbreak, and breathtaking writing, this is a story that will linger in reader's minds long after you've turned the final page.

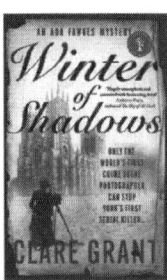

Winter of Shadows, Clare Grant
In the midwinter of 1862 in York, a young woman is found dead by the river, her body marked by a sinister act of mutilation. The mysterious death spreads fear, for this is not the first corpse to be discovered. Speculation grows there is a killer stalking the city's medieval streets.

This glorious historical crime thriller, described by Ambrose Parry as, 'hugely atmospheric', introduces the character of Ada Fawkes, the country's only crime scene photographer, who you won't forget in a hurry.

The God Secret, Yves Laliberté
When a deadly biological attack is narrowly thwarted by Royal Canadian Mounted Police agent Kristen Vale, she uncovers a chilling pattern of crimes. Joined by medieval historian Quentin DeFoix, Vale follows a trail of cryptic symbols, ancient torture devices, and forgotten iconography from the Dark Ages. As the body count rises, the pair must decipher a centuries-old mystery known only as The God Secret – before the next wave of terror is unleashed.

For the first time in English, Book One of the best-selling French-Canadian literary phenomenon, *The God Secret*.

***The Scotsman*, Rob McClure**
Chic Cowan will do anything to find his daughter's killer…even sacrifice his own sanity…and maybe he wasn't all that sane to start with…

Set during the turbulence of a divided America, a plot that engages with what 'woke' means, and the realities of policing, *The Scotsman* is the blistering debut from a new Tartan Noir talent. This is *Rebus* meets *Taken*.

***Cast No Shadow*, Nick Quantrill**
Podcaster Yaz Moy is stuck in small town purgatory with no way out. That is until someone approaches her with a story that could be the key to fulfilling her big city dreams. Yaz is forced to decide what matters more – her safety or the truth. And she's willing to risk it all…

"Hull's answer to Ian Rankin" – Hull Daily Mail

***CrimeBits: 100 Opening Gambits for Great Thrillers & Linked Mystery Puzzles*, selected and introduced by Lee Child & ed. Luca Veste**
A unique, interactive puzzle book including 100 first pages of thrillers, the best selected by the world-famous crime author Lee Child. Each page is linked to a puzzle, ranging from crosswords to wordsearches to mystery logic puzzles created by a *L.A. Times* puzzle setter Robin Stears.

***CrimeBits 2: 100 Opening Gambits for Great Thrillers & Linked Mystery Puzzles*, selected and introduced by Val McDermid & ed. Luca Veste**
The sequel to Lee Child's *CrimeBits* but this time selected by Val McDermid. A unique, interactive puzzle book including 100 first pages of thrillers. Each page is linked to a puzzle, ranging from crosswords to wordsearches to mystery logic puzzles created by a *L.A. Times* puzzle setter Robin Stears.

***The Wykehamist*, Alexandra Strnad**
Lucian is The Wykehamist, a bright, handsome, charming, and privately educated young man, who glides through life effortlessly. But when his life begins to unravel following his arrest in Hong Kong, journalist Clementine cannot resist the urge to rediscover the man who has been her obsession for so long...

Saltburn meets *American Psycho* in this shocking debut crime novel from Alexandra Strnad.

***Zigzag Girl*, Ruth Setton**
A twisty contemporary mystery with a touch of magic, set in Atlantic City and the eerie New Jersey Pine Barrens. Lucy Moon, a brilliant young magician with a mysterious past, works in the town's theatre, staging performances of enchantment and conjure. But one night, during the 'Sawing a Woman in Half' trick, Lucy discovers her friend's body in the box, dead. As Lucy digs deeper, she uncovers a trail of murders and suspects.